PRETTY LITTLE GIRLS
An Agent Victoria Heslin Thriller – Book 2

JENIFER RUFF

BOOKS BY JENIFER RUFF

PRETTY LITTLE GIRLS
An Agent Victoria Heslin Thriller
Book 2

JENIFER RUFF

Copyright © 2019 Greyt Companion Press
ISBN-13: 978-1-7339570-3-8
Written by Jenifer Ruff
Edited by Dan Alatorre
Cover design by Tim Barber, Dissect Designs
All the characters in this book are fictional. Any resemblance to actual people living or dead is a coincidence.

Visit the author's website for more information.
www.Jenruff.com

Until you know who you can trust, you trust no one.

Chapter One

Ava trudged up the hill towards the woods behind her apartment complex, following her dog. She glanced at her watch again as she tugged the leash, pulling Max away from whatever he was sniffing. "Crap, why did you let me hit the snooze button five times, Max?" Puffs of white breath formed in front of her as she wrapped his leash around her wrist and picked up her pace. "Because a warm bed is heaven, Ava. That's why."

Max trotted straight through a mud puddle; Ava jumped over it. "You have an answer for everything, don't you, boy? Can you give me a good one for Mr. Parker when I'm late for the third time this month?"

Wearing a large puffy coat, Ronald drove toward her on the maintenance golf cart, brooms and shovels bouncing along in the back. She waved at him. He was nice enough, but as she hurried onto the trail into the woods, she hoped he wouldn't follow like he did that day last summer.

The blanket of crisp leaves crunched under her feet. Max strained against the leash, flung his head into the bushes, and nuzzled his nose into a mound of decaying vegetation, going after every strange and wonderful outdoorsy scent. Ava peered back over her shoulder and was relieved to see Ronald driving in the opposite direction. Groaning against the cold, she jogged in place, one hand in the pocket of her coat. She had to admit, the chilly air was invigorating, and it would make her morning coffee so much more enjoyable, even though she'd have to take it to go. Why did Mr. Parker care so much about her being late anyway? She always got her work done.

Wheezing, Max hauled her forward, deeper into the woods. Once he caught the scent of something interesting in the wild—a deer or its droppings, a discarded hamburger wrapper—he was determined to get to it.

"No, come on. Are you trying to get me fired? Max, stop! We need to turn around."

He lurched ahead, ears erect and nose twitching, dragging her off the worn path.

"Max, no!"

A large tree trunk stretched alongside the trail, covered in moss. Max lunged to inspect it, his entire body wagging with excitement.

Ava's phone buzzed from inside her coat pocket. *Don't be Parker, don't be Parker.* She reached for her phone. *Please let this be one of the days when he has a doctor's appointment for his weird skin condition.*

She glanced at the screen. Jared. She didn't have time for ex-boyfriend's antics right now.

The leash went slack. Max whimpered. His front paw was lifted and his tail pointed. Ava moved closer to see what he'd discovered on the other side of the log.

Ava blinked. Her mouth dropped open. Her phone fell from her hand as she screamed. She stumbled backwards, tugging on Max, unable to tear her eyes away.

Is she . . .? Is she . . .?

The young girl didn't belong there, underdressed, unmoving, alone on the ground.

She had dark brown hair and pale skin. Her gray sweat pants and pink flannel shirt were wet from the morning's frosty mist. Leaves were tangled in her hair and strewn across her body. But it was her beautiful brown eyes staring blankly at the cold, gray sky that shook Ava to the core.

Ava screamed again as Max stretched forward and licked something off the corpse's chin.

♦ ♦ ♦

FBI Medical Examiner Dr. Rebecca Boswell didn't care if it was still November. As soon as the Thanksgiving dishes were washed, Christmas was on. An acoustic version of Deck the Halls blasted through the autopsy room as she studied the slender girl on the steel gurney. No identification on her—another Jane Doe, number 2537 to be exact—and this one was unusually young, sixteen at most. The ME lifted the girl's eyelids, revealing bloodshot brown eyes. A linear ligature mark circled her neck. Even before doing an internal exam, Rebecca was confident that the girl was a victim of foul play. No doubt she had been suffocated.

She pressed a button on her recorder.

"Jane Doe. Caucasian female, possibly of Eastern European descent. Very slender. Height five-foot-four, weight one hundred and two pounds. Long, dark hair."

An exceptionally lovely, symmetrical, face. Would have grown up to be a stunner.

"She's wearing eye makeup and blush. Aside from ruptured capillaries—consistent with asphyxiation, will confirm— her skin is smooth and clear. She has pink gel polish on recently groomed nails and matching polish on her toenails."

3

Youth today—in such a rush to grow up.

"Blood trailing from the corners of her mouth and over her chin, suggesting an internal injury."

She leaned over the table and gently pulled open the girl's lips. "Examination of the mouth indicates…" Rebecca's gut wrenched as she jerked backwards, gasping. In ten years of autopsies, she'd never done that before. Rebecca squeezed her eyes shut, letting her sadness turn to rage and then back to professionalism. She opened the girl's lips again and continued her examination. "The subject's tongue…" The ME swallowed hard. "…has been cut out." She turned off the recorder and took a deep breath, gazing at the child. "You didn't deserve that, honey. No matter what you did."

Rebecca removed her gloves and filled a cup with water. She gulped it down, crushed the cup, and slammed it into the trash can. She took another deep breath, wiped her forehead, donned new gloves, and returned to her work.

"Bleeding minimal, no inflammation, indicating the tongue was removed post-mortem." That, at least, offered Rebecca a small morsel of relief. She'd seen tongues cut out before, although never in such a girl. Whoever did it could be a unique kind of messed-up and wanted a souvenir. However, there was a more likely, uglier explanation. Someone was sending a message—keep your mouth closed, don't talk. But to whom?

What were you involved with before you died?

Rebecca cleared her throat. "Healthy, straight teeth, but no signs of previous dental work." *No fillings or caps to trace.*

After making dental impressions, she turned Jane Doe over to study her backside. At first glance, because the back of the girl's neck was covered by an array of silky hair, she thought she saw a

4

brown tattoo. When she swept the hair away for a closer inspection, she frowned. It wasn't a normal tattoo.

"Dark, well-defined scar, two inches in diameter, at the base of her neck at her T1 vertebrae—a circle with marks around the perimeter and an infinity symbol inside, most likely made by a small branding iron."

The brand was unusual, but could mean anything—an impulsive pact made with girlfriends, a boyfriend's favorite symbol—but seeing that the girl had likely been murdered, Rebecca wondered if the marking was gang related.

Serenaded by *Carol of the Bells*, Dr. Boswell pushed her braids over her shoulder, snapped digital pictures, and measured the bruises across Jane Doe number 2537's arms and neck. She collected scrapings from under the girl's finger nails, combed through her hair, and applied tape over her body to collect fibers. After she finished collecting external evidence, she washed the girl's body. She'd been found in urine and feces, a sign she'd lost control of her bodily functions. Might have been sick, or terrified, or a result of dying. It's possible Rebecca wouldn't be able to discover which. Lastly, before beginning the internal exam, Dr. Boswell printed the girl's fingers.

The internal exam took her over an hour. With a tap of her foot she recorded the summary of her findings.

"Abnormal findings in the internal exam included evidence of healed fractures, minor, but on multiple bones. Vaginal bruising and tears indicated recent, rough sexual activity. No semen found."

Rebecca neatly stitched the body back together, minus its vital organs. She exercised her lungs belting out *Gloria in Excelsis Deo* as she returned Jane Doe to cold storage.

"Jane Doe Number 2537 is only a temporary designation. Mark my words, poor girl, we're going to find out who you are and who did this to you." Dr. Boswell slid the heavy, steel drawer into place.

The ME washed up, anxious to load the photo of the brand into the computer and hopefully find a match in the FBI's database of tattoos and symbols. After the search had run its course, nothing turned up that looked like the mark on the back of the corpse's neck.

Curious, the ME called Special Agent Dante Rivera. A quick glance in one of the mirrors confirmed her full lips still held a hint of shimmer and her hot pink scrubs were great with her skin color. No reason not to look and feel good when she spoke to him, even over the phone. They hadn't been on a date yet, but she was a patient woman.

"Good afternoon, Dr. Boswell," Rivera answered, always the gentleman.

"Good afternoon, Agent Rivera. I just finished the autopsy of a teen-aged Jane Doe. She was suffocated. Her tongue was removed post-mortem."

Rivera grunted. "Such a nice world we live in."

"Isn't that the truth?" Rebecca sighed. As much as she wanted to flirt with him, the circumstances of their interactions rarely allowed for it. "What prompted my call was an interesting burn mark on the back of her neck. A brand."

"Like cattle?"

"Unfortunately, yes. I was hoping it might help identify her or give us a clue as to who killed her. I checked in the FBI database, and there wasn't a match. I also sent a picture to your phone. In case there's a chance you've seen something like it before. I know you've worked with some gang cases in the past."

"You know that, huh?"

Alone in the autopsy room, she smiled. "Yes."

6

"Okay." She heard the echoey noises of being switched to speaker phone, and a few seconds passed before he spoke again. "I'm looking at it right now. Can't say it looks familiar, but I'll ask around."

"Thanks, Rivera. I'm sending her prints and her dental images out. Such a young girl. And the final indignity is that as far as we know, no one has reported her missing. No one is looking for her."

Chapter Two

Sofia was a beautiful, graceful girl. She had vivid blue eyes and thick, dark lashes. Her mouth held a natural pout, even when she was terrified. In her petite, red dress, she stared out through the floor-to-ceiling window, squinting. She couldn't see the skyscrapers, only thousands of tiny lights blurring together in the darkness.

Anastasia joined her at the window. She was just as stunning. Light brown hair, emerald-green eyes with specks of copper, full lips, and an upturned nose. "Sexy and childishly innocent," according to their boss. The childish part wasn't hard to accomplish, especially not when she started working for him. She had only been thirteen.

Anastasia placed her hand against the glass and leaned into it. "Big view city skyline. I wish you see it clearly." She often dropped her articles and mixed up a few words when she spoke English. The girls were forbidden to speak their native language.

They'd worked in many nice homes, and this condo with its enormous televisions, sleek furniture, and modern art was no exception. A buzzed exuberance vibrated through the home along with the bass in the sound system. A new group of men burst in, all wearing Panther jerseys.

"Super Bowl bound, baby!" shouted the loudest, slapping a big bald guy on the back. "I knew they were going. I called it at the beginning of the season, did I not?"

The bald guy draped his arm over his friend's shoulder. "Don't jinx them, man. There's lots of games left."

With big smiles, and long swigs of beer, the hardcore fans broke into a chant. "We're number one! We're number one!"

"Are they some of the players?" Sofia asked Svet.

Her bodyguard huffed. "Hardly. They're just a group of traders who probably take roids."

Sofia sat on the couch and stretched one of her long, slim legs over the lap of a guy who could have passed for an NFL lineman. She gently stroked his bulging biceps with her light pink nails. He was an ugly white dude with a crooked nose and a neat, close-shaven beard, clearly intended to cover his acne scars. Even though he was much older than her, he was younger than most of her customers. Best of all, he was having a hard time making eye contact, focusing on his drink instead. It didn't happen often that a man was uncomfortable, but when it did, she appreciated it. He would be gentle. Chances were good he wouldn't hurt her.

The man patted her behind. "She looks really young, Mikey."

Mikey, just as large but not as ugly, responded with a laugh, his hand cupping Anastasia's breast. "Don't worry about her." He finished his beer and set the iced mug on one of his fancy glass tables. "They cost a small fortune. They probably take home more than we do."

Sofia cringed inside. He was wrong. So very wrong. She made nothing. If she had been earning money to send back to her mother and siblings in Ukraine, there would have at least been an upside to the miserable circumstances of her life. Yet, she knew better than to correct him. She couldn't trust any men with the truth. She'd tried before. Just because someone seemed kind, didn't mean they could be trusted. The last time she'd thought she could trust someone, he'd betrayed her. She'd been locked in a closet for days with only water to drink and a pot for relieving herself. So, no matter how sensitive the huge man with the bent nose seemed, she had to assume he was just like all the rest— stone-cold and uncaring to her plight.

She shrugged it off, forcing her sweetest, most genuine-looking smile. Batting her eyelashes, she shook her head slightly, pretending she couldn't understand his words. He offered her a drink, pointing to his own bottle and then the mini-bar across the room. "No, thank you," she said, adding an extra thick layer to her existing accent.

Svet carefully surveyed the rooms from a corner, wearing a silk suit and a scary, stern expression. A giant man, he had a thick neck, square jaw, and puffed out chest. He would force a quick stop to anything or anyone that might permanently scar the girls' faces or bodies, but that wasn't his real purpose. He followed them closely at every party as a constant reminder that there was no escape.

With guards, constant threats, no money, and little idea of how things worked in America, the girls believed they had no chance of successfully getting away. Meanwhile, there was a never-ending stream of men ready and willing to hand over cash and take advantage of them.

The ugly man took Sofia into a bedroom. Closing her eyes, she moaned softly in the practiced way she'd been taught. It helped each ordeal end quicker. She put her actions on autopilot and let her mind travel to another place. She asked herself the questions that had been circling through her mind since her best friend Sasha disappeared two days ago. Where was she? Locked inside a dark closet with only a bottle of water and a bucket? Had she been taken to a different city? Would Sofia ever see her again? Sasha was too brave for her own good, and that might be the reason she had disappeared. Sofia said a silent prayer that her friend was still alive . . . somewhere.

She closed her eyes and moaned.

If Sasha didn't come back, Sofia would have to be the brave one.

Chapter Three

Magda pulled her employer's Lexus up to the South Charlotte Mall behind a Porsche SUV and a flashy BMW Coupe. Tiny white holiday lights were already strung around the bare trees on each side of the mall's main entrance. In the center, a tall pine with silver and gold ornaments the size of bowling balls rose to the roof line of the building.

A valet parking attendant rushed toward her car. Magda held up a finger. "One second, please. I don't need parking. I'm only dropping off."

Emma brushed another coat of gloss on her lips and bared her teeth in the visor mirror. Her thorough once-over finished; she opened the passenger side door.

"Wait." Magda placed her hand on Emma's arm. "I don't see your friends. Where are they?"

Emma shook off Magda's hand and rolled her eyes. "They're inside. Waiting for me."

"Are you sure? I shouldn't drop you off until I know they're here."

"They're here. See? Emma shoved her phone in front of Magda's face, then pulled it away just as quickly. "I'm already late."

"You're meeting Tiffany and Nicole?"

Emma sighed, heavy and loud, as she got out of the car. "Yes. I'm meeting Tiffany and Nicole."

"All right. Be safe."

Emma slammed the door.

Magda lifted her eyes skyward, silently asking God for strength, before watching Emma walk away. The teen wore tight stretchy red pants and a draping black top with cut-outs in each shoulder. Magda wished she could reverse the girl's age back to when Emma was sweet and friendly and enjoyed spending time with her nanny. Despite Magda's best efforts to help raise a decent human being, Emma's attitude was turning out to be more like her mother's and father's. Magda had evolved into a personal assistant and chauffeur, while the sweet Emma had become a sullen teen who grew a bit more disrespectful every day.

"You can't stay here, ma'am." The parking attendant frowned at her. "You have to move." She held up her hand and offered a slight smile. "Sorry. Going now." She put the car in gear and drove off. Maybe Emma was simply angry with her parents again. That was probably it. The constant threat of divorce hung heavy in the air at the Manning home. It made sense that Emma was taking her frustration out on Magda, who was always available.

◆ ◆ ◆

Emma strutted to the center of the mall, past the big Christmas tree and the Santa station and straight to the bathroom near the food court. She had to pee, even though she'd just gone before leaving her house. Nerves did that to her. After exiting a stall, she stopped at the mirror. Pulling her long, straight, reddish hair forward on her shoulders, she slowly turned to her right and then to her left, studying herself again. She pursed her lips and sucked her cheeks in, so her face looked thinner, more angular. She was pretty, everyone told her so. Her newly straightened and bonded teeth looked amazing. She had long dark lashes and beautiful brown eyes that popped thanks to expertly applied eyeliner and eyeshadow. But she wanted to look *really* pretty, and she needed to look older. If Damian found out how young she really was, he might be angry. And worse, he might not be interested in her any more.

She gripped her phone. Only a few more minutes before she would finally meet him in person. This was it. She squared her shoulders and marched out of the bathroom with the saunter of a runway model, shoulders back and neck extended. Her stomach fluttered and her legs were a little weak, but years of performances at the Children's Theater had taught her how to conceal nervous excitement. She passed the Coppa Coffee and Tea store. Maybe she and Damian would come back and have a latte together. She really liked the Chai tea lattes there. If Damian didn't already have a plan for hanging out, she would suggest it. But probably he did, since he was older and seemed so confident and sure of himself. Would he look the same as he did in the pictures he'd sent over the internet? Or had he photoshopped those to make him look like a movie star? In a short time, she would know for sure.

She slowed her pace so as not to arrive early. But what if she was late and he left because he figured she wasn't coming? She sped up again.

The escalator took her down to the parking garage where they had arranged to meet. She hadn't thought twice about the odd choice of a location. Despite her nerves, she had to look nonchalant and cool, like meeting Damian was no big deal. Wouldn't it be great if one of her classmates saw her with him—

maybe some of the older girls from her school? They would be impressed.

With her coat wrapped over her hands, she leaned back against the wall, then stood up straight, then leaned back again, unable to decide which pose was better. Fidgeting with her hands, she pretended to read a mall directory. What if he blew her off? What if he'd never intended to come? She shifted her purse to her opposite shoulder. It was a little heavier than usual because Damian had asked her to bring her MacBook along. She had no idea why. Maybe he wanted to show her some new game.

"Emma?"

She turned around at the raspy voice and her stomach flipped over. Damian walked toward her. Hard to believe, but he was even more handsome in real life.

"Hi." She giggled as her nerves threatened to turn her into a silly child.

Damian's skin was the color of Emma's perfect spray tan. He had a beautiful smile, and his hair was cut in a cool way, neat and not messy. His outfit was perfection—olive-colored jeans, a navy shirt, and a North Face jacket—and it looked *so* good on him. He looked like he played football or rugby. Not too big, but strong enough to protect them if necessary.

She expected him to walk over to her, but he stopped a few yards away and glanced around. He had one hand inside his coat pocket. For a second, she worried he had changed his mind about hanging out with her. But then his smile grew bigger. "How are you?"

"I'm fine. And you?" Her answer was automatic, the same response she would offer a teacher or one of her parents' friends. She needed to do better, but her mind was racing, part of it wondering why he hadn't come closer. She walked toward him

15

until she was a more normal distance away. She cocked her head and batted her eyelashes until she could think of something clever to say.

"Hope you haven't been waiting long." He glanced up toward the escalator as he spoke. There was no one coming down.

"Me? No. I just got here, like seconds before you did."

He nodded. "You look really nice."

His smile made her tingle inside. There was nothing creepy or immature about the way he looked at her. She could tell he approved, and his gaze made her confidence soar. "Thanks," she said, shifting her weight, and moving her coat into one hand so she could put the other on her hip.

"I forgot the mall would be so nuts with Christmas shopping starting already. It took forever to find a parking spot."

"Yeah. Me, too." Heat rushed to her face with her lie.

"Since it's so crowded, what do you say we go to the Starbucks down the street? That one usually has booths and tables open around this time. We can jump in my car, it's a little cold for walking."

The Starbucks was close to her neighborhood. What if her mother went to the grocery store and then grabbed a latté and saw them? Nah. Her mother never did the grocery shopping anymore, Magda did it. But here's who did visit that Starbucks—Emma's friends. She would love them to see her with Damian.

"Sure," she said, in as natural and confident a manner as she could muster, already imagining how she would casually wave to any of the girls from school who might see her. How great would it be if a few girls from her field hockey team were there?

Emma headed toward the exit.

"Wait. This way." Damian gestured to the other end of the entry with one hand, the other hadn't left his pocket.

"Why? There's an exit over here."

He smiled. "Just come this way."

"Okay." She caught up to him, walking alongside him as he led her on a roundabout route through the garage.

"Sorry. Forgot where I parked." He laughed, occasionally looking up toward the corners of the parking structure as they weaved through and around dozens of cars.

Strange that he'd already forgotten when he only arrived minutes ago, but he must have been nervous, too. Emma barely gave it a thought, so concerned was she with her walk and her hair, worrying about looking old enough, and feeling grateful her orthodontist had taken her braces off a few months earlier than planned.

Chapter Four

Agent Victoria Heslin set her suitcase down and stroked each of her seven dogs in turn as they clamored for her attention. "Sorry, my darlings. We're not going for a hike today. I have to take a trip."

Ned leaned against the kitchen counter, smiling at her over a steaming cup of coffee. "Eddie's been moping since he saw your suitcase come out. He barely touched his breakfast."

"Poor Eddie." She rubbed the big greyhound's ears. "You can't come with me, baby. But I'll miss you."

"We'll miss you, too." Ned ran a hand through his tousled hair. Barefoot as always, he cut an athletic image in the morning light.

Victoria let out a heavy sigh and met his gaze.

Ned laughed. "They'll be fine. We have our routine down. I've got this."

"Thanks for doing this on such short notice. I owe you big time—again."

"It's my job." He grinned, tucking his hand into the pocket of his faded jeans. "But according to you, the list of favors you owe me is getting pretty long."

"Well... maybe we'll cash a few in when I get back. Deal?"

Ned pushed his way through the pack of wagging tails and placed his hands on her shoulders. He kissed her deeply. She opened her eyes and he stepped back, grasping her hands in his.

"Something else to look forward to." She glanced at her watch. "Darn. I'm going to miss my flight if I don't get going."

"Take care of yourself. Oh, and catch the bad guys."

"Will do." She smiled again before sliding her arms into her FBI jacket and walking out, trailed by the pack of dogs. "I'll call you later." She entered the garage and got into her black Suburban. Ned waved at her from the door, blocking the dogs' escape. Waving back, she pulled out of the garage and drove down the long driveway of her estate. The first rays of sunlight were just peeking over the horizon as she rolled through the large iron gate.

Time to call her boss and find out exactly what she was getting into.

"Listen, Victoria." Larry Murphy's firm voice gave no indication of the early morning hour. "This is official business—but it has a personal side. Kind of a favor."

"Happy to help, boss. Is this for your FBI counterpart in Charlotte?"

"Nope. Now and then I'll get a call from a friend. You know, when you're a SAC at the FBI, that's going to happen. This time, one of my wife's college sorority sisters asked for me to look into something. It's early in the process, might be nothing."

"But could be something."

"Exactly."

"Well, I'm just wrapping up paperwork from our last case. I'm—"

"The subject of the investigation is Emma Manning, a fourteen-year old girl. She disappeared from a Charlotte shopping mall last night. There's no strong evidence to suggest she's been abducted. But it would be good to have someone look at the whole situation immediately—someone who knows what they're doing. You know, in case she's not just a runaway. The Charlotte PD is on it already, as much as they can be at this point."

"Who's my contact?"

"Detective Martin Connelly. I'll send you his phone number. He'll be expecting you. Listen . . .it might be . . . it might be a trying situation."

"How so?"

"The girl's mother is begging for all the help they can get."

"That's expected. And the father?"

"Let's just say he might not be as receptive to detectives poking around in his business."

"Got it. Well, I understand firsthand the stress of a loved one going missing. How about I help the local PD find out what happened and see if I can assist the parents in handling the situation. Sound good?"

"Yes. I sent you a photo of the girl."

"I saw it." A professional photo of a teen with a pretty face, perfect teeth, and almost red hair with golden highlights. There were hints of adolescence in her dimpled cheeks but a stronger sense of blossoming maturity in her confident pose—one leg bent, one hand on her hip, head slightly tilted, playing it up to the camera.

"Sorry to send you during Carolina's Football Festival weekend. Might want to avoid the stadium area. I heard it's chaos."

"What's football festival weekend?"

"It's a first-time-ever thing. My wife calls it pigskin-fan frenzy weekend." Murphy laughed. "Two top-ranked college teams are playing on Saturday. After that, the Carolina Panthers play at home on Monday Night Football. There's a whole schedule of events surrounding it. ESPN's coverage has been wall to wall. Catch a game if you can and you can thank me for it later."

Not likely. "Thanks, boss. I'll give you an update once I have something to report."

"Safe travels, Victoria."

◆ ◆ ◆

As her plane landed, she double tapped her phone to close out of the mystery novel she was reading and noted the time. Less than an hour in the air from DC to Charlotte. At the terminal, she bought a sandwich in case her day got so busy she didn't have a chance to eat later.

The temperature in Charlotte was forty-five degrees, though it would warm up for the afternoon. She put on her jacket before leaving the airport. Following the signs for the rental car area across the street, she looked both ways and stepped into the crosswalk.

To her left, a white Maserati pulled out from behind a minivan and drove toward her with no signs of slowing.

Does he not see me?

She threw herself backwards as the driver slammed on his brakes and came to a screeching halt.

Shaken, and imagining how close he'd come to hitting her, she glared at the man behind the wheel, his eyes hidden behind sunglasses.

He waved, shaking his head and mouthing "sorry."

21

Once she had her rental car, she sent a message to let Detective Connelly know she was on her way to the Charlotte PD headquarters.

The Charlotte roads had no trace of litter. Medians with neatly trimmed grass and rows of perennial fall flowers were nearly everywhere. Scanning street signs so she wouldn't miss her turn, she passed out-of-state cars with football flags flying from painted windows. Uptown—that's what the woman at the rental car place told Victoria they called *downtown*—a few men and women wearing suits walked hurriedly on the sidewalks, but most of the crowd heading in and out of bars wore college team T-shirts and sweatshirts.

She drove through a network of skyscrapers and parked at police headquarters. After adjusting her ponytail, she walked inside, and stopped at the desk. "Hi. I'm here to meet Detective Martin Connelly."

The receptionist had the wrinkles of a long-time employee with a tired attitude to prove it. She held up one finger as she pressed a button on the console of blinking lights in front of her. "Charlotte police department. Hold please." Beside her, another officer worked the incoming barrage of calls.

Victoria turned and smiled at the person waiting next to her. She sent Ned a message to say hello and let him know she had arrived safely.

Several more phone lines were put on hold before the woman could address Victoria again. "Sorry for the wait . . . for?"

"Detective Martin Connelly."

The woman pressed a few buttons, and finally said, "He isn't here."

Victoria drew a deep breath, tapping her toe against the floor.

The phone rang again, and the woman at the front desk turned away.

"Agent Heslin?" asked a man who looked to be in his late thirties, walking toward her.

She caught a flash of black and silver as he slipped something into his pocket. Their eyes locked. There was something vaguely familiar about him, but she couldn't put her finger on it. His brown hair was thick with a bit of loose curl. His lively green eyes were quick to smile above dimpled cheeks in his round, boyish face. Under his dress shirt, his stomach was more round than flat.

"I'm Detective Marty Connelly, agent." He said *Mahhty,* like he was originally from the Boston area. The detective moved his unopened can of Coke from his right hand to his left, wiping his palm on his pants before extending his hand to greet her. "Glad you could come down to lend a hand. Hope you didn't have to wait long."

"No. Just got here." She stepped away from the busy front desk.

"Need anything to drink or . . . whatever?"

"I'm good."

"Well, if you're ready, we can go visit the girl's parents, and I'll fill you in on the way."

"I'm ready." She opened her arms. "Let's go."

He started walking and she fell in beside him.

"How was your flight from DC?" he asked, holding the door open for her.

"Fine." Victoria tilted her head. "You look familiar. Have you worked with the FBI recently?"

Connelly's smile grew. "Not with anyone from your neck of the woods."

"I thought I might have seen you before."

"I would have remembered you if we'd ever met before. I must have one of those faces. That's good for a cop, don't you think? Easily forgotten."

"I suppose it is." Victoria laughed as she lifted her hands behind her back to stretch. A light breeze caught her hair. A walk outside would have been nice rather than getting back into a car.

"Heard someone called in some favors to get you. You're a kidnapping expert?"

"I've had my share of experience."

"Hope it won't need to apply here, but just in case, it's nice to have you." He smiled as he led her toward the police cruisers and unmarked cars lined up behind the building.

"So, you're the primary assigned to this case?" She released her hands and extended her arms forward, still needing to get out the kinks from traveling.

"Yes. If it turns out to be a case." He smiled again. "It could end up being nothing more than a spoiled runaway situation."

"Right. Honestly, I hope so. It'd be the best thing for the family at this point."

"Exactly. So, how long you been with the Feds?"

"Eight years."

Martin let out a low whistle. "Eight fun years, huh?"

"I don't know if I'd call it fun, but I do love my job. Those eight years have gone by fast."

"This family has friends in high places." Connelly clicked the key fob for one of the unmarked sedans and stopped to open his door. "Guess that's why you're here."

Victoria opened the passenger side. "I hope I can help make a difference, once we figure out what we're dealing with. Fill me in."

"Well, first off, it hasn't even been twenty-four hours since Emma Manning disappeared." Connelly placed his soda in the center console and strapped on his seat belt as Victoria sat. "No leads yet."

"What are the chances she ran away?" Victoria asked, securing her own seat belt.

"The mother says zero, and she's got it pretty good at home, nothing to run away from, as far as I can see." Connelly started the car. "But the girl's not completely innocent. She told the woman that works for them she was meeting two of her friends. Those friends swear they never had plans and didn't have any idea who she might have been secretly meeting."

"Someone she didn't want her family or friends to know about."

"That's what I think." He looked behind him to back out of the tight spot.

"Who talked to the friends?"

"Me. That's what I spent most of the morning doing. I met with the parents late last night and then talked to Emma's closest friends this morning at her school, a very exclusive, private one."

Victoria studied the crowds as they drove through the city. "And you think they were being truthful?"

"I do. I put some pressure on them, wanted to be sure she wasn't bunking in someone's posh guest room. They didn't seem to be hiding anything. We can circle back to them if she doesn't come home. But right now, just can't waste too many resources without even knowing there's any foul play involved."

"I get the balancing act, but we need something in the first 24 hours."

"So that's why I've been up most of the night working this. One thing worth mentioning—the missing girl was featured in a newspaper article about a month ago."

"An article about what?"

"A trip she took to Jamaica, something sponsored by her school. You know the kind—touted as a volunteer opportunity, but really it's just a boondoggle for padding college applications."

"That's kind of cynical."

He grinned. "Just calling it like I see it."

"I'm sure they do some good there."

"Like bring a few sacks of their old clothes?" He laughed. "I saw the picture. One of the girls had a scuba mask in her hand."

"Did the article have Emma's photo in it?"

"Sure did. Big photo of her wearing a halter top thing. All of the girls' names were listed."

"Anyone might have seen her."

"Yep." At an uptown intersection, he smiled at the agent. "What do you like to do in Virginia?"

"Well, I've got seven dogs."

"Seven? On purpose?"

"Yep. We like to hike. My boyfriend and I do a lot of outdoor activities with the dogs."

Hearing herself say "boyfriend" out loud surprised her. She wasn't sure if Ned was her boyfriend. Probably not—or not yet anyway. But saying the actual word was strange—and nice. "What about a boyfriend for Emma? Did her friends know if there was anyone?"

"They say she doesn't have one. Hiking, huh? I don't know a lot about hiking in the area. We have a National White Water Center here. That place has some trails. And there's Crowder's Mountain with an amazing view at the top." He flipped back the top of his soda and took a few gulps. "Do you like to eat?"

"Doesn't everyone?"

"So, what kind of food do you like? Because over there— that's the best pizza in the city." He wagged his finger to the right and then swung his hand to the opposite side of the car. "And to the left, that place has the best burgers and milkshakes."

Victoria glanced at the restaurants. "What about Emma's cell phone?"

Connelly laughed. "Turned off. And the find my iPhone feature was disabled. The mother said that had been an ongoing issue, the daughter not leaving it on." He pointed again. "If you like wings—that's a good place there. Not the best, but really good—if you like 'em hot, that is. You like 'em hot?"

"Sure," Victoria responded, absent any enthusiasm. "Any history of running away?"

"Nope. That there is the best place for a draft brew, unless you prefer dark, then the best is a little brewery on the other side of town."

As they drove, Connelly continued pointing things out on every street, making Victoria wonder if she'd accidentally ordered a guided tour of the best casual dining places in the city and if it was too late to tell him she was a vegetarian. She devoted most of her attention to her phone and scanning through Emma Manning's social media pages.

"Over there, that's the mall Emma disappeared from."

Victoria studied the enormous building with protrusions in every direction. It was surrounded by other stores: Crate & Barrel, a fancy shoe store, a wine bar, upscale eateries, a modern hotel, and condos with tall glass windows and iron balconies.

"See that place? The Cowfish. They've got the best hamburgers. I recommend the Texas Longhorn."

She smiled. "A few miles ago, Shake Shack had the best hamburgers."

"Yeah. These are the other best hamburgers." He laughed. "Her neighborhood isn't far from here."

"Has anyone looked through the surveillance videos yet?"

"Yes. Already did it." He grinned. "I'm good, aren't I? Fast."

Victoria let out a small laugh. "The videos didn't show anything?"

"We know exactly when she was dropped off. We can trail her exact route, she wasn't there long—fifteen minutes, maybe. The surveillance cameras show her walking to the restroom alone, then to a lobby in the parking garage. She meets someone down there, but whoever it is never stepped into the view of a camera. They exchange a few words, maybe she's acting a little shy or nervous, but from our analysis of the body language, it appeared she liked and trusted whoever she was with. She starts walking, then, bam!" He snapped his fingers. "Just like that, she disappears. None of the other cameras in the parking garage picked her up."

An uneasy feeling rose in Victoria's gut. "Whoever she was with knew exactly how to avoid every camera in the garage."

"Yeah, I suppose it's possible. Or, it's just a coincidence."

"I'd like to walk the area, see how easy it would be to go undetected. I also want to see the videos. If we can't figure out what she's saying, at least I can get a feel for the body language myself."

"Sure. I'll send you the video after we meet with the parents. One of my guys made a clip of all the parts from yesterday with her on it."

Connelly slowed the car for a turn. "Here's the neighborhood. Might want to brace yourself to meet the parents. The father is a successful real estate developer. Lotsa money. They think they're all that. Think they hold all the power."

"No worries." Victoria smiled inside, realizing she'd just used one of Ned's phrases and also because "lotsa money" was a relative term. Martin apparently hadn't researched her and had no idea of her family background. Good. That's how she wanted it. Sometimes people treated her differently when they found out she was an heiress.

Connelly pulled the car up to a brick, one room gate house in front of the neighborhood. A sign in front of it read, "All guests and deliveries must stop here."

A guard stepped out to greet them. His hand hovered above a tablet. "Hello, Detective. Welcome back."

"Thank you. I'm with Agent Victoria Heslin, here all the way from our country's capital."

"I don't actually live in DC," Victoria said.

"Oh. My bad." Connelly held up his hand. "Anyway, here to see the Mannings again."

"I sure hope their daughter turns up soon." The guard tapped the stylus on the tablet before returning to the gate house. Connelly finished his drink while they waited for the tall black gates to slide open.

Chapter Five

The Mannings' house was a large, white, brick structure set deep within the quiet neighborhood. The house stretched from one end of the lot to the other, with Medieval-style spires atop multiple roof lines.

A three-tiered fountain sat in front of a pristine circular driveway, surrounded by a horseshoe-shaped arrangement of bushes and ornamental plants. Not a single weed marred the lush grass there or in any of the adjacent lawns. A Porsche Cayenne was parked under a *porte cochere*.

The doorbell was answered by a woman with black hair and olive skin, in her early sixties, holding a dust mop in one hand. She looked tired, with shadowy circles under her eyes, but her face lit up when she saw Connelly. "Detective! Glad you're back. Anything?"

"Not yet," Connelly said. "Agent Heslin, this is Magda Peres. Emma Manning's . . . nanny?"

"I used to be Emma's nanny." Magda tucked an errant strand of hair behind her ear. "Now I'm more of a house assistant."

Victoria shook Magda's hand. "Hoping I can be of some assistance."

"Thank you for coming." Magda's lined forehead conveyed her worry. She stepped back to open the door all the way. "Come in. Please."

The interior was open and spacious. Tall windows revealed a back yard that could have been a resort. An outdoor entertainment area with a tiki-style roof housed a huge curved television. Beyond a patio and pool stretched a large fenced yard, but no sign of pets. *No curious animals running to see who is at the front door. What a waste of an excellent yard.*

"Can I get you something to drink?" Magda asked, setting the mop aside. "Coffee? Flat or sparkling water? Sweet tea?"

"I'd love a glass of regular water." Victoria smiled. "Thank you."

"I'll take one, too." Connelly took off his coat and slung it over his arm. "Thanks."

Inside a living room with heavy cream-colored chairs, a well-dressed, slender woman stood up from a Chesterfield couch. Walking stiff and straight, she approached them with a frown.

"You're who Larry Murphy sent?" she asked, much to Victoria's surprise. In situations like this, Victoria was used to people being grateful for her presence.

"Yes. I'm Agent Victoria Heslin with the FBI."

The woman responded with a sigh. "I'm Patricia Manning." She waved her hand towards an adjoining room. A large diamond graced her finger. "And that's my husband, Tripp."

Through the arched doorway, a trim, handsome man with short dark hair, graying at the temples, paced in front of a large desk. He was in his early fifties, about the same age as his wife. He held a phone to his ear and stopped moving to stare at Victoria from head to toe in a way that made her uncomfortable. There was

31

no other sign of a welcome. An uneaten sandwich and large, red strawberries sat on a plate on his desk.

Patricia massaged her temples as she inspected the agent. "Do you have any experience with kidnappings?"

"I do. Experience and a string of successes, all of which resulted in safe return of the victim, and the kidnappers either apprehended or . . . deceased." She didn't share that her initial expertise in the area came from poring over the files of her own mother's kidnapping—what went wrong and if there had been any way it could have ended differently.

"There isn't any solid evidence that Emma has been kidnapped, but while we've got Agent Heslin here to help, I'll let her take the lead," Connelly said. "She'll see if there's anything else we could be doing to help get Emma back home."

Patricia narrowed her eyes at Magda as she set down a tray holding water glasses. "And I expect you've met our assistant. She's the one who dropped Emma at the mall yesterday without checking to make sure her friends were there."

Patricia's haughty attitude irked Victoria. Fear, stress, and lack of sleep could make any worried parent sound curt and aggressive, but something here was off.

Magda stood with her head bowed, wringing her hands. "She didn't send me a message to pick her up and didn't answer her phone, so I called the friends she was supposed to be with. They didn't know anything about meeting her at the mall."

"Did anything happen at home, recently?" Victoria asked. "An argument?"

"No." Patricia's voice was firm. Magda turned to look out the window.

"And there's been no communication of any sort?" Victoria picked up one of the water glasses and held it between her hands. "From your daughter or anyone else?"

"None. And I know what you're thinking." Patricia's voice rose with each word, her head moving side to side in short, angry movements. "But she wouldn't run away. She has varsity field hockey play-off games this week. There is no way she would miss those."

Victoria took a sip of water and set the glass back down. "I don't have enough information to decide what I think happened yet." She removed her tablet from her coat pocket to take notes and looked from Connelly to Patricia. "Did Emma have credit cards or ATM cards that have been used?"

Patricia leaned against the back of a chair, frowning at Victoria. "It would certainly help this whole situation if you could communicate with the detectives so we're not wasting time rehashing the same information. Time that could be spent searching for my daughter and whoever has her."

Victoria inhaled deeply, forgiving Patricia's behavior and again contributing it to a parent's shock and terror. "I understand, but bear with me, please. You may have to answer some of the same questions again. Even if I've already heard the answers second hand from the detectives. What makes you think someone has her?"

"I just said, she wouldn't run away."

No, but there are a lot of things in between running away and being abducted. Partying with friends, an unscheduled sleepover to push a few parental buttons.

Detective Connelly crossed his arms and turned to Victoria. "Emma has a few credit cards and a debit card. None of them have been used. We're monitoring them."

33

"Good. Thank you." Victoria thought through the information they had so far. "Have you contacted the media yet?"

The detective answered. "Not—"

"He hasn't." Tripp entered the room, head held high. "Because we asked him not to. Not yet."

"And why would that be?" Victoria asked, genuinely puzzled.

"Just in case she did run away, we don't need the whole city to—"

"She did not run away!" Patricia shouted, slapping her hand against the chair.

Scowling, Tripp walked to the picture window at the front of the house and stared out toward Connelly's car in the driveway. "Glad you brought an unmarked car. Nosy neighbors."

Wouldn't want the neighbors thinking you're in any trouble, would you?

He turned from the window. "Let's take this into the kitchen."

Inside the gleaming, white kitchen, he took a seat. The others sat down around him.

Victoria set her water down. "I suggest we get pictures of Emma broadcast on the local news as soon as possible."

Tripp frowned. "I'd prefer the whole city and whole country not—"

"I really don't care how you think it makes you look." Patricia's mouth twisted into an ugly expression.

"How it makes *me* look?" Tripp narrowed his eyes, staring at his wife. "*You're* her mother."

"I just want her found, and then we can figure out who is to blame."

Emotions could quickly run high and ruin an interview. Victoria had seen people at their worst. It was best to keep the Mannings focused and not venting at each other. "We'll need some recent pictures of Emma," she said, setting her business card down on the table. "Specifically, if you have ones where she is wearing whatever coat or shirt she might have been wearing when she went to the mall."

"I know what she was wearing," Magda said. "I'll try to find some photos."

"Thank you." Victoria now had an inkling that any questions about Emma might be better answered by Magda, but asking a parent first was the respectful thing to do. She turned to Patricia. "Detective Connelly said you weren't able to locate her laptop when he was here this morning. Have you had any luck finding it since?"

Patricia shook her head. "It's not here. She must have taken it with her."

"That's unfortunate," Victoria said. Their best source of information was missing with Emma. If she'd been kidnapped, there was a good chance that someone—a sexual predator most likely—had been communicating with her online. "Who is your email provider?"

"Spectrum Cable," Tripp answered. "Emma had a Gmail account and an email for school."

"Write those addresses down for us, please," Victoria said. "And before we leave, I want to set up traces on your cell phones, in case you get a ransom call. Make sure you answer any calls that come in, known or unknown."

"We're already doing that," Tripp snapped. "We're not incompetent idiots."

Victoria kept her response to herself, but stole a quick glance at Connelly, who was barely masking his displeasure. It was going to be a long evening.

"Good." Victoria took a sip of her water and set it back down on the tray. "We need to be prepared in case a ransom call does come and they expect a quick turn over. If they just want your money, we should know very soon."

"We know," Patricia replied, her voice cool. "And we'll be prepared to pay them whatever they ask."

"If your daughter was abducted, her kidnapper is probably known to her. That is usually the case." Victoria chose her words carefully. "So, we'll need a list of your contacts, particularly anyone you might have conflicts with."

"A list of all your enemies." Patricia sneered at her husband. "That's going to take quite some time."

Victoria faced Patricia. "And yours as well."

Patricia threw her head back and laughed.

Victoria pretended not to notice. Stress like Emma's family was experiencing could make people act strangely. "Is there anything in your life we should know about now? Gambling debts, problems with the law, drugs, enemies, affairs. Tell us now so we don't have to waste time digging it up on our own."

"You see, Patricia." Tripp's voice grew deeper. "Do you really want our lives turned upside down, without even knowing if she might just be off with new friends somewhere? I told you, the private investigator will be able to do more for us than the police. That's all we need right now. You didn't have to start calling in the brigades."

He reached for her arm. She pulled away from him, standing up to pace in a corner of the room. Her husband watched her, looking just as angry, rubbing the back of his neck.

There was something going on with this couple's marriage, but Victoria had yet to determine if it had anything to do with their daughter's disappearance. Their cooperation was critical. "May I remind you that lying or withholding information from a federal agent is a federal crime."

Patricia stopped pacing. "I don't see how our personal lives are relevant to you doing your job. She could be tied up in the back of some sociopath's trunk right now, and all you're doing is—"

Connelly put his hands out. "We're working on finding your daughter. And I did suggest to you this morning that you also hire a PI. It can't hurt."

"If it turns out your daughter's life *is* on the line," Victoria said, "we need to know everything that might pertain to her situation. Any persons who might have a reason to hurt your family, we need to know who they are."

Patricia huffed. "My husband has a little problem he can't seem to get under control."

Tripp shouted. "You want to subject us to all this?"

"Whatever it is—sir, ma'am—" Victoria looked each in the eye in turn as she spoke. "—we can find out about it on our own, but it will be far better for your daughter if you tell us."

Patricia aimed her steely gaze at her husband. "You tell them." She straightened her spine and lifted her chin, storming from the kitchen.

Tripp ran his hand through his hair, looking angry and uncomfortable as his wife stomped away.

"Mr. Manning, what is it you need to tell us?" Connelly's voice was soft and encouraging.

Tripp glared at the detective and agent in turn, as if fine-tuning his hostility gave him the upper hand.

Victoria pressed her fingernails into her palms. *Remember, you're here to get his daughter back.*

Tripp looked off to the side, addressing the vent above the stainless cooktop. "She's talking about extra-marital affairs. And there might have been a few mistakes along the way."

"What do you mean by mistakes?" Connelly asked.

"A few women claimed I fathered their children."

Victoria cringed at his callous use of the word mistake. *If that's how he referenced his biological offspring, how did he feel about Emma?*

"As you can imagine, Patricia didn't appreciate the betrayals. They've caused quite a strain on our relationship."

Really? No surprise there, buddy.

"Nor does she appreciate the ongoing cost of paying child support."

So, they were more than just claims. If I had to say one positive thing about this man, at least he's paying child support.

"Sir, I appreciate the difficulty this causes you." Connelly removed a pen and a small pad from his pocket. "I want you to know, we'll be discreet and do our best not to cause you and your family any embarrassment. Now, if you would, I'll need their names."

♦ ♦ ♦

After Connelly checked the monitoring equipment on the Mannings' home and cell phones, he and Victoria headed uptown to retrieve her rental.

The iron gate opened as they exited the neighborhood. She hadn't noticed it on the way in, but it slid open like the one at the end of her own driveway.

Has Ned already fed the dogs dinner? Of course he has. He fed them at six like always. Wonder which ones he took on his run.

"We've done a lot of work," Connelly said. "Considering."

"Considering what?"

"Considering we don't know if there was any foul play involved. A lot of work for a kid who may be sleeping off a late night-party session with a new boyfriend that mom and dad don't know about. I've seen it before."

Victoria gave no sign of having heard him. She held her hands tightly together on her lap. When her mother was kidnapped, a detective initially suggested Abigail Heslin might be out for a walk somewhere. As if her mother would ever leave their dogs alone with no one to check on them for an entire day. Then the insinuations abounded. Victoria wasn't supposed to hear them, but she did. Her mother had left due to an affair with her physician, or her dogs' trainer—the list went on. All preposterous suggestions without a grain of truth to them, but fodder the media pounced on—until the ransom call finally came through.

However, as much as she didn't want to admit it, Connelly had a point. If the Mannings didn't have friends in high places, would Victoria or anyone else be here helping? *Is it even necessary for me to be here?* With no evidence of a forced abduction and Emma missing barely 24 hours, the wheels were well in motion to find her. In that respect, Emma was a lucky girl.

"You've done a good job covering all the bases."

"Thanks," Connelly said, lowering his window. "Glad I was able to get a good start because as soon as something else comes up, I'm gonna get pulled. You know how it is. We're short staffed, overworked, and underpaid. What else is new? I'm glad you're here for now. So, what would you bet if you had to?"

"Bet on what?"

"Did she get kidnapped or did she run away?" Connelly stretched out his arm and pointed. "See that place on the right? That's Roosters. Best coconut cake in the world."

Victoria looked at the restaurant. Coconut cake sounded amazing for some reason. "I'm not a betting woman."

"Way I see it—" Connelly alternated looking at the road ahead and back at Victoria, "—we've got three possibilities."

"Let's hear them."

"If she *were* kidnapped, one, it could be a random crazy person. Two, it could be for money. Or, three, it could be to hurt her father, or the family. But if I had to bet—because I've been known to make a friendly bet or two—based on what I've seen of the family—I'd say someone wants to hurt them."

"It's also possible she was tricked or lured into something by a secret boyfriend."

"To be sexually exploited or something? Nah. There are sex trafficking rings in North Carolina, don't get me wrong, but they target runaways, kids in the foster care system. Doesn't happen to girls like her—too risky to take her. And, you know—no reason to run away. She's got everything."

"Kids don't run away from homes because they're poor, they run away because they need to escape something. Rich kids can need to escape, too. We don't know what her home life is like yet. We don't know about her self-esteem or her self-image, or her relationship with her parents." *Although I think Murphy would have mentioned something if the family was unusually dysfunctional. Assuming he knew.*

Connelly stopped at a light and rubbed his neck. "Right. Maybe no one took her. Maybe she just had enough of those parents and nanny breathing down her neck."

"Magda seems nice enough," Victoria said. "The father didn't want any publicity, which is strange. Usually parents want any help they can get, regardless of how it makes them look."

"Right." Connelly grinned, strumming one hand over the steering wheel as they waited for the light to turn green. "Wonder what else Tripp Manning's background search will turn up."

"Let me see what our intelligence analysts can do to help get us ahead of this. I'm pretty sure one of them can lend me a hand."

"That sounds good. I'll work the email server angle for as long as I can. We have a guy who's a pro with that. And I can get one or two people to help with the tip line once it's set up. I'll follow up on any legit leads."

Victoria hoped their research wouldn't be necessary, and Emma would come home on her own before the end of the night.

Chapter Six

Emma's neck jerked to the side and she woke to blackness. Her eyes were open but she couldn't see anything, not even shadows, only a uniform darkness. A heavy fog clouded her brain, like she'd been sleeping for days. Her mounting terror forced her alert.

A piece of cloth pulled tightly around her head and brushed her eyelashes. *I'm blindfolded!*

She tried to scream, but only a muffled grunt escaped her covered mouth. Her hands were held together by metal cuffs. She felt a firm, rigid pressure digging into her skin. Pinching, squeezing, under her knees and back and against her sides—flesh, muscle, and bone.

Someone is carrying me!

Her body jolted with each step.

She heard the soft thud and click of a car door closing, the stranger's scuffing footsteps, and her own frantic breathing through her nose. The man smelled like cigarettes and cologne. She struggled and her dangling legs hit and dragged against something, scraping her skin through her pants.

Arms like steel gripped her harder. "Stop moving, girl."

The man's tone was deep, with a heavy accent. His words were sharp. 'Stop' was more like stup. 'Moving' was said with a K at the end, like movink. She studied French at school and had visited Germany, Italy, and Japan, but whatever his native language, it didn't have a familiar ring to it. She only knew it sounded harsh and European. Like German, but not quite.

She tried to squirm out of his arms. He squeezed her tight, clamping her against his chest. She moaned and was sure he was close to crushing her ribs. Tears soaked her blindfold and streamed out from underneath.

He stopped walking and let go of her shoulder. Metal clanked against metal. A dragging scrape, and then they were inside, the air much warmer. He moved forward again in giant steps, jostling her around like a sack of potatoes as he lurched downward. With no warning, he released his grasp, dropping her onto a hard floor.

Squeezing her arm with a big, meaty hand as she scrambled to her feet, the man yanked her blindfold off. She blinked under the flickering tubes of fluorescent light. He was bigger and scarier than she had imagined, built like a grizzly bear with a buzz cut and the square jaw of a professional fighter. Afraid to take her eyes off him, but needing to see where they were, she quickly took in the large, mostly empty space. Cinderblock walls with no windows. Exposed pipes, ducts, and wires crisscrossed the ceiling. The odor of dust and mildew permeated the air—the way her mountain home smelled when no one had used it in months, except much worse.

Her heart was racing and goosebumps covered her body. *How did I get here? What happened to Damian?*

With a grunt, her kidnapper grabbed her hands and removed the cuffs. Emma stepped away from him, and this time, he let her. She yanked away strips of tape, pulled tangled strands of hair from her mouth, and screamed, "Help me! Help me!" as long and loud as she could.

No one came. The absurdly strong man only stared at her and laughed, intensifying her fear.

She searched for an escape. *Did he kill Damian? Is he going to kill me?*

The man lit a cigarette, caught up to Emma with a few long strides, and pushed her toward one wall. She hurried forward to avoid his touch. Her head ached and her stomach was queasy, like she'd just stumbled off a roller coaster. She stroked her wrists, sore and tender from where cuffs had pinched the skin and rubbed the bone.

"Stop." He tossed a bundle of something at her chest. It fell onto the stained floor.

"Put those on."

She grimaced at the clothes. A navy, green, and white plaid skirt with a white collared shirt, similar to the uniforms she'd seen catholic elementary school girls wearing at the school near her house.

She shuddered and wrapped her arms around her body. *I'm not taking off my clothes. I can't. I can't.* She looked around for anything that might give her an answer as to what she should do. "Where's my bag?" Unless she was playing field hockey, she was never more than a few feet away from her phone. She needed it now more than ever.

The man grabbed Emma's arm and yanked it back so hard it took her breath away. Before she could let out a scream, he slapped her on the side of her face. Emma gasped and staggered backward. In her entire fourteen years of life, no one had ever struck her like that. She'd been knocked around in games, but this

44

was so different. Overwhelmed with fear, shock, and humiliation, she burst into uncontrollable tears.

The man pointed to the clothes and growled. "Put them on."

With her hand shielding her burning cheek, she stooped to pick up the clothes. "Where do I—"

"Shut up! Put on the clothes!" His gruff, uncaring voice jarred her already heightened senses. He took a drag of his cigarette and stared with a callous, indifferent gaze.

She turned her back and crouched down to change, hiding her body by folding it smaller.

He jerked her around to face him. "Right here. Hurry up."

Shivering, she peeled off her pants and slid the skirt up over her hips. It barely covered her butt. She could feel the man watching her as she removed her blouse and pulled on the tight shirt. She wiped at her tears and her finger came away covered in runny eye makeup.

Will my parents be able to find me? Do they even know I've been taken? Nightmare scenarios raced through her mind—rape, torture, being left to die. Fear hollowed her stomach and trembled violently inside her chest. She bent forward to hug her torso and cover her abdomen.

Across the room, the door clanged open. A man with a confident gait walked down the stairs and approached them. He had slightly hollowed cheeks and sunken eyes. His clothing, a silver-gray suit above expensive leather shoes, made the most of his trim frame. He dressed like he could be one of her father's business associates.

Thank God! Someone to help me!

"I've been kidnapped," Emma cried, rushing toward him. "Help me!" She'd only gone a few steps when her kidnapper grabbed her arm and jerked her back.

The man in the suit threw his hands up in an exaggerated fashion. "What? Kidnapped? Are you sure?" He lowered his hands and smirked.

Emma's heart sunk. Fresh tears streamed.

He turned to her captor. "What did you do with Sasha?" He and the muscle-bound brute shared the same accent, but his voice was smoother, more sophisticated.

"I left her in Virginia. In the woods." Her kidnapper was taller and heavier, but the way he dipped his head and waited for a response showed the newcomer was in charge.

"Virginia?" He glared at the big man. "Why?"

"Had to go there for something. Thought it would be a good place."

"It might be as good a place as any." The older man cocked his head in a crazy, leering way reminding Emma of an evil Willy Wonka. "Or it might not. Let's hope it was." In frightening silence, he continued to stare. Then he turned to Emma, looking her over with a deep frown. Her throat constricted with fear. He moved closer until he stood only inches away. His dark, gleaming eyes held no hint of compassion. "What have we here? This one looks well cared for, yes?"

"She does."

"She reminds me of someone, but I'm not sure who." The older man cupped his hand around her chin and turned her head from side to side.

Emma cringed and pulled way.

He grabbed her hair and yanked her head back, sending sharp pain from her scalp down to her toes. "Looks like someone needs to learn how to behave. I'll touch you whenever and wherever I want to touch you."

Emma gasped.

"Let me go," she cried. "Please let me go!"

He kept on pulling. The pain was blinding. Either her hair would rip out or her neck would snap. Just when she thought she would pass out, he stopped pulling and ran his fingers through her hair.

"Why are you doing this?" Emma cried.

He stared at her. "Because this is what I do."

"Just call my dad," she pleaded. "He'll pay you whatever you want to get me back safe."

"Will he now? You're sure about that? I don't think so, little girl." His smirk returned, creepier than his scowl.

"He will. My parents are rich and will do anything to get me back. I promise."

Anger flashed in the older man's eyes. "Where did she come from?"

The hulking man shrugged. "Ask Damian."

The man in charge pointed at Emma. "You work for me now and you can call me Stephen. You do what I say, when I say it. That means, I say it, you do it." He enunciated the last sentence slowly. "I say it, you do it. I say it, you do it." He spoke quickly, jumbling the words together and Emma was certain the man was insane. "Simple enough, right? But . . . but, I know you're wondering now—how could you not? You're wondering what happens if I say it and you don't do it?" He smiled. "What happens then? Answer me."

47

She stared back at him, her teeth chattering from fear. "Answer me!"

Emma cringed. "I—I don't know," she said, her voice breaking.

His smile disappeared. "And I assure you, my dear, you do not want to find out." He stepped away from her. "Does she, Svet?"

"No," Svet grunted.

"She's not quite party girl material, but not submissive enough to be a motel girl. Not yet. We can change that. Clean up her face and take pictures. I'll put them on the website. But we're not going to sell her to anyone yet, understood?"

"Yeah."

"Then give her a little taste of what happens if she won't cooperate. We don't want her tiring out her little brain and up all night just wondering and wondering." He stared at Emma again, scowling, then turned to Svet. "If she can't behave, I don't have to tell you what to do, do I?"

"If she's a mistake, I'll handle it. Also, I dropped her phone and laptop in a dumpster."

"Good. I'm going to hot yoga. Take care of her." Stephen broke into a song. Emma recognized the tune, but some of the words were different and horrifying. "Welcome to my house. You don't get to go out." Singing, he spun around and walked away.

Emma's mouth quivered.

Svet squeezed Emma's arm and pulled her forward.

"Please let me go. Please. Just call my dad, he'll give you whatever you want."

He dragged Emma toward another door. He shoved her inside the room and pushed her down on a mattress. "Have you ever been with a man before?" His tone was low and raspy, menacing, as he unbuckled his belt.

"Wh—what?" Her voice broke, her lips trembling along with her chattering teeth. She struggled with all her might to free herself from his grip. But she had no chance.

From the top of the stairs, Stephen belted out a song like a malevolent lunatic in an insane asylum. "Sometimes your world changes, right before your eyes! You never really know what's gonna happen!"

◆ ◆ ◆

Sofia turned the page in her book, trying to stay focused on the fictional lives it contained inside. In the windowless basement, there was rarely any indication that the outside world existed. No mingling of voices, no whoosh of passing trucks or honking of cars, just the occasional hum and rattle of the exposed pipes. Until now.

Someone's high-pitched screaming and begging filtered through the adjacent wall.

A new girl. Lungs like a wailing siren. Definitely American.

The American girls had a harder time accepting their miserable fate. And they always paid for it. Sofia daydreamed about being brave, talking back to Stephen, refusing Svet's commands—but bravery resulted in beatings or worse. She wanted to be alive when the tables turned.

Keep watch. Be alert. No one knows the exact day or the hour.

One of her grandpa's favorite expressions about how Christ could damn them all to an eternity of agony or free them to the wonders of heaven at any moment. Repeating the saying was his way of reminding his grandchildren to behave, to stop doing

49

whatever they were doing to aggravate him. Believing Christ might return to earth at any moment gave her something to look forward to. Everyone who had hurt her would tumble straight into the burning, stinking pits of hell. She didn't know when it would be, but it had to happen. Some people deserved their punishments sooner rather than later.

Ragged, breathless shouts of "no," "please," and "stop," traveled through the walls—the new girl still begging and pleading between wrenching sobs. *If the new girl thinks Svet is rough, she has no idea what's coming.*

Turning over on her cot, Sofia grabbed her iPod, stuffed her earbuds into her ears, and turned up her music. A few feet away, Anastasia slept on her side with a pillow covering her head. Mercifully, it was getting harder for Sofia to remember the vivid details of her first days. Her memories were numbing. She'd only been thirteen.

Stephen was charming. Ms. Bois—that wasn't her real name and she forbid them to call her anything else—was stylish and beautiful. Together, the evil duo tricked everyone. They seemed legit as they recruited girls to audition for their modeling agency, sharing photos and runway videos of their current models. They promised sums of money almost unimaginable for Sofia's family, and a glamorous life in America. Sofia was already feverishly hooked even before Stephen explained—in an oh-so-caring voice—the sorts of things she could buy once she started earning money. Washing machines, clothes dryers, microwaves, things that would drastically change her family's home life.

Like she was sharing special secrets, Ms. Bois whispered about facials and massages, celebrity-like benefits that would further enhance their incredible beauty. They were to be pampered like movie stars. Truly, it was Ms. Bois who had missed her calling. She should have been an actress in the movies. She was the master of effortless lies, the greatest pretender of all time, the ultimate ice queen incapable of compassion. She was meaner than Satan. Thank God they rarely saw her anymore.

And Stephen—he had to be insane. Not sound of mind—as her grandfather used to say about the crazy lady who lived alone across the street and occasionally ran outside in her pajamas, yelling random things—*where are all the birds, who took the birds?*—and shaking her fists at the sky. But unlike the old crazy lady, Stephen could fool anyone when he wanted.

The days before Sofia arrived in the United States were the most exciting days of her young life, full of eagerness and anticipation. All because she had no idea what was in store.

"You're going to love it there," Ms. Bois cooed before they left Ukraine.

Now, Sofia laughed aloud at the naïve, wide-eyed girl who arrived in the land of opportunities with five other girls, including Sasha and Anastasia, each of them believing they were the luckiest people in the world.

At the airport, their dreams quickly shattered. Petar and Svet herded the girls into a van like animals bound for the slaughterhouse. They delivered them to a dingy, underground room.

Stephen had burst into song, making the crazy lady from across the street seem quite sane in comparison. "Ukraine seems like a dream to you now!" He grinned as he sang, scaring the girls out of their wits.

"Bringing you here cost us a lot of money," Ms. Bois said, her voice harsh and unrecognizable, acting like everything that had transpired had been the girls' idea. "You must pay us back first, before you earn any money of your own."

There was never another mention of modeling.

Another shriek penetrated the walls, barely perceptible above her music.

Sofia cried so much those first weeks, through assault after assault until every bit of her body ached from the abuse and she couldn't believe there was a tear left untapped. The threats never ceased, but for three long years she endured and survived. And in all that time, she had yet to see anyone earn their freedom. She'd seen two murders—one girl strangled, one shot in the heart—to teach the others a lesson. Some just disappeared, like Sasha. But none of them were saved, as far as she knew.

No one knows the exact day or hour. Nothing lasts forever.

Sofia cooperated to stay alive. Compliant on the outside, tough and growing harder on the inside.

With a half-hearted shrug, she picked up a magazine and thumbed through it. She stopped at an advertisement. A beautiful woman pressing her forehead against her palm, eyes closed, her face a miserable grimace. The caption read: *Do you suffer from migraines? Get the help and relief you need.*

Sofia carefully tore into the paper, cutting around the word *help.*

She dropped the scrap onto the floor under the cot.

Her own little trail of crumbs.

Would the new girl's mother know something bad happened to her?

Sofia's exhausted, hard-working mother never knew. "I'm going to make you proud," Sofia had said, taking in the worry, but also the hope in her mother's eyes during their final farewell.

I still will. Once this all ends.

Tentatively, she pulled one earplug away from her ear.

The new girl's voice had grown raspy and weak, but she still sobbed and yelled out for help that would never come.

God, she's a feisty one. She still doesn't get that her whole life has changed. Maybe it's hard for her to believe, but the sooner she figures it out and toughens up, the better off she'll be.

Svet might pull out a back tooth, cut off part of a toe. He knew little things that wouldn't show but hurt like bloody hell. After he'd run out of tricks, if the new girl still wouldn't cooperate, or if she wasn't very pretty, she'd be drugged with meth or heroin and used up in the dark behind a motel room door that opened and closed with a never-ending stream of customers. That would be her miserable existence until she died of sickness or overdose. That's how it worked. The motel girls never lasted very long. Thank God she wasn't one of them.

Yet if she hadn't been so beautiful, she'd be home with her family right now, complaining with her brothers about their cramped cottage and too many chores, but happier than she'd ever realized.

For a long time, over a year, it had been just the three of them—her, Anastasia, and Sasha—moving place to place, never more than a week in the same location, enduring shameful and perverted horrors behind closed bedroom doors. But now it was only her and Anastasia. Perhaps the American was meant to replace Sasha.

Where are you, Sasha?

Sofia squeezed her eyes shut as she heard confused pleas and a final blood-curdling scream.

The branding.

Yep, the new girl was here to stay.

Chapter Seven

Resting on her cot, Sofia finally set her book aside and edged forward to study the newest arrival. She squinted to take in the details she craved. Her eyesight wasn't so great anymore. She needed glasses, but that wasn't going to happen. Stephen said it was her fault for reading so much.

She inhaled a light scent, something floral with vanilla mixed in, barely detectable over the odor of freshly burnt flesh and sweat. Long, straight, smooth hair hung in sections over the new girl's back and shoulder. It was tangled, but clean and voluminous, as they said in the magazine ads. Beautiful highlighted streaks of gold blended with light reds and light browns. Sofia resisted the urge to reach out and stroke it.

The girl had been lying face down on Sasha's cot for fifteen minutes, ever since Svet called her a whore, shoved her into the room, and locked them in again. Her shoulders lifted and dropped with great, gulping sobs. Her legs were tan and muscular. She must have run track or maybe played tennis. At least she spoke English fluently and would always know what the people around her were saying. That would make a difference for her. Although . . . sometimes it was best not knowing what was about to take place. Everything that happened was bad, but the less time spent worrying about specifics, the better.

The new girl finally lifted her head and looked around. Her face was a puffy, splotched mess. A dribble of blood ran from one corner of her mouth. She blinked, staring at Sofia, the still-sleeping Anastasia, then back to Sofia. She reached toward the back of her neck but didn't touch it. "Where am I?"

So many questions. Sofia set her book aside and shrugged. "It's not the Ritz-Carlton. What's your name?"

"I'm Emma Manning, and I want to go home right now. Can you help me?

"No. You were taken, as we all were."

"We can't get out?"

"Obviously not, or we wouldn't be here." *How stupid is this girl?*

Emma's eyes floated down to Sofia's book. *Fifty Shades of Gray.* Svet had given it to her. He thought he was being funny because it was about sexual fetishes. Sofia enjoyed reading. Her grandpa gave her books whenever he could. Now, with nothing else to do during the day besides ballet videos, she read anything she could get her hands on. Every page, sentence, and word, even the tiny print on the bottom of magazine ads.

Sofia crossed her arms. "The book before this one was *The Count of Monte Cristo.*" *About someone else with real problems*

Emma sniffed and wiped her nose with her hand.

The American was pretty, but not beautiful. A smattering of freckles covered her face. She hadn't been tricked into modeling, unless she was very gullible with an inflated opinion of her looks. But she didn't look strung out or neglected either. If she wasn't special enough to be a party girl, what was she supposed to be? *"How did *you* end up here?"* Sofia asked.

55

"I don't know." Emma sat up all the way, rubbing her eyes. "I met someone named Damian online. Then we finally met in person at the mall. He gave me a drink and—" She coughed and choked around a sob before she could continue. "—now I'm here."

"Ahh. Damian." Sofia smiled, glad to know he was still around. She hadn't seen him since they arrived back in Charlotte.

"Why did he do this to me?"

Anastasia sat up, arched her back, and reached her arms toward the ceiling. "Money, sex, power. Reason everyone do bad things."

"Excuse her English." Sofia rolled her eyes toward the grimy pipes on the ceiling. She had no idea why Anastasia hadn't learned to speak as well as she had. They'd both had some English previously in school. Maybe it was because Anastasia spent most of her days sleeping. That was how she coped. "Damian gets paid to bring you here. But he can't quit, either. It's not his fault. Damian is one of the nice ones." He brought them smoothies and chocolate, magazines that were left behind at his gym, and the books that had helped Sofia with her English and made the passage of time in hidden locations bearable. He'd taken them to the movies and shopping for new clothes and makeup several times. He'd never once hurt them. One of his hands was useless and mangled—almost always tucked into a pocket—and somehow it made him seem more like them. Beautiful at first glance but hiding a secret.

Emma closed her eyes and scrunched her face together. "That man—"

"That was Svet," Sofia said.

"He—he took pictures of me after... after he—" her voice broke as she sobbed.

56

"We know what he did." Anastasia's voice was a gentle whisper. "Don't think about or you turn crazy."

"He told me if I didn't do everything he said, he would post them on the internet for everyone to see."

Sofia shrugged. "He might. We don't know everything he does."

"I can't believe this is happening," Emma cried. "It's like a horrible, horrible bad dream."

"It's nightmare." Anastasia stretched her slender arms out wide. "But much real. You see small cut anywhere? Like wrists?"

"Huh?" Emma asked.

Anastasia approached Emma. She grasped her arm and examined it closely from wrist to her shoulder.

"What are you looking for?" Emma asked.

Anastasia studied Emma's other arm in the same manner. "While you is drugged . . . they say they put in chip. But not sure if true. We don't see."

"I don't understand," Emma said.

"A microchip for tracking." Sofia raised her voice until she was almost yelling, as if that would help Emma understand. "So they'll always know where to find you."

Emma looked around the room like a rat trapped in a small cage, her eyes roaming from corner to corner, floor to ceiling.

No way to scratch your way out of here.

"Where are you from?" Emma wiped tears across her cheek. "Your accent?"

"Ukraine," Anastasia answered. "Us both is from Ukraine." She ran her fingers through her hair and pulled it on top of her head with an elastic band.

Emma winced as she stood up.

"You'll get used to it," Sofia said. "That stinging pain between your legs. It won't hurt so much. Eventually." Which was sort of a lie because there were plenty of things to come that would hurt much worse. Some people got off on feeling pain, while others perversely enjoyed dishing it out. Even after years of working for Stephen, she couldn't rule out the possibility of unpleasant surprises.

Emma limped to the door and pulled on the handle. It didn't budge.

"It's always locked," Sofia said

Emma was crying again. She rested her back against the door. "How long have you been here?"

Neither Sofia or Anastasia answered. Sometimes it was better to let the bad news sink in gradually, a little at a time.

Emma scanned the room again. "What if we have to go to the bathroom?"

"It's not always like this." Sofia heard the apologetic tone in her voice as the indignity of their current location hit her. They'd left the basement and returned many times in the past few months, never staying more than a few days, thank goodness. It *was* one of the worst locations. "There's a bathroom with a shower on the other side of this basement. You can knock and ask to use it. If no one is out there and you can't wait, there's a bucket in the corner."

"What?" Emma's eyes grew wide and her mouth dropped open. She stood there, face frozen in horror. After all that had happened to her, all she'd just recently experienced—kidnapping, rape, beatings, having her virginity stolen—Sofia didn't know for sure that Emma had been a virgin, but it seemed likely —after all that, the girl appeared most shocked about having to relieve herself in a bucket.

58

"You too good for that?" Sofia glared, which also helped bring Emma's face into focus. "Then I hope you can hold it a very long time." She flipped her book back over and struggled to make sense of the words. She hadn't intended to be so uncompassionate. The new girl was scared, and it wasn't her fault that she was now, presumably, Sasha's replacement. It was extremely unlikely that she'd gone and raised her hand and knowingly volunteered to become a sex slave. Yet Sofia couldn't seem to stop the stream of critical, unkind thoughts from swirling through her mind and slipping off her tongue.

She returned her attention to her book and read the same paragraph four times. The words were temporarily meaningless and unconnected. When her anger eventually dissipated, she was able to concentrate again. Only when she was immersed in a book was she able to completely forget about her circumstances. At the sound of trudging footsteps, she looked up and saw Emma stumbling toward the bucket. Emma covered her nose and mouth with her hand and spun around, managed a few steps back, and doubled over, retching.

"No!" shouted Anastasia.

Emma vomited on the floor.

Sofia rolled her eyes. "Great. Just effing great. Just what we needed in here. So glad you could join us."

Chapter Eight

Victoria checked into the Hampton Inn, not far from the mall where Emma was last seen. The lobby had a complimentary candy bar, and she couldn't resist filling a small bag with some of her favorites.

The hotel clerk handed over a key card. "You're lucky we had a cancellation for this suite. We've been fully booked for weeks."

"I believe it. I had to travel last minute. Finding a room was a challenge. Glad something became available."

"A lot of people are visiting Charlotte right now for the football games and events." She smiled. "Don't go uptown unless you have to."

"Yes. I've heard." Victoria smiled back.

Inside her suite, she kicked off her shoes and stretched out on top of the bed. She chewed on a piece of red licorice, rubbed her eyes, and groaned.

The Mannings are a challenge.

Although she loved all aspects of her job—profiling, investigating, analyzing, apprehending criminals, and helping make sure the worst of them never walked free again—she was relieved to have some time alone. Of course, alone had always been best when it included her dogs, and now—Ned. She missed all of them. She checked the time, wanting to give Ned a call to see how he was doing, but she still had some work to finish.

She got up to adjust the heat and a whoosh of warm air pushed through the vents. Thinking about what had been done so far, and what else could be done to help bring Emma Manning home, she set her laptop on the writing desk in the living room and logged on. She had two emails from Magda. The first contained the nanny's account of Emma's activities from the last week. The second consisted of photos. She'd also included a link to the recent newspaper article featuring Emma and a few other girls from her school on their trip to Jamaica.

Victoria looked everything over and then typed a note to Sam Miller, one of the intelligence analysts in her office, and one of her favorite colleagues.

Emma Manning, age 14, disappeared yesterday afternoon around 5:30 pm from a mall in Charlotte, NC. Can you find any useful information using her images?

If anyone could work magic, it was Sam. He'd been a big help on her last case, never failing to provide the agents with information to move their investigation forward. He was always in a good mood, never flustered. In that way, Detective Connelly and the intelligence analyst seemed to have some similar traits.

After she hit send with Emma's photos attached, Victoria opened an email from Connelly with the surveillance video. She watched Emma walk through the mall, studying the girl's body language, building her understanding of the young teen. She tried to read her lips in the lobby of the underground garage. She caught a few words, but nothing to indicate who she was with or where they were going. Mostly Emma smiled, giggled, looked self-conscious—all normal behaviors for a fourteen-year old girl. Perhaps another round of questioning Emma's friends might turn up a lead. Someone might remember her mentioning a new friend from another school, or a new crush.

That was all Victoria could do for now. The Mannings were preparing to liquidate assets in the event they received a ransom demand. With the parents' permission, Connelly and his crew were going to access the family's emails, which would hopefully reveal a treasure trove of information.

It was a good head start. She hoped it would be enough.

Victoria stripped and stepped into a hot shower. She scrubbed her face and let the hot water cascade over her shoulders, washing away the long day of traveling, and the lingering unpleasant feelings that came from spending time with the girl's parents. She didn't like them. It felt good to admit that to herself, but she wanted to help Emma just the same.

After her shower, she dressed and returned to her laptop, pulling up the live video feeds coming from her home's security system. She switched from room to room, watching her dogs sleeping like the dead, some sprawled across their beds and others on the furniture. She discovered Ned reading a book on her couch. Eddie's head rested on Ned's leg. Victoria picked up her phone to call him but kept watching, unable to keep herself from just admiring him for a bit. He wore shorts with a sweatshirt. His long, muscular legs were stretched out on an ottoman. One hand held his book open, the other absentmindedly patted Eddie's neck.

This was wrong, watching him. Smiling, she quickly closed her laptop and called him.

"Hi. How is it going there?" She hit the light switch and plunged her room into darkness.

"Good. Dogs had sardines, kale, and pasta with their dinner and chased each other around the yard. We're ready to hit the sack for the night."

"Um, I happened to check my security videos a second ago. Looks like they're already out."

"Hey—were you spying on us?"

"Maybe . . . not intentionally." A warmth crept across her cheeks. "But you do look awfully handsome in your sweatshirt."

"Hope I didn't pick my nose while you were watching."

"I wouldn't have told you I was watching if you did." She laughed. "I would have wiped the memory from my mind and pretended it never happened. But you know, I see some awful things with my job, your nose-picking wouldn't have a chance of making my worst-things list."

"Good to know." He chuckled. "How about you? Everything okay there?"

"I'm picturing your eye brows lifting right now, the way they do whenever you ask a question. Did you know that? Your mouth also turns up into an irresistible smile."

"Irresistible, you say? I'm going to start asking more questions."

Smiling at the confident tease in his voice, she slipped under the covers, curling her legs underneath her, and pulling the top sheet up to her chin. This playful banter and the accompanying giddiness were all new for her. She looked forward to more of it in the future. "I'm helping on a case that might not even be a case yet. If it resolves itself, it's possible I could be on my way home tomorrow."

"Excellent. But do what you have to do. One step at a time until it's over. Hey, great football there this weekend. Maybe they give out complimentary tickets to FBI agents. You know, like they give the police discounts to Disney."

"It's not my thing. A little overwhelming. Hope you don't fantasize about taking me to watch football with you."

"No, I promise, that's— that's not what I fantasize about."

"I'm aware of the games, though. Impossible not to be. Lots of coverage on the news. All the uptown hotels are full. I was lucky to get a room here. It worked out though. The place I'm staying at happens to be right near—um—right where I need to be."

"Can't tell me or you'll have to kill me?"

"No. Nothing like that." She laughed and curled her toes up under the covers. "I can tell you, but it's not what I want to talk about. You and the dogs are like my happy place. I don't want to mess it up talking about work."

"Got it."

"Did you work at the clinic today?"

"Yes. Busy day eliminating reproductive capabilities. A few animals came in thinking I was their friend. Not sure if they thought so when they left. Janice still hasn't figured out the computer system but she's incredibly determined."

Victoria laughed again. "I love that you volunteer there. Have I told you that enough?"

"Tell me again. I'm listening."

"I'm picturing that irresistible smile again." Victoria's own smile stretched farther. Speaking to Ned was the next best thing to being with him.

They talked about nothing important, random things, just what she needed, and then said goodnight. She turned on the television. When the picture came to life, a group of emaciated donkeys huddled together behind a fence.

A male reporter's solemn voice captioned the scene. "Barnyard of horrors discovered in Cleveland County."

Victoria raised her head, propping herself up on her elbows.

"Animal rescuers from the Hopeful Heart Rescue have taken in a herd of miniature donkeys and need your help. The group says it's one of the worst cases of neglect they have ever encountered."

Victoria grabbed her phone off the nightstand.

"Getting any of them adopted in their current conditions will be difficult. People interested in adopting them are asked to email the organization."

Victoria snapped a picture of the information on the television.

The donkey rescue story cut to a tanned female news anchor. "A local student is missing after a trip to the Charlotte Mall to meet friends."

Three different photos of a smiling Emma Manning appeared on the screen.

"Anyone who has seen the missing girl since yesterday, please call the tip line below."

◆ ◆ ◆

The tenth grader had a looming Algebra exam on Monday and no chance of passing it. He attempted to reread the chapters and study the notes he jotted down in class. It shouldn't be so hard, but it was. Might as well have been Chinese. Needing to distract himself so he didn't go to bed feeling doomed, he grabbed his remote and turned on the television to play a video game.

Before he switched the input, a reporter's serious tone said something about a fourteen-year old girl from Charlotte and images of someone who looked about his age filled the screen. Something about her made him pause. She was sort of pretty, in that snobby, private school girl way—yeah, she went to Charlotte Day School, that was obvious from the insignia on her field hockey uniform, but why were her pictures on the news? It took him a few seconds to register the rest of the information.

Emma Manning. Missing. Long straight reddish-brown hair. Black shirt. Burgundy pants. Black ankle boots. Have you seen her?

The images struck a familiar chord. He had seen her all right. He was sure of it! Not her face exactly, but the hair, the clothes, someone just her size. He grabbed his phone and captured a picture of the number to call on the bottom of the screen.

Then he needed time to think. What did he remember? He'd seen the missing girl on Thursday night at Resling Corporate Park. It was growing dark, but the street lights had yet to come on. That was his signal to go home because it wouldn't be too much longer before his mother got home from her shift at work and put something in the microwave for their dinner.

The buildings in that complex were empty. *For Lease* banners hung across the fronts. The empty parking lot was perfect for skateboarding. He'd just failed on a heel flip over stairs and fallen hard. His whole right side stung. He was leaning against a railing waiting for the pain to subside, holding his skateboard under his arm, when a dark sedan drove past and parked across the lot in the shadows between the vacant buildings.

A big, muscle-bound, bouncer-type guy emerged and hoisted a girl out of the back. The guy was too old to be the girl's boyfriend, too young to be her Dad, but he could have been an older brother. The girl's head lolled back like she was drunk or drugged . . . or dead. Her black shirt fell down her shoulder. There may have been something covering her face, but he wasn't sure because as she lifted her head, the man turned, blocking the view. He could say for certain that the big guy had a buzz-cut and wore a dark sweatshirt and jeans . . . maybe. But most clearly, he remembered the girl's black boots flopping beneath her like a puppet as the man carried her toward the building, until the flopping changed to kicking. That's when a cold tingle spread over his scalp and he knew something strange was happening.

A second car arrived moments later. A BMW. An old dude climbed out. Around his father's age. He wore a suit.

What make of car did the first guy have? The cops might want to know that, too. It was nothing special or he would have remembered, like he remembered the beamer. So, it had to be one of those makes and models that practically everyone drove. Honda? Hyundai? Mazda?

Would he be on the news? Was there a reward? Pleased with himself, which made up for all the bad feelings generated by the upcoming Algebra test, he dialed the tip line number.

Chapter Nine

Victoria slept poorly, waking from and returning to a bad dream. In the dream, she was on vacation, hiking somewhere far from home. Eddie, her sweetest and goofiest dog, ran off the trail after a squirrel and never came back. She stayed in the woods until the sky turned an inky black, calling his name over and over until her voice was no more than a raspy, croak. Eventually she had to drive home, heartbroken because he was out there alone somewhere—cold, hungry, afraid, and would never find his way back to her. The dream seemed very real and continued to unsettle her long after she woke with the rising sun.

Before getting out of bed, she checked through new messages and emails on her phone, deleting anything she didn't need. There were no new messages from Connelly, so she sent him one. *Any news?*

When she started the day away from home, she often experienced a bit of homesickness in the mornings. Entering the bathroom minus a canine entourage, their absence hit her in a wave of melancholy. *Perhaps I'll find out today that Emma returned to her family, and I'll be on my way back to Virginia.*

She dressed in work-out clothes, put a towel down on the carpet, and scrolled through her YouTube feed of exercise videos.

She selected a Navy Seals ultimate-mat-workout and hit play. On top of the dresser, the television played the local news on mute. When she looked up from her phone, the words *Breaking News* flashed across the bottom of the screen. She paused her exercise video, shifted her attention to the news, and turned up the volume.

A blonde woman was reporting. "Employees at three separate Charlotte locations found handwritten notes with bomb threats. The threats appear to have been delivered overnight. With an estimate of over a hundred thousand people visiting for the upcoming sporting events, local authorities are taking this threat very seriously."

Victoria wiped her brow with one of the hotel's hand towels.

The report switched to a live press conference and Victoria went back to doing crunches. There wasn't much more that could throw a city into panic and chaos than multiple bomb threats on a weekend with major organized events. For Charlotte authorities, today would be an all-hands-on-deck kind of day.

Detective Connelly hadn't responded to Victoria's message by the time she left the hotel for a run. Quite possibly, he had been pulled into helping with the enhanced security measures. Under a cloudy sky with fog billowing through the streets, she ran around the perimeter of the South Charlotte Mall. An employee unlocked the front doors and she entered with a group of mall walkers.

She found her way to the giant Christmas display in the center of the mall and took the escalator to the lobby below.

She stood where she remembered Emma standing and studied the area.

Where did Emma go from there? Was she lured? Tricked?

Victoria would be angry if the girl had run away or gone to stay with a new friend and not told anyone, causing all this stress and worry and wasting valuable resources. However, that scenario would still be her number one preference. Any other possibility made her shudder for poor Emma Manning. A disturbing memory from a previous case flashed through her mind—a girl in the trunk of a car. She pushed it away.

She left the lobby and walked through the surrounding parking garage. Had Connelly or one of his colleagues tracked all the cars that left the parking garage shortly after Emma was seen in the lobby? That's what she would have done. Surveillance cameras were clearly visible hanging below the ceiling. Avoiding all of them would require a precise and convoluted orchestration of steps, but it was certainly possible.

She checked her messages. Still no word from Connelly, but Ned had sent her a photo of the dogs staring up at him with their big round eyes while he prepared breakfast. Feeling lucky and missing all of them, she ran another mile to an empty office-parking area.

A car slowed down as it passed. Hanging his head and shoulders out the window, a teen yelled to her. "You can run after me anytime!" Hoots and laughter followed as the car sped away.

It happened. Even when people knew she was an agent.

She sprinted across the length of the lot, took a quick break, and sprinted back, pushing through the burn in her muscles and lungs. She repeated the exercise three more times, and ended sucking in giant gulps of breath with sweat beading every inch of her body. Having done enough, she returned to her hotel room to shower, dress, and call Sam.

"Good morning. How's Charlotte?" As always, Sam was gracious and pleasant, like a hotel concierge, even though, no matter the day or time, he had multiple agents making demands and urgent requests. Everyone in the bureau wanted their information as soon as possible. She didn't know how Sam dealt with the constant stress, but he did it well. Victoria made a mental note to send him a gift of some sort, anonymously, something to let him know how much his work was appreciated.

"Charlotte is fine," she said, pulling on clean socks. "Bomb threats this morning."

"I heard. I grew up near there, you know. It's changed a lot. Grew like wildfire."

"I didn't know that about you. Well, I'm not sure if I'll be here very long." There were voices and shouting in the background, her home office was already busy. Murphy's voice rose above the others. Then she heard Rivera. "Sounds hectic there."

"Hold on one second." More muffled sounds filled the wait until Sam returned. "Agent Rivera says hello."

"Tell him I said hello back, please." She wondered if Rivera had been assigned to a new case yet. "Any chance you have some time?"

"I don't have time—I make time—and I can make as much as you need."

She couldn't help but smile. "Did you see my email from last night?"

"Yes. Your search is already up and running." Victoria heard another commotion in the background and thought Sam might have to go. Instead, he asked, "Do you have a forensics person scanning her social media?"

"Her phone and laptop are missing, but the detective on the case has people accessing her calls, emails, and social media."

"Okay. I'll call you immediately if I find anything, meanwhile, just let me know if there's anything else I can help with."

71

"Thanks, Sam. You're awesome. Have a good day."

She brushed her blonde hair back and gathered it in a ponytail, placing her cap over her head. After a quick breakfast at the hotel's buffet, she drove her rental car back to the Mannings' house, leaving a message for Detective Connelly on the way. He still hadn't responded to her earlier text. For all she knew, Emma might already be back home, punished for the foreseeable future, but safe and sound. Surely Connelly would have let Victoria know if that was the case, but maybe not. Maybe he had too many other things going on now, thanks to the recent bomb threats.

A Channel 14 news van was parked to the side of the Mannings' gated neighborhood. A reporter stood at the end of the drive, using the neighborhood entrance as his backdrop.

Victoria waited for the news team to wrap up their segment, then checked in with the guard on duty. He signed her in and opened the gate.

A long trailer with landscaping equipment occupied the road in front of the Mannings' house. In the circular driveway, Connelly was stepping out of his car. He waited for Victoria to park, made eye contact, and shook his head. "I've got no new news. Let's see if the parents have heard anything," he said, walking alongside her. They passed two men edging the flower beds. A third man drove a riding mower.

Victoria found it interesting that there were no other cars in the driveway. No other friends, family, or neighbors gathering to offer the family support. Usually they swarmed like flies, some of them purely nosy, but offering to help in any way and arranging for meals to be delivered to the family.

Connelly rubbed his eyes. "Sorry I didn't get back to you. We had a briefing uptown and I didn't have time to check in with the Mannings yet. That's what I'm doing now. Hoping for closure on this."

Magda opened the door again. She saw them and her eyes lit up. "Do you know where Emma is?"

"No, unfortunately, we don't." All hopes that Emma was home had just been dashed. "No word from her here, then?"

"No. Nothing." Magda reached toward her neck and clutched the collar of her shirt. "What about from the tip line?"

"I've got people monitoring it." Connelly wiped his feet on the doormat. "The thing about tip lines is that we get hundreds of callers. Some well-meaning, some that get off on intentionally wasting our time with false information, plus a whole assortment of whack jobs who actually believe the bizarre theories they want us to pursue. It's a lot of work to comb through all of them, but I'll be notified the second they have a promising lead."

"Come in." Magda stepped aside. "The Mannings are meeting with a private investigator in the dining room."

The dining room was decorated in shades of silver, white, and gray. A contemporary painting with a sparse outline of a horse hung in the center of one wall. Tripp and Patricia didn't strike Victoria as animal lovers. They were seated on opposite sides of a large table, an abstract sculpture centerpiece between them. The other man stood up as she and Connelly entered. He was somewhere in his mid-thirties, with hair styled to fall in soft layers over one side of his forehead, and the carved jaw of a model. He wore an expensive-looking navy suit cut perfectly to his proportions, and a crisp white pin-striped shirt. If he was indeed the private investigator, his appearance said he was able to charge top-notch fees. Or maybe he was like Victoria, lucky enough to do what he loved without ever having to worry about income.

The Mannings made no attempt at introductions, so the stranger smiled, not a big teeth-flashing smile, but professional and courteous, and introduced himself. "Hi. I'm Jay Adams. Private investigator."

"Special agent Victoria Heslin with the FBI."

"Detective Martin Connelly, CMPD."

"Nice to meet you both." Adams resumed his seat as Victoria and Connelly pulled back chairs.

"Glad you're both here," Patricia said, her tone managing to convey the opposite. She gave Victoria the same scrutinizing once-over from the day before. "You can tell our investigator what you have and haven't done."

"I don't want to get in your way, but I'll do whatever I can to supplement your investigation," Adams said.

"Okay, then. Let's get started." Connelly took out a small notepad and rattled off a list of people he had already interviewed, and the information gained.

Adams's Rolex rubbed against his legal pad as he quickly scribbled short-hand notes, nodding occasionally. He asked a few questions and Connelly answered them. Outside the dining room window, one of the men from the yard crew pulled weeds without looking up or inside.

"This cannot be happening." Patricia tugged on her ring. "Someone has to know something." She twisted her hands together. "Someone should talk to Emma's coach. And her English teacher. I think she's very close with her English teacher."

Patricia suddenly whipped her head around. Victoria followed her gaze to the foyer. There was nothing there except a marble-topped console with a giant display of white flowers in an urn. Just as quickly as it arrived, Patricia's startled expression disappeared, replaced with her default frown. "What does our expert suggest we do next?" She directed the question at Victoria, emphasizing the word expert in a way that made it sound more sarcastic than sincere.

"We should start researching your contact lists."

"My enemy list." Tripp grunted. "That's what you called it yesterday." He rested his cheek against his hand, middle finger fully extended toward his temple. She imagined it wasn't intentional but couldn't be sure.

"It's best for us to start with anyone you've had personal or professional conflicts with." Victoria was certain that part of the list would be long.

"I agree." Adams set down his pen. "Those would be the people we'd want to talk to first if there was an abduction."

Victoria noted the "if" and expected Patricia to tell the PI off in her exasperated tone, but the woman only bowed her head. Apparently, it was okay for Adams to suggest the possibility her daughter may have run off on her own.

"Do you have the list for us?" Victoria asked.

"I've put your list together," Tripp said. "But I'd like to wait another day before you start interrogating people."

Patricia sat up straight. Her eyes darkened. "Another day?"

"Yes, Patricia." Just then, he looked more tired and worn out than angry. "One more day might give us a better idea of what's happened to our daughter."

Patricia slapped her hands on the table. She shoved back her chair, loudly scraping the wood floor. A random thought crossed Victoria's mind—odd that there wasn't some sort of felt pads on the bottom of the chairs.

"Do you realize what could happen to our daughter if we wait another day?" Patricia crossed her arms, still glaring at her husband. "I honestly cannot believe I married you!" With that, for the second time in two days, she stormed from the room, leaving Connelly and Victoria looking at each other and Adams staring down at his hands.

The awkward mood was interrupted by Victoria's phone vibrating inside her coat pocket. Grateful for the interruption, she took it out and glanced at the screen. "Excuse me. I need to take this." She lifted her chair up as she pushed it back and moved away from the table.

Crossing to the back of the house for privacy, she answered. "Hey, Sam."

"Hey, Victoria. I've got a hit on your girl."

"You did?" Victoria had an immense amount of faith in Sam's abilities, but she could hardly believe he had already found a hit on Emma's image amongst millions of photos.

"The software did. A useful hit, I should say. The girl and her friends posted a few lifetimes worth of photos on the internet. But . . . we used websites and key words known for links to prostitution and human trafficking, some of it on the dark web. It still meant scanning millions of images looking for a match in that database, but that's how we got one so quickly. Just posted to a website this morning."

"What's the site?"

"The site is CarolinaFestivalsexygirls.com."

Victoria groaned like the wind had been knocked out of her. It was terrible news. "These facial recognition packages are pretty infallible, right?"

"Rarely do they make a mistake. They're matching hundreds of data points. But it's not impossible."

"At least we know something now." A new to-do list began forming in her head. "Is there a phone number on the ad?"

"Yes. I'm tracing it as we speak. Looks like a voice over IP routed out of Romania."

"So . . . we can't track it?"

"Not right away. No identifying metadata, and a reverse image didn't return any results, as expected. But I'll trace the website address. If it's a U.S. hosted server, no problem tracking it."

"Okay. Thanks. I'm with the parents now. Call me as soon as you have something else."

"I always do. I'm sending you the website link."

Thinking through what she would say, Victoria walked back to the dining room. In her absence, Patricia had returned. Everyone looked her way. For a split second, Victoria caught Connelly's gaze with her solemn expression, communicating that the case had turned a dark corner. She weighed her words carefully, aware of how her news would impact Emma's family and the investigation. "One of my colleagues just found something relevant regarding Emma's disappearance. This will help us move forward. He's about to send it to me."

"Found something? What does that mean?" barked Patricia. "Is she okay? Did something happen to her?"

"What did they find?" Tripp leaned forward; his hands balled into fists on the table, ready for battle.

Victoria stared at her email, waiting for Sam's message. "One of our intelligence analysts found a picture of your daughter. It was loaded to a website this morning."

"What website?" Tripp asked.

"I should have it any second now." Sam's message popped up and Victoria opened the link. She scanned over a few images until she spotted Emma. She was dressed in a young girl's school uniform. Her eyes were wide with what Victoria could only guess was terror. Her mouth was partly open. Victoria set her phone down near the center of the table, unsure of who should see the image first.

Tripp scooped up the phone. He brought the screen closer, stared, then closed his eyes and dropped his head back.

"Give it to me." Patricia snatched the device from his hand. "Oh, God! Oh, God!" She glared at her husband.

Why was that one of her first reactions to the news?

Patricia shifted her anger toward Connelly. "The ad says all the girls are over eighteen. Emma is certainly not! We told you she was taken!"

"And that's why we're all here." Connelly said.

Patricia pushed the phone toward him. He shifted in his seat and his expression gave nothing away, but his face might have turned a shade paler.

"Are you familiar with this site?" Patricia asked, her voice shrill.

"I'm sure the site was created for this weekend and will be taken down in a few days," Adams said. "That's how these things work."

Victoria wondered how the private eye knew.

"Maybe it's an old picture that someone stole," Tripp suggested. "You know . . . where they've really only got girls past their prime but they entice Johns with photos they swipe off the internet."

"How can you ask that?" Patricia shouted. "What's wrong with you? Those aren't her clothes! She doesn't have any clothes like that! Whoever has her took that picture."

"There *are* prostitution sites that copy photos of attractive young girls and women they find on the internet, most of them do—" Victoria said in her kindest voice. "—but the timing—this photo was posted this morning—combined with you not recognizing the clothes she's wearing . . . all of that indicates this photo was not borrowed for this ad."

Patricia's hands hovered over the table and trembled. "She's only had her braces off less than a month. She just had her front teeth bonded last week. Those are the new teeth. Someone— some demented kidnapping prostitution ring has her."

"Now, listen—" Connelly lifted his hands in a gesture intended to calm. "—we still don't know for sure she's in danger. This could be some sort of stunt with a new boyfriend."

The detective's suggestion was possible, and they had to consider every angle, but Victoria never would have said it aloud. There was enough anger, tension, and confusion in the Manning house without adding to it. She narrowed her eyes at Connelly, willing him to shut up before he made things worse.

"She would never," spat out Patricia, her fingers stretching, curling into fists, and stretching again. "There is absolutely—you don't even know her."

"She doesn't need to be involved in any stunts to make money," Tripp added. "I take care of her."

Victoria concentrated on keeping her voice level amidst the escalating stress. "It doesn't matter if she was abducted or not, she's a minor, so being a part of this in any way—even if it's just her image being used—is forced coercion. We'll do everything we can to find her and get her home as soon as possible."

Tripp stood up and paced, pressing his fists against his forehead. "Can we stop the television coverage now. Now that we know someone has her . . . and . . ." He looked away, unable to finish his sentence.

"I wouldn't advise that. Someone might have seen her, someone might still see her," Adams said. "Whoever has her, if they see the ads on TV, they might decide she's worth more ransomed back to her family than . . ." He let his sentence trail off, unwilling to remind the parents that it appeared their daughter was being prostituted.

Victoria silently disagreed. What Adams said made sense, but it wasn't in the best interest of getting Emma back safely. She would wait to tell him why in private. They didn't need to be hashing everything out together in front of the family.

"Can we drop your pointless investigation into my contacts now?" Tripp asked.

His wife stared at him with her mouth hanging open. "Some of your contacts probably know exactly where she is." She sputtered and turned to Connelly. "Find her!"

"I'm going to call our intelligence agent back." Victoria got up from her chair. "I'll see if he's been able to track the website."

Connelly pushed away from the table at the same time. "I'm going to call headquarters."

"Just call the damn number for the site and get her back!" Patricia screamed. "Just do it. Why aren't you doing it? Good God. I can't believe this is actually happening."

"Even though her picture is in the ad, it doesn't mean that if someone calls that number, Emma shows up," Connelly explained. "Emma might not even be in the country anymore. The girl who shows up might not look anything like Emma. It's not like a John can call the Better Business Bureau and complain that they didn't get the prostitute they specifically asked for."

"Emma is not a prostitute!" Mrs. Manning shouted.

Connelly frowned. "I know—but . . . our best chance of finding her is to trace the website."

"Do you have anything you can take to help you calm down, Mrs. Manning?" Adams asked.

Victoria braced herself for Patricia to jump down his throat at the suggestion, but instead she pressed her lips together and left the room with her chin held high.

Seems to be a pattern.

"May I speak with you two privately a moment?" Victoria spoke quietly to Adams and Connelly.

The detective and the PI followed her into an office and Victoria shut the door behind them. They stood at the far end of the room in front of a marble fireplace.

"We have to be careful or we could lose her for good," Victoria said. "First, it would be best if we could kill the media ads."

"Why?" Adams asked. "Why not add a reward?"

Victoria bit into her bottom lip as her gaze traveled over neat stacks of papers on the desk and back to the men. "If we keep the pressure on and spook them, they could decide she's not worth the trouble and kill her. I don't want to chance that."

"She's right." Connelly leaned against the fireplace. "We've got to stop the ads. If they find out she's got parents who can throw their weight around, they might get rid of her to protect their operation."

"How are we going to get the media to drop the story?" Adams looked from Victoria to Connelly as he spoke, then returned to Victoria. "It's not just on the news, it's going viral everywhere, and that's without this latest information. All they've had to report so far is that she didn't come home yesterday."

Victoria crossed her arms. "I didn't have much luck on my last case with trusting reporters to hold back. Not with a sensational story."

"I'll see what our department can do," Connelly said.

"Do you have undercover informants that can help you track this group?" Victoria asked. "Because I can get some help from my office, but I want to know who is doing what. No sense in duplicating efforts."

"Yes." Connelly eyed the office door. "Although the bomb threats are going to change resource availability. Whoever has Emma, they'd be stupid not to get her as far from here as possible. And once she goes international—"

"She's gone and we're not going to find her," Adams said, finishing the detective's sentence.

The three stared at each other. "I've got to make some calls," Connelly finally said. "Excuse me."

"So do I." Victoria followed the detective out of the office, leaving Adams behind. She went out the back door and into a corner of the yard where she could be alone to call Sam.

"I didn't want to call you with only bad news," Sam said. "I'm not sure where the website is hosted yet, but it's not in the States. I've got someone working on it."

Victoria sighed. Getting information on the account would be a lot more difficult. Once the hosting country was identified, they'd need to serve a warrant. It could take days—maybe weeks—for the approvals, depending on the bureaucracies. And if it was an unfriendly country, it might never happen. "Okay. Thank you, Sam. Any information you can find about the website will be useful. It's all we've got at this point."

"I'll do my best."

Chapter Ten

Gray walls. Stagnant air. Little comfort.

Sofia was used to it by now.

Emma rocked forward and back on Sasha's cot, still crying. Sofia did her best to ignore her.

"I don't feel well," Emma muttered, looking up at Anastasia. The new girl had figured out where sympathy would and would not be found in the room.

"You need to stop crying," Sofia said, giving Emma a quick sideways glare. "It's not going to help."

Anastasia's hands were hidden under the frayed cuffs of her too large sweatshirt. She absentmindedly chewed on the edges. If she got really nervous, she would start pinching her earlobe. It happened often and as far as Sofia knew, Anastasia wasn't even aware she was doing it.

"Neither of you have a phone?" Emma asked.

Sofia laughed. "Are you kidding me?"

She heard heavy footsteps coming closer. The lock turned.

Emma scooted sideways to face the door and wrapped her arms around her legs.

Metal clanked against metal and Svet barged in. "Leaving in thirty minutes," he barked. He held a dry cleaner's bag with two black dresses inside. "Anastasia—shower first."

Anastasia gathered clothes and toiletries into her arms.

"Where are we going?" Emma asked.

"Not you." Svet responded without looking at Emma. "You're not going anywhere."

Emma whimpered.

Her cry got his attention. He sneered and loomed closer. "Remember, girl. I have pictures on my phone. You don't want nobody to see them, yes? I will put them on internet if you piss me off. No one can trace them, but everyone will see them." He emphasized 'everyone,' making the word sound sinister and complicit.

He reached toward Emma. There was something in his hand.

She jumped up from the cot and backed into the nearest wall.

Stupid girl, Sofia thought. *He'll get off on your fear.*

Svet laughed at her attempt to escape him. "If I want you, you can't hide. You're trapped. But I'm done with you. For now. Here." He rattled a container of pills. "Every day, take one."

Emma didn't move.

Sofia stepped forward. "I'll see to it."

"Make sure. Start today. They're counted." Svet handed Sofia the container. "She's no good if bleeding. No one wants to f—"

Sofia set the pills down on her cot. "I said I'll take care of it." When she spoke again, she made her voice as neutral as possible, hoping Svet would answer without thinking. "Is Sasha coming back?"

"Wouldn't you like to know?" He sneered and she realized her question had been futile. Svet would never miss an opportunity to be cruel. "Smells like crap in here," he said before leaving with Anastasia, closing and locking the door behind them.

"Who is Sasha?" Emma asked.

"A friend."

Emma stared at the bottle in Sofia's hand. "I'm not taking those."

"They won't hurt you. I've been taking them for three years. You can't get pregnant if you take them and you won't get your period either."

"I'm not taking them." She shook her head, like that would make a difference.

"Whatever," Sofia said. "But I promise you, the harder you make this for yourself, the worse it will be. Just be glad you're not going with us tonight. We have to work. Not that you could anyway, you look like a wreck."

"What kind of work?"

How dumb is she? "I think you know."

"It's better if I stay in the same place." Emma's voice quivered. "The police will find me soon."

Sofia snorted. "Don't hold your breath, sweetheart." But a tiny spark of hope had been steadily growing inside her since Emma arrived. Maybe the girl's family lived right in this city. Maybe they really were looking. *Wouldn't it be wonderful if Emma's words came true?*

Chapter Eleven

In a corner of the Mannings' freshly-cut back yard, Victoria sat on the edge of a garden chair and called Murphy to give him an update. From the little she knew about Celia Murphy, it was safe to assume she was bugging her husband for news on what Victoria was doing with regard to Emma's disappearance.

"Did you find the Mannings' daughter?" her boss asked.

"No. Not yet. But we had a breakthrough. Sam found her picture on a website for commercial sex. I'm guessing she was tricked or lured into it. But no proof yet."

Murphy groaned. "Damn. Oh, that's bad. Glad we took this seriously right away and sent you. Any location identifiers in the photo?"

"Sam is analyzing every pixel to find something, but there's a solid backdrop behind her, like a giant sheet. There are other girls in the ad. They all look under eighteen. All have the same sheet behind them."

"If the photo had been in a hotel room, we could have used the Traffickcam database to find out where it was taken." Murphy growled into the phone. "I'm thinking of my own kids. Whoever did this . . . I want to tear them to shreds with my own hands."

Victoria absentmindedly pulled a leaf from an overhanging branch and smoothed it between her fingers. "But why would they take *this* girl? She fits into the average age range for sex trafficking, but the usual target would be a runaway, someone in the foster care system, or with a history of abuse. Someone who might not be missed right away."

"Agree," Murphy said. "She doesn't fit the profile. Maybe this group doesn't even know who she is, they just randomly snatched her off the street because they saw an opportunity."

"If they don't know who they're taking, they won't last long in this business. So, I hope that's the case." *But I don't think so.* Victoria caught a flash of movement as the patio door opened.

"Charlotte PD should be more involved now," Murphy said. "Although they've also got the terrorist threat to deal with. We're sending some people to help with that."

Connelly emerged from the shadows and waved. Victoria held up a finger. "I'll stick around as long as I can be useful here. Unless you need me on another case."

"You're good for now," Murphy said. "And I appreciate you being there. Just do whatever you can. I know you will. I know how much it means to you, personally, to see a kidnapped victim returned home safely. Just keep me updated."

"Will do, boss."

She ended her call and met Connelly on the back patio. He crossed and uncrossed his legs as he typed on his phone. She plopped into the chair next to him. "Do you have a daughter, Connelly?"

"No. Why do you ask?"

"Your face when you saw the website."

"Oh." The corners of his mouth turned up, but there was only sadness in his eyes. "No daughters. But I've got nieces

87

around that age, friends with daughters. Seeing those ads hits a little close to home."

"I know."

"I'm going uptown now. The whole precinct has a briefing on the bomb scares. I'll call you tonight," he said. "Let you know where things stand."

"Oh. Okay. I might do a little snooping around some of the transit areas. See who might be willing to talk. And since we have the 'enemy list,' I can do some research. Make sure we're considering all angles."

"Excellent." Connelly tapped his toe while he was talking. "In fact—yeah . . . it would be a big help if you could focus on that list, maybe use your intelligence analysts and follow up on any leads. Thank you."

◆ ◆ ◆

Back in her hotel room, Victoria snapped a photo of each wall in the bedroom to put on the TraffickCam website. The site was created to help pinpoint the location of missing girls. In pay-for-sex advertisements, pimps often posted photographs of their victims in hotel rooms. All it took was one piece of artwork or a pattern on a duvet cover for an investigator to match a hotel room from the website to one in an ad. The more hotel photos on the site, the better the chance of identifying a location.

After uploading the pictures, she logged into the FBI's proxy server and began researching. Several names from the Mannings' recent past warranted further investigation. A local investor, a construction company, a rival developer—all had filed claims against Tripp's business. Next, she made an investigative check list they could use to make sure everything was being done. Had someone looked into the uniform Emma wore in the website picture? What stores sold them? Which school or schools used them? Had they found anything in the analysis of her phone records yet? Did anything come from accessing her emails on the internet provider's server? Were any of her friends ready to tell a different story now that she hadn't returned home?

She sent the list to Connelly since it was his case. She couldn't forge ahead without knowing who was doing what. There was no sense in duplicating efforts. If the Charlotte police didn't have the bandwidth to investigate, perhaps Jay Adams could.

A call to Connelly's cell resulted in his voicemail greeting. She opted to grab lunch and then drive down to the police headquarters to discuss the list of investigative items in person and make sure Connelly had them covered.

The uptown streets were busier than yesterday, bustling with people around the stadium. Outdoor stages had been set up for bands. Vendors sold souvenirs. Restaurants and bars advertised game-weekend specials. Mixed in with the crowds were uniformed officers and bomb-sniffing dogs. Charlotte authorities were being thorough with their safety precautions. She hoped it would be enough to keep everyone safe.

Catching sight of the city's bus station, she made a split-second decision to stop. She paid to park and walked to the edge of the terminal. She found a spot with a good view of the area, did her best to look like a bored woman waiting for a bus, and began observing. Transit terminals were good places to watch for signs of inappropriate relationships between men and girls. A much older man and a strung-out younger woman. Girls who appeared nervous or afraid. Girls with bruising around their necks—some Johns liked to choke girls until they passed out before raping them. If Victoria noticed a girl sending up warning signs, the agent could see who was hanging around the girl, who was watching her from a distance. That would be someone she should talk to, or follow.

89

Someone who might know a thing or two about what happened to Emma. She didn't expect them to know anything for free, but once Victoria took out a wad of her own personal cash, then they might remember something.

The station was swarming with people, most of them entering the city for the football game and related events. When a bus pulled away, she was surprised to see someone she recognized through the crowd. Jay Adams. From farther away, the PI cut a trim, athletic figure in his dress shirt and slacks. But the woman he was talking to—younger, a bit rough around the edges, in tight jeans and impractical heels—she didn't look to be his type.

Victoria didn't approach Adams. The woman might have been a paid informant whose trust he had earned. But Victoria was curious. Was Adams doing the same thing she was? If so, she thought he was a damn good PI and the Mannings were lucky to have hired him. Since he was from Charlotte, he might have a better idea of who had information.

Leaving Adams at the station, she moved on to the police headquarters. Inside, the same clerk from yesterday sat behind the front desk. A line of civilians waited. As Victoria approached, a woman in uniform stepped in front of her.

"Excuse me." Excitement sparkled in the young officer's bright eyes. "Are you the FBI agent working with Detective Connelly?"

"Yes. I'm Victoria Heslin. How did you know that?"

"I didn't, but I figured you might be just because well, word got around quick that you're very pretty. You perfectly fit the description I heard."

"Oh." Victoria laughed. "Someone is quite good with descriptions, then."

"Officer Roberta Jefferson." She smiled. "Do you know if the tip from the boy panned out? The one who saw her at Resling Corporate Park?"

"I'm not sure what you're referring to."

Roberta's face dropped. "I was working the tip line last night. A high school kid called in. He was sure he'd seen her. Same hair and outfit. He seemed credible. I was hoping it was legit." She raised her eyes toward the ceiling. "Then again, he also asked like five times if he could be on the television news, so maybe he just wanted a few minutes of fame. And he admitted hadn't really seen her face."

"I haven't heard anything about that tip."

"Guess it didn't pan out." She shrugged. "Shame. It was the best lead we got from the tip line. So far, anyway. Oh, well."

The officer walked away.

"Hold on." Victoria said. "Do you still have the information from that call?"

Roberta turned back. "Sure. I can forward you the email I sent Connelly. I've got my notes, too, if you want to see them. I'm going back to my desk now. Follow me?"

"Yes." Victoria followed the young woman up the stairs, weaving around desks until she stopped at one near the center of the room.

The officer flipped over a few pages in a notebook and pointed to lines of half-print, half-cursive, parts of it circled with asterisks next to them. "Here's what he told me. Gave me an address and everything."

Victoria leaned forward and ran her finger down the side of the notepad as she read. "These are good notes. You asked a lot of questions." And the caller had answered each with solid information.

"Sure. You know . . . just in case we couldn't get in touch with him again."

Victoria took out her phone. "I'm getting directions to the address." She typed and clicked until the information popped up. "It's only twenty miles away."

"Yeah. Not far at all."

"Do you know if Connelly is here?"

"He's not," Roberta said. "Wherever he is, if it's not work-related, I'm sure it has something to do with his mother. I mean . . . I don't know him all that well, but I've heard he just moved his mother to a new facility, it's like the country club of nursing homes, a really nice place, but she's having trouble adjusting."

Victoria called Connelly and this time he answered.

"Hi. It's Victoria. I'm at your headquarters looking for you."

"Hey. I was just dealing with some personal business."

"Everything okay?"

"My mother is in an assisted living facility, but she has Alzheimer's and needs someone with her at all times. A private care-giver." She could hear the sigh between his words. "The woman who was supposed to show up for a shift change didn't."

"Oh . . . I'm sorry."

"It's okay. I've got someone now."

"I'm calling because I think we've got a good tip."

"From the tip line?" Faint, muffled conversation in the background filtered through the phone.

"Yes. A teen thinks he saw Emma being carried into a building at an empty corporate park. It's not far from here."

"Really? Send me the address. I'll check it out."

"I just sent it. I'm going over there now to take a look."

"Can you wait for me?"

"We should go as soon as possible. The tip came in last night. I'll head out now and see if there's anything to it."

"Okay. But wait for me when you get there. Don't go into any buildings alone. You should have back-up, just in case."

He had a point. "Meet me there?"

"Yes. I just need ten minutes to finish something up and I'll be on my way. Call me when you're almost there. And wait for me."

"Okay." She was already on her way out the door. "I won't go in until you get there. Hurry." She waited to cross the street, then strode across the parking lot and got into her car.

As she eased into traffic, a familiar surge of adrenaline made her feel even more like the tip was a good one. Without a flashing light, she drove as fast as she dared. As she got farther away from the football stadium and uptown area events, traffic thinned. She arrived forty-five minutes later.

The large parking lot was empty of vehicles—a perfect place to skateboard, like the tipster said he was doing. Victoria parked toward the back, under the shade of mature trees, allowing her a wide range view. If anyone drove in or out, if anyone left any of the buildings from front doors, she would see them. She shut off the car, but barely had to wait before Connelly arrived. He stopped beside her, rolling down his window, engine running.

"I flew over here. Glad you waited."

Victoria pointed to a two-story, box-like brick structure with large windows. "That's the building."

Connelly studied the area. "Doesn't look like anyone's in there. No cars. Let's park on the other side. Over there." He pointed. "You have Kevlar and a weapon?"

"Weapon, but no vest."

"I've got one for you." He turned to stare at the building they would enter. After a few seconds he said, "Follow me."

Victoria started her car and followed Connelly to the far side of the building. She got out and he tossed her some equipment.

"I did some research," she said, strapping on the vest and studying the windows for any sign that someone might be inside. "The building should be deserted. All of the others are. Last tenants left six months ago. A company called Independence Financials."

Connelly grunted as he eased his vest over his shoulders.

"There are entrances on every side of the building," Victoria said. "We should go in through a back one."

They hurried around to the back of the building and stood by a locked door.

"Here, let me." Connelly stepped forward, taking a small pouch from his pocket. He removed a metal tool no more than three inches long and stuck it in the lock. He hunched over, maneuvered it around in the lock for a few seconds, then looked up. "That was easy."

He opened the door, yelled "Police!" and stood aside. Victoria met his eyes, Connelly nodded, and they burst in with their weapons ready.

Swathes of sunlight beamed through upper windows into an open area. The interior space was empty of everything except office cubicles. Closed doors lined the exterior walls.

So many places to hide.

Victoria pointed to Connelly and gestured for him to head to the left while she went in the opposite direction. After he acknowledged her plan with a nod, she crept forward, staying low. Stopping at the first door, she flung it open, moved aside, and peered in.

Clear.

On her way to the next room, she kept her eyes peeled for any signs of movement or sound as she checked the space between the rows of cubicles.

Across the floor, Connelly disappeared into a room, then reappeared. His eyes settled on hers for the briefest instant as he gave her a quick thumbs up.

Minutes later, they met directly across from their initial point of entry.

"All clear," Connelly said.

Victoria remained alert, listening and scanning. "Let's check upstairs."

They took the concrete stairwell up and emerged on another floor identical to the first. Outside the windows, clouds moved over the sun, plunging the interior into shadows. Connelly went left and Victoria went right.

They met again where they started. Connelly's shoulders were relaxed as he slid his gun into his holster. "There's no one here."

"We're not finished." Victoria kept her voice low. "There's a lower level to search. She could be tied up somewhere."

They went down two flights of stairs to the lower level. Victoria pulled a heavy metal door partway open with a noisy creak, and stood back, listening. The windowless basement was completely dark. Hearing nothing, she flicked on a row of light switches and headed down.

The lower level was mostly one large and unfinished space. But there were three doors on the opposite side. With Connelly following behind her, she stayed close to the wall, passing food wrappers, cigarette butts, empty soda cans, and a People magazine. She whispered, "Someone's been in the basement. There was no trash on the other floors."

At the first room, she was focused and ready, half-expecting to find Emma. *But she might not be alone.*

She opened the door. *Nothing.* She was disappointed to find a storage area with HVAC units, spiraling, silver ductwork, and pipes.

There were two more rooms to investigate.

The second door was slightly ajar. Connelly pushed it open and looked around. "Clear, but—there's something here." Victoria moved past him to see what was inside. A mattress covered by a sheet was lying on the floor against one wall. *The boy's tip was good after all.* She crouched to study it. Long hairs. Smears of blood. *This should be a goldmine for evidence.*

"One more room." Connelly was already heading toward the door in a half crouch, his muscles tensed and ready.

Hoping to find Emma, but prepared to encounter whoever was responsible for bringing her there, Victoria's heart was pounding as she drew closer to the final room.

The door was closed tight. Victoria met Connelly's gaze, she mouthed, "One, two, three," and they burst through prepared to shoot.

"There's no one," Connelly said, lowering his gun.

Victoria lowered her weapon and coughed as she was hit with a faint but foul smell reminiscent of a dank alley with human waste. Inside, three empty cots were haphazardly arranged. Underneath one of them was a paperback book. A row of paper grocery bags and gallon containers of water were lined up against one wall. In the far corner, a tall painter's bucket had a roll of toilet paper next to it.

Victoria's muscles tensed with her mounting anger.

Connelly's eyes roamed the room. "Someone was living here."

"And not by choice, or they would have used one of the bathroom facilities." Victoria picked up the book. *Fifty Shades of Gray.* She peered inside the grocery bags. "All trash. I see fast food containers, granola bar wrappers, apple cores."

"I see something." Connelly knelt to get closer to an object under the cot. He removed a tissue from his pocket and picked it up. "A pencil. Might have prints."

Victoria came closer. "That's not a pencil. It's eyeliner." She walked around the room, being careful not to touch anything. "If this is what I think it is, a pimp will move from city to city every few days with three or four girls. We might have just missed them."

"Looks that way," Connelly said, his brow furrowed as he walked the room. "I'll be right back. I'm going to call for a warrant. And I've got an evidence kit in my car."

"Okay. But we need to get forensics in here, have them bag and tag everything."

Connelly left and Victoria examined every inch of the room with a professional eye, moving in grid patterns. A tiny, whitish object caught her attention. She moved closer and crouched down.

A single tooth.

And next to it, a tiny scrap of torn black paper. She turned it over with her pen.

Help.

The silence was broken by the heavy door creaking and scraping across the concrete at the top of the stairs. Footsteps echoed from the other side of the basement, growing closer.

That was quick. "I found some things," Victoria called. "Can you give me a bag?"

No one answered. *Guess he didn't hear me.* She raised her voice. "Got the kit?"

The footsteps stopped, then started again, retreating, lighter and faster.

"Connelly?" Victoria stood up, tense and aware, and moved quickly to the door. Her skin tingled with the possibility of danger.

A tall, muscular man hurried up the stairs.

"FBI! Stop!" Adrenaline surging, Victoria pulled her gun and raced across the basement after him.

Moving at a surprising speed for his size, he hurled himself up the stairs.

"Stop!" Victoria shouted again.

At the top, he disappeared through the heavy metal door.

She bounded up the stairs, taking them three at a time, and sprinted across the lobby. Grabbing the main door, she pushed forward, expecting to hurl herself through the opening. The door didn't budge. Cursing, she tried again with more force. *It's locked from the outside!* She spun around, searching for a nearby exit. As fast as she could, she flipped the lock on a side door and burst out. *Move! Move! Move!* She pumped her arms hard toward the front of the building. The screech of a car peeling away cut through the prevailing quietness of the isolated area. By the time she rounded the corner of the building, a dark sedan was out of the corporate park and speeding down the cross road.

"Damn!" Heart pounding, she looked around. There was no one else. *Where's Connelly?*

Her chest still rising and falling with rapid breaths, she jogged to the front door, the one that wouldn't open. A heavy padlock with a keypad, the kind used by realtors for showings, secured the entrance. The man must have left it open upon entering the building and locked it after his exit.

She placed her hands on her legs and leaned forward, gasping. *Who was that? Why was he here?* Trying to sort out what had just happened and catch her breath, she went back inside. Connelly appeared in the lobby with a box of equipment in his arms.

"Did you see that guy?" she asked, her face still warm from her adrenaline rush.

"Someone was here?"

"White male, twenties, buzz cut, six feet three or taller, extremely muscular and fast. He had a big head start and locked the door on me."

"I didn't see him."

"If you didn't see him at your car, then he definitely came through the front door. Which means he had the combo for the lock. I had to race to a side door. That's how I lost him. By then, he was too far away for us to call in a useful description of the car." She glanced at the box in Connelly's hands. "Give me the kit. I'm going to print the door."

"You don't want to wait for the techs to do it?" Connelly asked as he handed her a plastic case.

"I'll do it." She wiped perspiration off her forehead as she headed back outside. At the front door, she concentrated on

99

spreading the printing dust, conscious of Connelly watching her while he made phone calls.

Finished with his calls, Connelly came back and stood looking over her shoulder.

"I see some loops and arches," she said. "They might do." She slid the partial print evidence into a bag and put it in the case.

"I'll take that." The detective tucked the kit back into the box.

They headed back down to the basement. The rush from the chase had dissipated and Victoria's body was calm again. "Who else knew we were coming here?"

"The parents. They put me on speaker because Adams was with them. They want him to be in the loop on everything."

"Why did you tell them?"

"They thought we weren't doing enough to find their daughter," Connelly said. "I wanted to let them know what we were doing. Magda probably heard, too. But, I'm not sure what you're getting at, because there's no way that would have given anyone much time to get out of here."

Victoria frowned. "It was enough." Although dozens of officers and employees in the police headquarters could also have heard about the tip and known someone might check it out.

She looked around again. "Did you call for a full-forensics sweep?"

"Yeah. They're on their way."

"Okay. Hey, did you see the list I sent you earlier?"

He stopped in the doorway. "The to-do-list? Yes. It's great. It will help us make sure nothing falls through the cracks. Speaking of to-do's, while I wait for forensics, would you go to the Mannings' house for me?"

"What for?" Victoria continued to study the room.

"Pick up Emma's hairbrush and toothbrush so we can compare hair fibers and DNA."

She wanted to stay and assist forensics, but being a good "team player" here was important. Connelly was finally asking her for specific help. "Sure," she said, putting aside her own agenda.

"I want to let them know she wasn't here. They'll be going nuts waiting for news. I can't imagine being in their shoes. It will help if they see you, hear it from you. You do a good job dealing with them."

"Okay. I'll go."

"I'll stay on site until the tech team arrives. Then I've got a department meeting I'm supposed to attend. The whole city is going bonkers—thousands of good Samaritans calling in to report suspicious vans, suspicious bags, suspicious people, thinking everything might be a bomb. Even calling in on the tip line we set up for Emma. We've got to check them all out in case, God forbid, one of them really is right. I'll call you later?"

"Yes. Call me as soon as the tech team finds anything."

From the doorway, she glanced around the room one last time, eyes settling on the putrid bucket. She scowled. "Whoever was living here, it wasn't by choice. We need to find them."

Chapter Twelve

"Shut the door," Tripp said to Adams.

Adams placed a hand against the door frame of Tripp's study. A flat-screen television adorned one wall, golf trophies and books lined the other. The man of the house took the only chair in the room.

"I only have a few minutes." Adams shifted his weight from one hip to the other. "There's something I have to—someone needs my help."

"That text you just got? You have a more important client?"

"It wasn't from another client."

Tripp bent over behind his desk and opened a drawer as he spoke. "Well, you're here now. This won't take long."

The PI stepped inside and closed the door.

"What I'm about to show you is for your eyes only." From a legal-sized folder, Tripp extracted a white business envelope. "Read the note."

The PI removed a single piece of white printer paper from the envelope. He unfolded it and read.

Tripp rested his arms on the desk and stared at the private detective.

Adams' expression gave nothing away as he placed the paper down on the desk. The two typed lines stared back at him.

I made it without your help. Now I want you to know what helpless feels like.

"Do you know who it's from?"

Tripp shook his head.

"When did you receive it?"

"About a month ago. It came in the mail."

"Why didn't you show it to the detectives?"

"Because of what they might find. I don't want it to be public record."

"It doesn't necessarily—"

"Look, I might know who it came from. One of two women from years ago. One was a lot older, one a lot younger. I don't discriminate on age. But I don't want Patricia to know. She can't know. I will categorically deny I ever met these women if it comes to that, but I don't want her to even hear about them."

"Okay. That's a different matter." The PI rubbed his chin. "And technically, you're my client. But, if I find out who wrote this letter and that it has anything to do with your daughter's disappearance—"

"We'll cross that bridge if we come to it."

"So, what is it, exactly, you want from me?" Adams asked.

"I'll give you some more names. They're not on the list I gave the detective. One of the women . . . we had a summer fling. Turns out she thought it was more significant than I did because we had a few casual dinners, you know—before the main event. She tried to stay in touch. Told me she was pregnant."

Adams crossed his arms.

"I know . . . I know . . ." His leather chair creaked as Tripp leaned way back, folding his hands in his lap. "Should have used protection. Guess I don't like to, never did. Anyway, I ignored her. I was sure she was either lying to me in the first place or got an abortion. So, I don't know why she would have a problem with me today, but who knows."

"Was that the last you heard from her? What about the others?"

"There might have been additional attempts to communicate with me. I don't remember exactly. It took me a while to even remember their names. Hell…if I didn't have such a good memory…" Tripp selected a piece of stationery from another drawer, wrote on it, and pushed it toward Adams. "Find out if any of these women wrote that letter. And if it has anything to do with my daughter's disappearance. And be discreet."

Adams dipped his head. "That's my job."

Chapter Thirteen

Not far from the entrance to the Mannings' neighborhood, Victoria saw Adams' white Audi leave through the gate. Acting on an impulse, she made a split-second decision to follow him. The forensics team wouldn't need the hairbrush and toothbrush until they returned to the lab. The Mannings would have to wait a bit longer to hear Emma had not been found. Following Adams was more important. She wanted to know what he might be doing for the Mannings on the side. She had a hunch there was something else in play, something the family was doing their best to keep under wraps.

Adams' first stop was a shopping center. The parking lot was full, with cars circling for spots and following shoppers to their vehicles. The only open space was for a UPS store, with a sign that said ten minutes only on it. Adams pulled in.

Cheater.

Victoria drove past, her head turned away. She idled behind another vehicle waiting to claim a spot and watched Adams in her rearview mirror. He got out of his Audi carrying a square cardboard box.

Guess I owe him an apology.

She barely had time to get turned around before he was heading back to his car and pulling out.

At the main road, a string of traffic prevented her from keeping up with him. She finally caught a break and was lucky to spot him making a right turn ahead.

After a few miles, Adams turned into an apartment complex.

Victoria drove past and parked in front of the next building, glad her dark blue rental was unobtrusive in make and color. Shielded between a van and a truck, she busied herself with arranging pretend objects on the passenger seat while she kept a careful eye on him.

Adams got out of his car. A teenage boy wearing a hoodie and athletic shorts, and carrying a drawstring bag, walked forward to meet him. The boy must have been waiting in front of the building and knew Adams was coming.

Adams used his hand to turn the boy's head to the side. After a few seconds, the boy jerked his head away. The PI stared up at one of the apartment buildings. They exchanged words. She couldn't see what Adams was saying, because his back was to her. He held up his hands and then placed them on his hips. The young man looked away, but stayed where he was, hands stuffed into the front pocket of his hoodie.

Then the teen handed something to Adams. Something small enough to fit in the palm of his hand. Adams took it, slid it into his pocket, and placed his hand on the young man's sleeve. They stayed like that for a few seconds, some sort of silent agreement occurring.

A few more words and then Adams beckoned toward his car. The young man followed, glancing over his shoulder at the building as he walked to the passenger side.

What was that about?

Victoria followed them to the drive-through of a Panera Bread. She parked in a spot for to-go orders. She would have loved to run inside and order a salad, but she wasn't about to lose them now. She had to know what this was about and where they were going. Instead, she pulled a bag of licorice from her purse, grabbed four slices, and chomped into all of them at once.

Adams handed a credit card to the woman working the window. A minute later, he accepted two bags and pulled away.

Their next stop was a hotel. Adams parked his Audi and they walked inside. The teen carried both the Panera bags and was still wearing his draw string bag on his back. Adams carried nothing.

Victoria curled her fingers tightly around the steering wheel. *Not good . . . not good . . .not good. Maybe the young man just looks young but isn't. Maybe it's a boyfriend. No . . . he's young. Definitely a minor. Doesn't even look old enough to drive.*

Victoria played devil's advocate with herself, trying to find a non-sinister explanation for what she was seeing. But the discrepancy between their ages, their dress, and their mannerisms made that difficult. Everything that came to mind made her blood boil. She sat stewing in her anger. Adams walked out alone only a minute or two after he'd gone inside. So perhaps Adams wasn't the customer. Didn't matter. An adult dropping a teen at a hotel was a red flag of a teen being pimped.

Her phone pinged with a new message. Connelly asked how the Mannings reacted to the news about not finding Emma.

Victoria didn't respond. She wanted to tell someone about Adams, but at this point, she didn't know who she could trust.

Adams got in his car and drove off. Victoria debated following, but the Mannings were waiting for news of their daughter. She selected their address from her phone and started the directions, which required her to head in the opposite direction from Adams.

What was going on with the PI? Did he leave the teen there for a customer? Did what I just saw have anything to do with Emma Manning's disappearance?

She called Sam and left a message. After spelling Adams's full name, she added, "Get me anything you can on him."

Chapter Fourteen

The temperature had dropped with the setting sun and a chilly wind blew strands of her hair as she rang the Mannings' doorbell. Following Adams had taken a little over an hour, but after what she'd seen, she was glad she'd made the detour. Her empty stomach tightened, a reminder she'd missed dinner. Connelly's mention of coconut cake from yesterday popped into her mind and disappeared just as quickly. Licorice followed by cake wasn't exactly a dinner of champions. She could do better. But now, she had to tell Emma's family that they hadn't found any conclusive evidence in the empty building. Not yet, anyway.

She wished she could tell the family they were close to finding Emma, but it wouldn't have been true. Closer maybe, but not much.

Magda answered the door with a sad smile and a nod. She held a rag and spray bottle in one hand.

"Still cleaning at this hour?"

"It helps me stay calm. I have to do something. I just feel so . . . "

"I understand completely." Without thinking about it, Victoria rested her hand on Magda's arm.

109

The corners of Magda's mouth lifted as her lips stayed pressed together, hardly a smile, but she appeared grateful for the tiny bit of comfort.

"Are the Mannings at home?" Victoria surveyed what she could see of the house. As before, everything was immaculate.

"Mrs. Manning just went upstairs to lie down. She's . . . she's not feeling well right now. Mr. Manning is in his office."

Magda led Victoria across the house. Through the kitchen doorway, Victoria spotted an almost empty liquor bottle on the counter. Magda followed the agent's gaze and frowned, but continued on.

"Agent Heslin is here," Magda announced at the open door to Tripp's office.

Dark circles rimmed his eyes. He stood up quickly and walked out to meet Victoria, eagerly studying her face for news. She kept her expression solemn.

"You didn't find her." His whole face had dropped. "Did you find anything?"

"Someone had been living inside the building. But whoever was there left before we arrived."

His expression contorted with anger. "So, do you even know if Emma was there?"

"Detective Connelly is still on site working with a forensic team to collect evidence. If your daughter was there, they'll know very soon. I came to get something they can use for a match. Her hairbrush and toothbrush."

"Oh!" Magda exclaimed from nearby. "A few weeks ago, all of the hairbrushes and toothbrushes in our house went missing. Everyone has new ones now."

"That's very strange." Victoria knitted her brows together.

"Yes. We didn't know what to think of it. I mean, how could something like that happen?" Magda asked. "Nothing else was missing. It happened on the same day a company was here cleaning windows. But why would they want those? I called the company and they said it had nothing to do with them."

"It was Emma playing some sort of prank." Tripp said.

"But she denied it," Magda responded. "She swore on her life she had nothing to do with it. And she was upset because apparently her hairbrush was special."

"Then it was one of her friends." Tripp dismissed Magda with his cool tone. "We have more important things to think about right now."

Magda turned and headed up the main stairway. Tripp followed her for a few strides then stopped, turning to Victoria as he pressed a hand against the banister. "What did you find in the building, exactly?"

"Hairs and fibers. Some trash that might have prints." She spared him hearing about the tooth and the blood-stained sheet they'd pulled off the mattress. "Mr. Manning, I have a few more questions for you."

"Let's go into my office," Tripp said, moving in that direction.

Magda appeared at the top of the stairs, so Victoria waited for the woman to come down. She handed Victoria a hairbrush and toothbrush inside a plastic storage bag.

"Thank you." Victoria placed the bag in her backpack and then followed Tripp's path.

Inside his office, he sat behind his desk with his hands steepled in front of him. He watched Victoria enter, but she could tell his thoughts were elsewhere. He didn't offer her a seat, which was fine with her.

111

Above the fireplace, the television played on mute. Emma Manning was one of the news stories, after the bomb threats and the football coverage. The words *Suspected Sex Trafficking Ring Abduction* scrolled underneath her picture.

Victoria frowned. *How did that happen?*

Tripp followed her gaze to the television. "When my daughter comes back, her life is ruined. What little girl wants everyone to know she was sex trafficked? We don't even know if that's the case, but it will forever be the perception."

Victoria swallowed around a lump forming in her throat. *At least he believes Emma will come home.*

There was no way the media outlets would back down now, not with this story. But the embarrassment it may cause was not Victoria's primary concern. The heightened coverage would put pressure on the abductors. The chances of them allowing Emma to be found alive and risk her revealing their operation or any of their identities were slim. If this kept up, they would kill her, if they hadn't already. The girl's best hope for survival might be that she was already far from Charlotte where the constant media coverage wouldn't be as much of a threat to whoever had her. But if she'd been taken out of the country, the chances of finding her were slim.

"What is it you need to ask me?" Tripp said.

Victoria stepped closer and touched her fingers to the edge of his desk. "How did you find Jay Adams?"

Tripp picked up a pen and tapped it. "He was recommended by a colleague."

"Have you used him before?"

"Yes." He cocked his head. "Why are you asking? Are you going to be needing an enemy list from him as well?"

She steeled herself against his sudden aggression—*it's the situation, don't hold it against him*— by focusing on what she'd come to find out. "We got a good tip, thanks to the media bulletins. But whoever was there appears to have left in a hurry, and might have known we were coming."

"So, you think—what?"

"Could be a coincidence. But in case it's not, I want to know how they knew. Where is Adams now?"

Tripp dropped the pen and strummed his fingers. His gaze traveled to a collection of trophies, then back to Victoria. "He doesn't give me a running play by play of his whereabouts, but I happen to know he had a personal issue to deal with."

"What did he need to take care of?" *Did it have anything to do with the young man and the hotel?*

"Come back in the morning and you can ask Adams whatever you want to ask him yourself." Tripp's eyes dropped to her chest and stayed there.

Her body stiffened and she clenched her jaw.

"He'll be following up on leads for me tomorrow." He continued to stare, clearly not caring if she caught him ogling or how it made her feel.

Narrowing her eyes, she asked, "What sort of leads is he following up for you?"

He turned to the television. A man wearing a Panthers NFL jersey was smiling inside a Chevrolet showroom. "If something comes of them, I'll share it with you and the detective."

Presumably, Tripp was a grieving, heart-sick father. But tolerating his patronizing, sometimes hostile attitude had become too much. He needed a firm reminder that hampering a federal agent's investigation was against the law. She hardened her

113

expression, about to let him have it. He exhaled loudly and spoke again.

"Adams was previously hired by my wife to follow me and document affairs I've had."

Victoria remained quiet, hoping he would continue. Someone working with Connelly had already followed up on the "mistakes" Tripp told them about yesterday. He was paying child support to two different women. In addition to Emma, he had a two-year-old son and a three-year-old daughter.

"I was careful. Very careful."

No idea what that's supposed to mean. Having affairs and fathering children unintentionally is hardly being 'careful'. She wasn't inclined to trust or believe anything he said.

Tripp leaned back in his chair, staring at his trophy shelf. He lifted his gaze toward the ceiling and swiveled his chair from side to side before he continued in a tone of resignation. "I have Adams tracking down two other women from my past. I'm talking way in the past. Before I met my wife."

Victoria processed the information. It didn't make sense. Were Emma's parents in denial about her situation? How could they be? Tripp saw the website photo; he watched the television coverage. Why would he think a former lover might be involved? And if he hadn't met Patricia yet, why did he need to keep the old relationships under wraps?

She cleared her throat. "I know this is difficult to hear, but at this time, it appears likely your daughter is somehow involved with a sex trafficking or prostitution ring."

"I know."

She stood stock-still, waiting. There had to be more.

"I'm sorry." Tripp stood up. He aimed the remote at the television and shut it off. "It's very late and believe it or not, I have

114

a call scheduled with a developer. As much as I enjoy your company—" His eyes lingered on her face, making her uncomfortable. "—you and I are going to have to put this talk off until tomorrow."

"I'm sorry, but that doesn't work for me. My priority is finding your daughter, not your work commitments. I need to know why you have Adams checking out these women. And why you didn't give Detective Connelly and me their names."

Tripp glared at her. "The women Adams is looking into. . . I don't want anyone to know about them. Especially not Patricia."

Maybe or maybe not. I would think she would care much less about relationships that occurred before they were married than the ones that happened after.

"The possibility exists that at least one of these women thinks she was pregnant with my child. If she does think that, I'm sure she's wrong."

Ah . . . he just doesn't want to pay child support to a third and fourth woman. "And why are you so sure they're wrong? Why do these women need to stay hidden?"

"Because they were prostitutes. Can you understand why that might not be well received?"

Chapter Fifteen

After replaying the conversation with Tripp Manning in her mind, Victoria had to focus on calming down. She dealt with plenty of criminals and disturbing people in her line of work, but Tripp rubbed her the wrong way. When he stared unapologetically at her breasts, it was all she could do not to tell him off. She had to remember to be professional, regardless. Not only was she representing the FBI, but she was also doing a favor for her boss. Still, for now, she wanted any thoughts of Tripp Manning and his seemingly endless string of affairs out of her head. She left the gated neighborhood, waving a combination of goodbye and thank you to the guard. Finally, she had time to call Ned without the possibility of being interrupted. Speaking to Ned was exactly what she needed to clear her mind.

"Hi. I'm so glad you answered," she said, turning onto a road lined with beautiful Crape Myrtle and Magnolia trees.

"Then I'm glad I did, too. You missing me? Or just your dogs?"

"I'm missing all of you." She hoped her sincerity came through loud and clear. "The day has flown. I haven't eaten anything since I grabbed a sandwich at lunch."

"Myrtle is already pacing in the kitchen to let me know it's time for their bedtime treats. These dogs sure know their routine. Hey, girl—"

Huh?

"Myrtle—it's Victoria on the phone."

Oh. He's talking to one of the dogs like she understands. She smiled. *Just like I do.*

"I'm putting you on speaker," he said.

"What about you? What did you do for dinner? There's no food at my house, is there? I would have stocked up for you if I hadn't had to leave with just a minute's notice. Please go ahead and order whatever you need with my card."

"You forgot to cancel the Farm Fresh delivery, so I ate that. As my appetizer."

"That's okay. I wouldn't have cancelled anyway. They need the business. Definitely eat it while I'm gone. I don't want it to go to waste." She sighed, loud enough that Ned heard her.

"What's wrong?"

"Nothing. It's just—I wish I was officially in charge here. If this were my case, we'd be making so much more progress."

A dog barked on Ned's end. "Can you take it over?"

The single bark was followed by an escalating chorus.

"No. I'm just supposed to be helping, sort of like a consult. But I don't know for sure if things are getting done." She slowed down and switched lanes to get around a group of bicyclists. "I guess I'm assuming they aren't because I'm not in the loop and the guy in charge isn't quite as intense as I'm used to."

"He's not taking the case seriously?"

"He's not doing anything wrong—maybe I'm just not impressed with his management skills. He's more suited to be a

117

travel agent than a hard-core detective." *So much for not talking about the case.* "And on top of that, the family hired a PI and I've got a terrible feeling about him right now. More than a feeling."

"Why?"

"Right from our first meeting he had me wondering. For a PI, he was well-groomed and very expensively dressed. A dichotomy of sorts."

"Someone could say that about you."

She huffed. "I suppose they could. I wanted to know what he was working on for the parents, so I followed him."

"You tailed the guy?"

"I did. I trust my intuition, not to mention my training. Now I have to figure out if what I saw is what I think it is. And if it's what I think it is, it's a big deal and I can't confront him until I have more evidence. Anyway, enough about me. Tell me something good. What are you going to do tomorrow? Big run day? Or big swim day?"

"Neither. I'm taking the day off. I hate to admit it, but I'm a little sore."

"Sore. How come?"

"I had a half-tri today, remember—"

She gasped. "Oh, my God! Ned! I'm so sorry! I'm the worst, worst, worst—" She was about to say girlfriend but stopped herself. Worst would suffice. She'd been self-absorbed, which wasn't like her, and was the opposite of the person she wanted to be.

Ned laughed. "Hey, it's no big deal. It was just a local one. If I was doing the Ironman and you forgot—well, then I might be pissed. But this wasn't anything big. I still managed to take Eddie and Izzy for a walk after."

"No. I feel terrible. Going on and on about myself."

"Look, my days are excellent. I wake up and I have complete control over my time. I get to make a big difference for people who otherwise couldn't afford pet care at the clinic. But it's safe to say your days are probably more interesting. I'm all for our conversations tipping towards whatever is more interesting."

"I promise that very little of what I do is interesting or glamorous. Please, tell me about your race." Victoria was still disappointed with herself for forgetting. "How did you do? Beat your time?"

"I did. The weather was perfect. I used a new bike and new shoes, always a risky move, but nothing went wrong. And I had a nice surprise at the end. Somehow—I'm sure you wouldn't know anything about this—my number raised five thousand bucks for the Compassion Clinic. Not too shabby. That pays for a lot of vet care."

So glad I filled out the donation forms for his clinic before I left, or I might have forgotten those as well! I've got to get better at this girlfriend thing.

Chapter Sixteen

After the party, Sofia was hungry and exhausted, her insides raw and stinging. She didn't know what time it was, but some of their parties lasted from late at night until just before sunup, and it was all she could to do to keep her eyes open. More than anything, she wanted to shower—and hoped she might get a chance before Svet locked them in the basement room again. Next to her in the van, Anastasia slumped against the seat, rubbing her hand gently over a blossoming bruise on her arm.

Svet turned into a neighborhood with large homes. The yards were expertly lit with spotlights and floodlights. He slowed in front of a stately, stone covered house. In Ukraine, it would have been a small-scale palace, but lots of their American customers lived in similar-sized homes. On both sides of the driveway, hundreds of purple and lavender clumps—they didn't look like flowers through Sofia's eyes but had to be—appeared in the headlight beams. This wasn't what she expected at the end of a long night. She nudged Anastasia and whispered, "Do you recognize this place?"

"Um . . . no . . . we are never here before."

Svet stopped in the driveway, but kept the engine running. He grabbed his phone, punched at the screen, and waited. "Here. Open garage door."

Oh, no. Not another party. Just when she believed they'd survived another night; they were expected to work again. Dreams of taking a shower were forgotten. She'd be eternally grateful if only she and Anastasia could return to their basement room and be left alone.

A few seconds later, one of the four garage doors slid up.

Inside, Stephen's BMW was parked in one of the spaces. Behind it, the girls' suitcases were lying toppled on the concrete floor.

Svet parked and exited the van. "Get out. Grab your stuff and bring it inside." He left them alone and disappeared through a door leading from the garage to the house.

"Where are we?" Anastasia asked, rolling her suitcase forward.

"No idea." Sofia kept her eyes on the entrance to the house. She didn't like the uncertainty. This wasn't how they did business. Svet never walked in before them and left them alone. Perhaps it wasn't another party. But then what were they doing in this nice home? And why was Stephen there, too?

She quickly unzipped her bag. Her stuff was tossed and tangled inside, mixed with Anastasia's. She moved some clothes aside and found their DVD player and exercise discs at the bottom. The book she'd been reading wasn't in there, but she hadn't liked it anyway. Sex wasn't something she wanted to think about if she didn't have to. She zipped her bag up and hurried into the house after Svet and Anastasia. The unexpected change in their routine had left her wide awake again.

121

Inside, they left their suitcases by the front door and followed the sound of Svet's voice across the house and into the backyard. Stephen stood on the patio talking to Svet, chain smoking like he did whenever he was angry. Beyond him, a pool with a cascading waterfall had been built with the same stones that formed some of the home's exterior walls. Tiny white lights were strung around the patio and yard.

In her sleeveless dress, Sofia shivered in the brisk, evening air. But it felt good to be outside—cool, clean, and invigorating. She squinted around the area, hoping to see Sasha.

Stephen stared at Anastasia, frowned, and turned to Svet. "What happened to her arm?"

Svet shrugged.

Anastasia wrapped her hand around the reddish-purple bruise.

Stephen glared at the big man. "One of your main responsibilities is preventing anyone from hurting the girls. Why do I need to remind you that they're the ones bringing in the money, not you?"

"She's fine." Svet said. "So, uh, is she here?"

Sofia was dying to ask who 'she' was. *Emma?* Also— where were they and why were they there? But she could only wonder because Stephen did not allow them to ask questions.

"She's not," Stephen replied. "But that could change any minute. I don't know where she is."

The 'she' in question wasn't Emma, or Stephen would have taken a whole different tone.

He turned to the girls and his voice was soothing, the way he sounded when he wanted them to believe he cared. "You're staying here for now. Help yourself to whatever food you can scrounge up in the cabinets and fridge. Then go downstairs and take your stuff with you. Find a bedroom to stay in and go to sleep. Your new friend is already down there. Make sure everything stays as you found it. Don't leave the basement. Exercise in the morning."

Sofia squinted, taking a last look at the blurred outline of a pool, a waterfall, and the tiny white lights before she and Anastasia walked back into the house and found the kitchen.

Behind white cabinet doors, matching containers with blue tops were stacked on top of each other. Boxes were lined up edge to edge. Cans formed perfect rows. The fridge held cartons of yogurt, some fruit, and water bottles. Barely saying a word to each other, the girls made quick work of eating. It was unusual for them to have this freedom in a kitchen.

Satiated, yet still alone, they took protein bars, packets of nuts, and a box of chocolates from the cabinets. They hid the food inside their suitcases, insurance for the next time they were miserably hungry.

"Let's find the basement," Sofia said, feeling like a thief looking for an escape route so she wouldn't be caught red-handed.

Anastasia opened the door to a bathroom and closed it again. She did the same with a closet.

Sofia followed Anastasia through the house. "When you went in with Svet, did he say whose house this is?"

"He not say. But look." Anastasia pointed to a life-sized portrait on the dining room wall. A slim woman with red hair. A haughty expression and the hint of a mysterious smile all rolled into one. They would have thought the woman was beautiful if they didn't already know her.

It was a portrait of Ms. Bois.

Chapter Seventeen

Following up on the women from Tripp's past brought Adams to an area of town he hadn't seen in years. Not since he'd traveled to a nearby high school to play a basketball game with his school team.

He drained the last of his morning coffee, parked, and walked up to the apartment he'd come to visit. The address was the last one on record, but the woman he was looking for seemed to have disappeared. The doorbell hung from a broken wire, so he knocked.

A scruffy man answered the door with a T-shirt stretched over his beer belly.

"Sorry to bother you," Adams said. "I'm looking for Linda Wood. This is her last address on record."

"Who are you?" the man asked.

"I'm a private investigator. Jay Adams." He waited while the man rubbed his unshaven chin.

"Don't know nothin' about a Linda Wood. She don't live here. But there's some old ladies who have lived in this place forever. Always watching me come and go. Minding everyone's business. If the lady you're looking for used to live here, try asking one of them."

"Thank you," Adams said. "Where can I find one of these ladies?"

The man pointed. "See that door with the Home Sweet Home sign? That's one of 'em." He turned to Adams. "I might need a PI. How much you cost?"

"Depends on the job." Adams smiled and reached for his card.

The man looked Adams up and down. "Never mind. I doubt I can pay whatever it is you're asking. You look a little high-brow for my wallet."

"If you change your mind and want to discuss it, here's my card." Adams handed his card to the man. "I've been known to discount my fees. Thanks for your help."

Several of the porches and balconies functioned as storage areas piled with junk. A man on one balcony caught his attention. A hoodie covered his face in shadows. He was carrying two stuffed black garbage bags.

The porch of the apartment with the painted Home Sweet Home sign had potted plants and an assortment of rabbit statues. He rang the doorbell and waited. From somewhere between the apartments came a heated argument between two men.

An elderly woman opened the door and peered at him suspiciously through the screen. Her apron and house coat appeared to be as old as she was.

"Hi," Adams said. "I'm looking for Linda Wood." The smell of whatever she was cooking wafted through the screen. *Chicken soup?*

The woman cocked her head to the side and frowned at him. Putting himself in her shoes, Adams smiled, attempting to look as kind and harmless as possible.

"Are you a cop?"

"Private investigator. My client is looking for Ms. Linda Wood. One of your neighbors suggested you might have known her."

She placed her hand against the doorframe and leaned closer. "I knew her. But you're about five years too late."

"Do you know where she might be now?"

"Sure do. Six feet under. I was there when she was buried. You want to visit her grave?"

Adams was surprised and angry at himself for not discovering her obituary with his research. But if there was one, how could he have missed it? In any case, Linda Wood had not sent the threatening letter.

"Died young, she did. Before her time should'a come. Cemetery is over there on the other side of the highway," said the woman. "And Linda's got one of the biggest tombstones in the place. You'd think she'd been the president of something. Fancy casket, too. Not the economy ones. Wish she'd been alive to have seen it. She would have been real proud and real surprised. I can't imagine how it got paid for."

◆ ◆ ◆

The sun glinted through Victoria's windshield and she pulled the visor down. From a safe distance, she watched Adams talking to an elderly woman on her doorstep. The apartment complex was older than the one where he picked up the boy yesterday. *Are his visits related to Emma Manning's investigation and the leads Tripp gave him, or something else?*

Sam called. Victoria answered immediately, as if Adams might be able to hear the soft vibration of her phone and she needed to silence it.

"Hey," she said. "I'm in my car, playing spy again."

"I'm sure you've had some training for that. Jay Adams again?"

"Yes. I followed him from the Mannings' neighborhood this morning."

"I found out a few things about your PI."

"What did you find?" She took a sip of coffee from her to-go cup. She couldn't wait to hear what Sam had discovered.

"I knew the name was familiar, but it's a common one, of course. His father used to be the mayor and is currently a major investor in several Charlotte endeavors—a minor league sports team and two restaurants."

Another call came in.

"Hold on, Sam. Sorry, I've got to take this call. Let me call you back, okay?"

"Sure thing."

Victoria had done some of her own research earlier and found the owner of the vacant building she and Connelly had investigated. A company in India called Kolmon. They owned corporate buildings all over the world that they leased or resold. A local realty company helped find the tenants and handled the rental agreements. The realtor was calling her back.

Victoria hung up and accepted the new call. She identified herself and explained she needed a few minutes of the realtor's time regarding one of her listings.

"I'll head back to my office as soon as I'm finished at this property," the realtor said. "I'll be there in less than an hour. But then I've got another appointment at three that unfortunately cannot be rescheduled. So hopefully we'll be finished by then. You have the address?"

Victoria kept her eyes on Adams, who was heading straight to his vehicle. "I do. Thank you. I'll see you soon."

Victoria typed the realtor's office address into her phone, grateful that the woman was concerned and willing to help without even knowing the seriousness of the issue. Busy people were rarely receptive to questioning that interrupted their workday. And guilty people rarely cooperated without first being served a warrant. Lonely people were a whole different story. Some of the elderly offered cookies and tea and treated the agent's visit like a social call.

Minutes later, Adams drove out of the apartment complex and Victoria did, too. As much as she wanted to know where the PI would go next, she had another angle to explore with the realtor. Slowing to a stop at a yellow light, she called Connelly.

"Hey, Victoria." He was breathing loudly.

"Hi. I've got an interview lined up with someone who might be able to help us."

"In five hundred feet, right turn on West Moreland Road," her phone instructed.

"Is this related to the info you sent me last night about Tripp Manning's alleged lovers?"

"No. And they aren't alleged lovers. He's the one who told me about them."

A row of cars with the word Clemson and orange tiger paws painted on the windows honked their horns.

"Because I'm not seeing how they could be relevant now," Connelly said. "Let Adams chase them down."

That might be what I've just watched him do. The irony hit her—she'd been investigating the investigator. She would tell Connelly about Adams soon, but not until she had a better idea of what he was doing. A little more time and patience.

She kept her voice calm. "This is something different." The light turned green and she hit the gas pedal harder than necessary.

"What is it?"

She filled him in on her research. "The realtor's name is Allison Greenwood. I'm on my way to meet her now."

In the next lane, a man hung out the window of one of the Clemson cars and yelled to the car behind him, distracting her for a second.

"A realtor?" Connelly asked. "You think she'll know anything?"

"I think someone should find out. It's her listing. I imagine she visits the building occasionally. I'll let you know if I learn anything worth an additional look."

"I'm at the lab, trying to find out why the print analysis hasn't been done. I'll give them a few more minutes and then head over and join you."

Victoria stopped at a gas station and took her time filling her tank and purchasing a bottle of water before continuing to her destination.

Sitting in her car outside the realtor's office, she drummed her fingers across the steering wheel. She could handle being away from home, as long as she was making a difference. But when she was just killing time, she was reminded of all that was waiting for her at home. Mainly, Ned and her dogs. There was also her father. She should visit him once she was back, take him up on his frequent offers to meet for lunch. Maybe she could bring Ned with her. Or was it too soon? She'd never had a guy she wanted her Dad to meet. Plenty of male dogs, but no humans. Her work and her dogs consumed her life, never allowing time for a serious relationship—until now. For once, she felt like a normal person.

She took a few sips of water, glanced at her watch, and called Ned.

"Hey there," he said. The sound of his voice, the voice usually accompanied by his warm smile, made her heart skip a beat.

"Hi. I'm just calling to say hello." *And this time, I'm going to ask about him first.* "How is your day going so far?"

"Good. I'm just hanging out with the dogs right now. Going to watch a game later. My sister and her husband might come over to watch with me, if that's okay."

"Of course, it's okay!" She really liked the idea of his family coming over. She just wished she could be there, too. *Once we get Emma back . . .*

"What's going on there?"

"Nothing right now. I'm just waiting on someone. But there's something I meant to talk to you about yesterday and I forgot."

"Uh, oh. That doesn't sound good. Did one of the dogs complain about me? Did Eddie say I was skimping on his meals?"

She laughed, almost told him no before realizing how ridiculous that would be, and laughed again. "Any chance you learned about livestock in vet school?"

An S-class Mercedes sedan parallel parked in front of her.

"Farm animals?" Ned asked. "Like chickens and pigs?"

An elegant woman with long, straight red hair and pale skin exited the Mercedes wearing a black sheath dress.

"Miniature donkeys," Victoria said, watching the woman through her front windshield. "Would you be able to care for sick donkeys?" If he said yes, then he was getting a well-deserved salary bump for sure.

Without glancing toward Victoria's rental, the woman sauntered away on high heels with balance-a-book-on-her-head posture.

"Sure, with some research," Ned said. "I'm no expert, but I have a buddy who specialized in equine health I could consult with. You know someone with a sick donkey?"

As soon as the woman disappeared inside the office, Connelly arrived and parked across from Victoria.

"I'm so sorry, Ned. I thought I had more time, but now I have to go. I'm following up on a potential lead. Can I call you back later?"

"No problem."

She listened for any sign of annoyance but didn't detect any. His easy-going nature was one of the things she appreciated most about him, along with his love for animals, his kindness, his intellect, his discipline, and his incredibly fit body. And he seemed to get that things with her would need to move slowly. "Tonight? After your family leaves?"

"Sure. I'll be here. No worries."

She waited for him to say goodbye before hanging up, feeling a twinge of guilt. Next time she called she would make sure she had more time so she wouldn't be ending the call abruptly again.

Victoria put her phone away and got out of her car. The detective waved. As she walked over to meet him, he popped the last piece of a bagel into his mouth.

"Any break with the evidence from the basement?" she asked.

He shook his head. "Nope."

"Did they find prints on the trash or the book?"

"Yes. They lifted some from the foil wrappers and scanned them." He ran his tongue over his teeth like there might be something stuck on them. "No matches."

"What databases did you use?"

"All of them."

"Why don't you send them over to me, we've got experts . . ."

"So do we."

Victoria frowned. His tone made her realize she'd overstepped. Her comment had come off as condescending. She could hear his phone buzzing, but she had several more questions about the investigation. "Did you access her emails yet?"

"Someone is working on it." Connelly thrust his hand into his coat pocket to retrieve his phone.

"Still working on it? That could be your best lead. Why haven't—"

He held up a finger for Victoria and lifted his phone to his head. "Detective Connelly."

Victoria blew out a breath, checking her frustration at the door as they entered the office. At the reception desk, Connelly was still listening to whoever was on the other end of his phone. "Allison Greenwood, please," Victoria said.

The middle-aged receptionist smiled at Victoria. "Sure." Then the woman turned to Connelly. "And welcome back."

Connelly finished his call and grinned. "You have a good memory."

"Thank you," the woman said, beaming. "As a matter of fact, I do. And in case you don't—Miss Greenwood's office is down the hall." Still smiling, she pointed in the general direction. "First door on the right."

"I was once a client," Connelly explained to Victoria as he walked down the hallway.

"You know the realtor we're meeting?" Victoria asked.

Connelly shrugged and kept moving. "We've met."

"But you didn't remember her name earlier?"

They had reached Allison Greenwood's office, and there wasn't time for him to answer.

Inside the bright, white space, the same striking woman with the perfect posture stood up from behind a desk and greeted them with a polished smile. Close up, Victoria could tell the woman was in her mid-thirties. Attractive and exceptionally well-maintained. After introductions were made, the realtor asked if she could offer them anything to drink, appearing as gracious as she was beautiful.

"No, thank you," Victoria said.

"If you'll excuse me for just one minute," Miss Greenwood said as she walked around the desk, "I just got in and there's one thing I need to take care of." The realtor's gaze locked with Connelly's for just a second longer than Victoria considered normal, but she said nothing to suggest she had met him before.

Once the realtor left the room, Victoria whispered, "Not sure she remembers who you are."

Connelly made a sad, comical, clown-face. "Well thank you very much for rubbing that in. I guess I'm easy to forget." Without missing a beat, his confident, laid-back smile reappeared.

"So, she wasn't *your* realtor, then?"

Connelly's face twitched. The soft but unmistakable buzz of a vibrating phone filled the quiet office. Connelly was still holding a phone in his hand. That screen remained dark. The buzz was coming from his coat pocket.

"You need to get that?" Victoria asked.

He responded without checking the phone. "No, it's my personal line."

Victoria wondered if it was related to his mother again. Having to take care of aging parents was stressful. She hoped he wasn't the one having to pay for her assisted living facility and private care on his police salary.

Ms. Greenwood returned, barely a minute after she left the room. "Sorry about that, so how can I help you?" She smoothed her dress against the back of her legs and gracefully sat.

Victoria answered. "We have some questions about one of the office buildings you're offering for lease in Resling Corporate Park."

"Sure. Which one?" She scooted forward and hit a few buttons on her keyboard.

"It's the eight thousand building."

The realtor tilted her head to the side. "Are you interested in renting the property for one of the police units?" Her tone indicated she knew they weren't.

"No. We're interested as part of an ongoing investigation," Connelly said.

"Got it. All right, in that case, what can I tell you? Let's see. It's been on the market for over a year. Haven't had much interest in the property since it came available. A few months ago, I was hoping Amazon might want the land to build on, but they aren't interested in another Charlotte area location right now."

"When did you last visit the property and go inside?" Connelly asked.

"Oh, it's been awhile. Like I said, not much interest. Just give me a few seconds here and I can tell you exactly," she said, focusing on her laptop. "Okay. Four weeks ago. I showed the property to a corporate client from New Jersey. Is there something specific you'd like to know?"

Victoria doubted that whoever was living in the basement had been there that long. There would have been more trash. But it was possible. Maybe whoever was down there cleaned up every few days. "Did you go down to the bottom level when you were there?"

"The basement? No. The client wasn't excited about the property. It was one of several I showed them. We didn't stay long. I don't know if I've ever been down to the bottom floor of that property. Why do you ask? Maybe if I knew what you were looking for, I could be more helpful."

"We found evidence of squatters there," Connelly said.

Victoria frowned. *Squatters would not have locked themselves in one room with a bucket.*

"Really? That's not going to help it sell." Miss Greenwood looked concerned. "Well, I guess it's been cold lately. I suppose, as long as there's no harm done . . .Was there any damage?"

"No. Nothing vandalized," Connelly said. "A forensics team was out there yesterday and collected evidence."

"They were?" Ms. Greenwood asked. "Did they have a code to get in, or did they break in . . . never mind. I better go out there today and have a look. Might have to put different locks on."

"We're done there." The detective tapped his thigh. "But we might have someone watching the property in case whoever was there returns."

"Okay. I understand." The realtor glanced at her watch. Her tight, professional smile returned.

"Did anyone else go out there to show the place?" Victoria asked.

"Nope. That's unusual by the way—so few showings. It's a fluke. But location is everything. Most businesses don't want to be isolated." The realtor stood up. "I'm afraid I have to leave soon for another appointment. But, please, if there's any way I can help you, just let me know. You've got my number."

Victoria and Connelly exchanged a brief look. She wasn't sure what he was thinking. The interview had not been particularly helpful so far, but she had nothing left to ask. "Thank you for your time."

"Yes, thank you," Connelly said. "We'll let you know if there are any additional issues with the property."

Victoria and Connelly walked out together.

"That was a waste," Connelly said. "I have to get back uptown." He gave her a dismissive wave as he walked to his car.

Victoria followed. *Not every lead will pan out, you still have to track down each and every one.* "Look, I know this isn't my case. But I really care about getting Emma Manning home. And I can't help if I don't have a better idea of what you're doing."

"We're all very grateful for your help. You've been great. Especially with finding that website. If I didn't thank you enough already, I should have."

"I wasn't looking for a thank you, Connelly." Victoria stood with her hands on her hips. "I need to know what is and isn't being done. I'm happy to fill in wherever needed."

His phone rang again.

"That's great. I really appreciate that. I do." He smiled, but his jaw looked tight. His phone kept ringing. "Okay. Let me call you once I get to my office and I'll send you an updated case list. Gotta go. Try that fried chicken I told you about, if you haven't already." He got into his car and shut the door.

Victoria wondered if his personal issues were impeding on his professional duties.

Chapter Eighteen

Stephen stood on the patio admiring the landscaped back yard. On the distant horizon, acres of plush green golf course met the hazy sky.

Svet had left and his brother, Petar, arrived to replace him. Petar joined Stephen on the patio. "N—n—nice digs." He leaned against one of the chairs around the firepit. "So, are you g-g-gonna tell me what that was about yesterday?"

Stephen puffed his cigarette. His eyes settled on the tattoos covering Petar's arms—a snake, a skull, and a mermaid with enormous breasts. "You're the one who needs to tell me. What did you see?"

The bodyguard lit his own cigarette and spoke to his boss without looking at him. "Just one FBI woman."

"What was she doing? And don't make me drag this out of you with a hundred questions. Listening to you try to sputter out words requires more patience than I have right now."

Petar swallowed. "I dunno."

Stephen glared at him.

"Looking around?" Petar inhaled and blew out a ribbon of smoke. "Sh-sh-he yelled out something to me. I took off. W-why didn't you tell me you left with the new girl? I thought I was supposed to watch her."

"I didn't have time to tell you. Isn't that obvious? I had just enough time to get her out of there. Did you change the plates on your car?"

"Yeah." Petar swallowed, staring out towards the pool. "Just did. W-w-what are the girls doing here?"

"If you mean, why are they here—they're here because I told Svet to bring them here. If you mean what are they doing at this very minute—I sedated our most recent addition. Sofia and Anastasia are watching television."

There were no landlines in the house and the girls didn't have access to a cell phone. As long as the local girl was sedated, he wasn't worried about them going anywhere. Anastasia and Sofia could be trusted. Years of threatening them—*I'll always find you and I'll slaughter your families if you try to leave, if you don't do as I say*—had taken their toll. Although, he'd thought the same about Sasha until she'd outright refused a new customer's request, kicked him where it counted when he tried to force her, and then screamed for help.

"Sh-sh-sh—" Petar gulped. "Should I get them some food?"

Stephen sat down on one of the recliners and stretched his legs over the thick cushions. "They can fend for themselves with whatever food is in the house. Just keep an eye on them, make sure the girl doesn't wake up." His phone rang. Petar walked into the house as he answered.

"What happened?" Allison always got right to the point.

"We had to vacate your building. And good thing we did. An FBI agent came sniffing around."

"That would be Agent Heslin. Who was staying there?"

"Sofia and Anastasia. And a new girl."

"A new one?"

"Damian brought her. She's a local."

"Please tell me it's not the missing girl on television. Emma . . . something or other."

Stephen was surprised and impressed that Allison had surmised correctly.

"Damian brought her. And I'm going to have a memorable chat with him about it. Believe me."

"I'm glad you got everyone and most everything out in time. But that girl cannot—"

"How do you know we got out in time?"

"I tried to call you earlier. Detective Connelly and that agent came to poke around and ask questions. Now I know why. Emma Manning."

Stephen sat up to grind his cigarette butt on the glass side table.

"So where are the girls now?"

He leaned back on the cushions again. "A friend's house."

"A friend?"

"A friend with a house that's way too big for just her. A friend who must have so many other places to stay that she didn't even come home last night."

Allison inhaled like she was about to dive underwater and stay there. "Where are they, Stephen?"

"Don't lose your professional demeanor. It's unbecoming. They're in one of your guest rooms."

"What? Emma Manning, too? No! Absolutely not. I have neighbors! A neighborhood association." Stephen knew Allison was in her office because she was only hissing, not shouting. Her rage came through the phone just the same.

"Miss Manning is drugged. She has no idea where she is, where she's been, or where she's going. Your nearest neighbors are acres away. If they see anything, they'll think you're having a few girlfriends to stay."

She scoffed. "No one would ever believe that. Why didn't you take them to your condo?"

"Why would I? You have extra space and a view of the golf course. Though I might have taken them somewhere else, had you answered your phone when I called you."

"You could have taken them to a hotel! Get them out of my house. Did anyone see them go in?"

"No one saw us. Our cars are in your garage."

"How the hell did—never mind. Listen to me, I have a new place for them. A place they can stay permanently."

"You mean we would buy the place?"

"We should have someone else buy or lease it for us. It would put an end to these fire-drill evacuations. It's an empty commercial property near the stadium. Used to be a club. It won't sell. It's run down and the owners won't come down on the price, but I'll get them to come around. It will be a good location for business. There are living quarters upstairs. You can take the girls there now, until they leave Charlotte. In that area, even if someone notices them, they won't care."

"I'm not moving again. We're staying here until after the games, then we're off to Winston-Salem."

"No. No. No. Absolutely, not. This new spot will be closer to—"

"This is close enough." He adjusted the lumbar pillow behind him. "It's a wonderful place for me to meditate. You know, Allison, until now, I don't think I ever fully appreciated the set-up you have. Our arrangement has certainly worked out well for you.

141

For the most part, you get to live in the lap of luxury and keep your distance from the whole ugly operation."

"Or I wouldn't be able to do what I do for us." Something snapped on Allison's end of the phone. "If I have to be anywhere near those girls, I'm going to need a bigger cut."

"If our business is suffering, you suffer, too."

"Business is hardly suffering, Stephen. You don't have enough girls to handle all the calls with this event in town. But if you think you can offer clients a girl whose picture is all over the news, you've lost it."

Stephen laughed.

"Did you hear me? Do not put that girl on the market here. We need to get her to the Dominican Republic where she'll disappear. I don't care who you sell her to there, just make sure she never sees the light of day in this country again."

"Don't forget, Allison, this is my business. I started it and I know what I'm doing. But you've piqued my interest with the business property near the stadium." He sat up to light another cigarette, then leaned back again on the striped chaise lounge and closed his eyes. "I was thinking, when we get back from Winston, I might want to buy myself a nice place like yours."

"I'm heading over to the place to make sure it's safe—the spot I want you to move to. And then we'll talk again. Those girls need to get out of my house. And don't let them touch anything. I mean it. And for the record—I was away on business last night, not that I need to explain my private life to you."

Allison hung up.

She was freaking out, showing the cracks in her facade of control. He had expected no less. In her perfectionist mind, she had a reputation to uphold—sexy, powerful business woman who donated generously to the community. If the world ever found out she was a key player in a human trafficking ring—well, that would derail her carefully-constructed persona before she knew what hit her.

How fun would it be to bring down Allison?

Maybe someday he'd find out. She wouldn't be the first colleague he'd had to murder. *Mr. Jones tried to cheat me and didn't realize how carefully I tracked our earnings.* But for right now, she was useful and he benefitted from her ambitions. Bottom line—she was an asset.

Allison was right about the American girl, though. Little Miss Manning was an escalating liability. Because of her, the FBI was on their trail. Something had to be done about the situation.

There was nothing easier and more lucrative than selling girls for sex. A bag of drugs could only be sold once. One and done. A young girl could fetch thousands of dollars an hour and be sold over and over again. A recyclable product with unlimited earning potential. If he picked the right girls and paid off a few business allies to look out for him, no one gave them any trouble. But if he took the wrong girl . . .

He leaned his head against the pillow and smoked another cigarette before making his next phone call. "Hello, my friend."

"Stephen! I was gonna call you. I, uh—listen—"

"Shut up."

"I mean, uh—I've got to know—you don't have Emma Manning, do you?"

Anger pulled at the corners of Stephen's mouth as he spoke. "It appears you've forgotten why I'm paying you."

The man on the other end of the line gulped. "This is a whole different game you've stepped into. First I have—"

Stephen frowned. "Whatever you're going to do to get the cops, the FBI, and the media off our trail—do it now!"

"So, you do have her? I need to know—"

Stephen hung up. He opened the Peace and Calm Meditation App on his phone and selected the gentle sounds of rainfall before placing the phone down on the chaise. He closed his eyes, but his mind raced. What was the point of a home like Allison's if he couldn't relax here?

A faint chirping noise sounded through the recorded rain. At first, he thought it came from the App, but soon realized it originated somewhere in the bushes. He stood, cocking his head to listen, and then strolled toward the sound.

A bird was lying on the ground, uselessly flapping one broken wing. Stephen picked the animal up and peered at it. The bird struggled and Stephen tightened his grasp. The chirping intensified into a high-pitched screech as he clenched his fist and the space surrounding the bird became smaller. He grinned at the desperate fight for survival erupting inside his hand. The tension in his shoulders relieved a bit more with the shattering of each fragile bone.

The bird's head flopped to one side, lifeless. Stephen dropped it on the ground and booted it out of sight.

Returning to the chaise, he kicked off his shoes and sat down, wiping blood and gore onto the blue-striped cushion.

He turned off the fake rain, closed his eyes, and laid his head back.

◆ ◆ ◆

Perched on the edge of her office chair, Allison took a sip of her coffee, eyes glued on the local news coverage. *Spoiled little Emma Manning.* Her disappearance had caused quite a stir, although it had recently taken a back seat to the bomb threat news.

How nice to have so many people worried about you, so many people concerned with your well-being.

Allison crushed her empty cup, tossed it into the trash, and shut off the television. She scooped up her key fob and stood. What a difference from the rusty old key she carried as a child, the one that opened a one-room apartment crawling with roaches. The frail latchkey kid with the frizzy red hair had disappeared without leaving a trace, just like Emma Manning. Allison's money brought power. The power to teach people a lesson if they crossed her.

"I'm going to check on one of our properties." She cruised by the front desk in her high heels. "I won't be back today."

"Miss Greenwood, wait." The receptionist craned her neck. "Aren't representatives from the Kline Company meeting you here later?"

"I pushed that back. Something came up." Her smile was forced. She couldn't escape the unpleasant knowledge of those girls in her house. The space she'd tried to keep separate from the ugly realities of her current and past life. She wanted them out.

Inside her Mercedes, Allison gripped the steering wheel hard, still reeling from her conversation with Stephen. *Does he not realize just how much he owes me? When I first met him—showing him the tacky condos he asked to see—he expected me to believe he recruited models. Ha! Considered himself an 'entertainment services entrepreneur.' What a joke! All he had was a few foreign girls from poor families and none of them were lasting under his living conditions.*

She braked hard to avoid blowing through a red light. The sudden stop sent her lurching forward against her seatbelt.

I'm the one who got him to branch out with a higher quality product.

She'd elevated Stephen from dime-a-dozen pimp to a provider of luxury entertainment services. His upgraded girls really could be models. And why? Because *she'd* taught him how to maintain them—hair, nails, nice clothes, ballet and stretching videos daily, keeping them underfed, making sure they never got pregnant or caught a disease.

Now he deals with doctors, lawyers, business leaders and entrepreneurs in upscale homes—because I knew people in the Carolinas who were willing and able to pay.

He'd be nothing without me. And he repays me by taking them to my house!

She inched from one block to the next, her engine purring quietly. Fans in town for the football games and events had added to traffic and each stoplight took ages, almost doubling her driving time. But she wasn't complaining. With the games came a flood of demand for commercial sex. A demand that often exceeded their supply. Too bad Emma couldn't earn her keep.

Allison returned to fuming about Stephen's attitude until she arrived at the potential new site for housing their girls.

The building was a nondescript two-story rectangle with vinyl siding and a smattering of litter in place of landscaping. Situated on the outskirts of uptown and walking distance from the stadium, the location was ideal.

A few cars were parked around the building, game attendees willing to walk over a mile and risk a car break-in rather than pay for parking. She drove around to the back, trying to keep her Mercedes somewhat hidden.

Using a code, she unlocked the front entrance and looked over her shoulder before going in. Her gaze was drawn first to the grimy windows. Dark walls, dust, neglect. The space needed cleaning and airing out, but . . . location was everything. With some inexpensive tweaks, the interior could be good enough for their needs. For next to nothing, they could erect dividers to create small rooms. They could order beds, linens, and a few massage tables to put in the front.

She climbed the narrow stairs without touching the railing. The second floor was even darker, with almost no natural light, perfect for keeping the motel girls hidden. She opened the doors to two windowless storage areas—*perfect*—and a small bathroom with a shower.

As she approached the last room, she had decided they needed to buy the place and was already thinking about finagling the deal of the century. The door opened on rusty hinges. She stared inside. Positioned high in the wall like a prison cell, a small window let in a shaft of light, showcasing the fine cloud of dust motes floating above a chipped nightstand. Allison took in the room, her chest tightened and her shoulders slumped as her professional shell slowly dissolved. The bedding was gone, but a lumpy, stained mattress sat on top of a metal frame. The paint was a sunny yellow color, out of place with the rest of the rooms. Opposite the window, thumbtacks pinned a torn poster to the wall.

Allison gripped her purse and sneered.

Someone's futile attempt to make it look homey and nice.

It's sad.

Pathetic.

It looked just like the room she grew up in.

A horrible memory assaulted her.

She was back in her childhood bedroom. Years ago. She was about to start her homework, pulling her English book from her bag, when a low whistle made her spin around. She hadn't heard the man come down the hallway and into her room. Her mother wasn't home.

He leered at her. "How much you charging?"

Every muscle in her body tensed with rage. "Nothing you could afford," she had said, trying to be tough. She knew what he wanted. She knew how her mother made ends meet.

"Maybe not, but let's find out what you're worth." He rushed forward and grabbed her, spinning her around and pushing her roughly against the wall.

She struggled as he hiked up her dress and thrust his pelvis against her. Every muscle in her body tensed with fear and anger. She could hardly believe what was happening.

He was so much bigger than her. So much stronger.

The more she struggled and screamed, the more he grunted and moaned.

"I'm not a whore!" she screamed over and over again.

There was nothing else she could do but endure.

When he was finished, the man stumbled back, grinning.

"Go away! Get out of here! Don't you ever touch me again," she had shrieked through her tears.

He tossed some cash on the floor and walked away, laughing, leaving her feeling more alone than she'd ever felt before.

Chapter Nineteen

Ms. Bois's basement was nothing like the one they'd left. There were two bedrooms, two bathrooms, a kitchen with a bar, and a television room. If the homeowner stayed away, they could live there happily for a long time.

Sofia dragged a heavy chair until it was a few feet away from the television.

Seated on a chair identical to the one Sofia moved, Anastasia wrapped her arms around her waist as she spoke. "Put back in same place before Ms. Bois gets here."

"I will. Can't see unless I'm close." Sofia wrapped a soft blanket around her shoulders, settling into the plush armchair to watch a program called *Pretty Little Liars*.

"Your eyesight is very worse." Anastasia's voice softened. "Sorry."

Sofia shrugged. "Is what it is."

Anastasia selected a chocolate candy and took a bite. "Her house, her pool, this is the life I thought we will have in America, you know . . . before."

"Why am I not surprised that Ms. Bois is actually living it?" Sofia huffed. "I wish my family could see this place. The giant beds with all the pillows. A shower the size of an entire room. All because of us. Because men want to be with us." She took a drink from the fancy bottled water she'd taken from the fridge. She'd seen an advertisement for the bottle in the magazines Damian brought them. *Water for people who demanded the absolute best.*

"I hope we come back here." Anastasia nibbled on another chocolate. "But I don't think so. Something happened."

"Definitely." Sofia lifted her butt a few inches and dragged the chair forward again. "Something strange is going on. Too bad the American can't tell us what happened while we were working."

Other than being dragged out of bed by Svet for a quick photo shoot in beach clothing, Emma had stayed in the bedroom by herself. Last they checked, she was sweating all over the impossibly-soft, clean linens. She was drugged. Her forehead was hot with fever, her skin flushed and damp. Sofia thought about checking on her, bringing her one of the special electrolyte-infused waters and making her take the birth control pill. She'd do it after the show ended.

"These girls do whatever wants and have lots of money for spending," Anastasia scoffed at the television. "They think they have problems. What do they know?"

"This show is old," Sofia said. "No one uses phones like that anymore."

Anastasia set down the box of chocolates. "I wonder if my family has cell phone now."

They were silent for a while, watching the show. Content. Anastasia hadn't tugged on her ear all day.

"How much of the show is real?" Anastasia asked as the program ended and switched to a commercial for moisturizing lotion.

"None of it is real. It's all pretend acting." Sofia finished her water and looked around for a trash can. She appreciated how clean the house was, wanted to keep it that way, and didn't want to anger Ms. Bois. She was always irritated, even without being provoked.

"I mean, is it how people live here? They come and go, no one tells them what to do."

Sofia shrugged. "If you really care to know, ask Emma."

Anastasia started chewing on the cuffs of her sweatshirt.

Sofia punched the arrow button on the remote to search for a new show. She wouldn't mind another episode of Pretty Little Liars if she could find one.

"—search continues for Charlotte teen, Emma Manning."

Sofia jumped to the edge of the chair, sending her water bottle tumbling to the floor. "Anastasia! Look. He's talking about Emma."

Anastasia was already leaning forward, staring wide-eyed at the television newscaster.

"Emma is a freshman at Charlotte Day School, an honor student who volunteers at the Charlotte Assistance Center and a member of the field hockey team." A picture of Emma in a sport uniform appeared on the screen.

As far as Sofia knew, no one had ever looked for her and Anastasia. Sure, her family had to be wondering what happened to her, why she hadn't written or sent them the money she had promised to send, but they had no idea what her life had become. No idea that the modeling agency was total BS. How could they? But people were looking for Emma. She was important enough to be on the television news.

The photo disappeared and the newscaster returned. "Authorities believe her disappearance might be related to a sex

151

trafficking ring. If you have any information, Call CMPD at the number on your screen."

Anastasia reached for Sofia's hand and squeezed it. In a hushed voice, Sofia said the number aloud and repeated it, nodding encouragement to Anastasia until her friend began reciting it with her. Clasping hands, they stared into each other's eyes, whispering the number over and over. The tip line was the most important piece of information they'd come across in years.

Chapter Twenty

Seated at the desk in her hotel suite, Victoria dropped her head into her hands to think. She didn't like how slowly the investigation was moving. Emma was still missing. The meeting with the realtor had been a bust. She wished she had stayed on Adams' trail.

Meanwhile, her personal life was on hold. She could leave Charlotte and go home today if she wanted. Murphy would be okay if she told him that's what she was doing.

The truth was, she didn't need this job, she didn't need any job. But she had good reasons for wanting to be part of the FBI. Bringing home missing loved ones was one way of delivering on her desire to protect others and herself. She didn't want to walk away from the investigation until they found Emma. Was it already too late? What if the media coverage had scared her abductors into getting rid of her? What if she'd been whisked out of the country the same day she disappeared? What if? What if? There was no way to know with the little information they had. Thoughts of Victoria's own mother strengthened her resolve. Since they didn't know Emma's fate, they had to continue on and keep faith that Emma could still be brought home.

Meanwhile, it felt like everyone involved might be hiding something. And maybe they were.

She grabbed her laptop and hit the start button. She'd already done some research on Tripp Manning. He owned a commercial real estate development company. On the surface, he did quite well. But the complicated structure of his multifaceted business sent up a warning signal. Was the structure necessary and simply beyond her business understanding? Or was it to disguise cash and money flow from prying eyes?

Normally she would ask one of the FBI's financial analysts, one with expertise in money laundering, to have a look. But the Mannings were Murphy's friends. Or, at the least, the wives were friends. Out of professional courtesy, she needed to tell Murphy first. He might already know what it was all about.

Murphy didn't answer his phone. She left a message.

What else was bothering her? Tripp's marital indiscretions. According to one of the few updates Connelly sent her, an officer had already interviewed both the women to whom Tripp paid child support. The women were cooperative. Both of them said they felt bad for the Mannings and what they must be going through. No red flags up, according to the officer.

Her phone rang. Connelly. She pressed the button and lifted the phone to her cheek. *Maybe working on his level for a while would help.* "No, I haven't tried the fried chicken yet, Connelly."

"Ha! Well, there's still time."

"Any news on the DNA tests?"

"Not yet. But they can take days, even prioritized."

"Let's take the tooth to Emma's dentist. I can do it. That would be a lot quicker. They can match it against dental records and we'll know if it's hers or not."

"Sure. Wish we'd thought to do that first. I'll have to try and get it back from the lab."

"What about the task force you mentioned? Are they on this now?"

"Yes. We just met."

A rush of embarrassment quickly changed to anger because he hadn't included her. *What does he think I'm here for?* She reined in her resentment and said, "Why wasn't I called?"

"It was a last-minute thing. We're getting pulled in multiple directions right now, case-wise. Most of us were already together uptown."

She pushed aside her frustration. "What's the update on accessing Emma's emails from the server?"

"It's been done. Nothing suspicious. If someone was communicating with her prior to her disappearance, they weren't using any traditional methods. Listen, Victoria, there's something new. The reason we met."

She could tell from his tone that the news wasn't good. "What is it?"

"We found another picture of Emma. We have good reason to believe she's no longer in the States."

Victoria's heart sank. "What did you find?"

"Another ad. Just posted. She was wearing a shirt from the Dominican Republic. And a Larimar necklace. That piece of jewelry is only sold there. As disappointing as it is, can't say I'm surprised. It's what I'd expect them to do."

"Send me the picture," Victoria said. She was surprised Connelly and his team, whoever they were, had found it first, rather than Sam. Maybe Sam had stopped running his search.

"Sending it now," Connelly responded. "I'm getting roped into other stuff and I'm trying to press back, but I've got to finish something here. Are you at your hotel?"

"I am."

"Can you help me out?"

"What do you need?"

"Would you go to the Manning's house and let them know what we've found? Show them the picture I sent you. Explain what we're facing now and help them understand the probability of getting their daughter back is low."

The type of visit agents and detectives wish they didn't have to make.

"Sure."

◆ ◆ ◆

A compact car in the Mannings' driveway had a magnet advertising The Pest Control Company. Victoria parked beside it and studied the new ad Connelly sent her. The caption read, *New and Fresh in Town.* Code for *virgins.*

Based on Emma's attire, Victoria's analysis would have also led her to conclude Emma was now in the Dominican Republic, a safe-haven for sex-traffickers. From Victoria's experience, the police there were paid next to nothing and had to be bribed to do their jobs.

Troubled, but not sure why, she walked to the house. Magda opened the door for her. Inside, Patricia sat alone in the kitchen, staring intently at a small television. Her face was made up, her hair done, her outfit meticulous—a true Southern woman even in the worst of times—but her eyes were red-rimmed and puffy and the wine bottle in front of her was almost drained.

A news anchor announced, "The demand for commercial sex is highest during large sports events that attract out of town visitors." A general announcement asking the public to be on the lookout for signs of human trafficking. No mother of a missing girl should have to hear it. Emma's mother had to be heartbroken and sick with fear and worry.

Victoria cleared her throat. Patricia turned and their eyes locked. "If some man visiting from out of town can find a girl and have sex with her—book an appointment just like getting a manicure and pedicure—why can't the police do the same thing?" Patricia demanded. "Save every girl? Arrest every pimp and customer? Why can't they do it?"

"I—we—they do. But the resources for sting operations, they're hard to come by. There's just so many girls, and when one is saved, another takes her place. As long as the demand continues there will always be girls to meet it. And so many of the girls, they won't press charges, they're afraid—"

"You only try to save them if someone is looking for them? Is that it?"

"No, that's—"

"Where is my daughter?" Patricia's mouth hung open.

Victoria hunched her shoulders, preparing for the verbal assault she knew was coming. Instead, Patricia collapsed into sobs.

And then, once the woman had recovered some composure, Victoria had to deliver her news.

◆ ◆ ◆

Drained after her time with the Mannings, Victoria drove to the nearby Charlotte mall. She needed to eat, and it wouldn't hurt to return to the place where Emma was last seen. Maybe whoever lured her from the mall was still lurking around, preparing to target their next victim.

She ordered at the food court and went outside, selecting a secluded table where she could talk on her phone without being overheard. She set her number in the metal holder so the server would know where to find her.

Live music was set up on the other side of the outdoor seating area. The band was taking a break, so instead of music, she listened to water cascading from the large, center fountain and the hum of conversations. Four teenage girls at the closest table were leaning forward, engrossed in discussion with the occasional shriek of laughter. They looked to be around Emma's age.

Victoria zipped up her coat. The evening was cool, but not cold, ideal weather for a brisk walk or run. She considered going into the mall after she ate and buying a gift for Ned. Maybe something for running or hiking.

Slipping her phone from her bag, she found a voicemail from Murphy. She listened. He didn't sound angry, but as always, his tone was firm.

"I need you to help get Emma Manning back, not investigate her parents. Lay off that angle for now."

She would follow her boss's orders. At least for the time being. There were other places she could focus. Several things about the investigation didn't feel right.

She took out her phone and studied the new ad again, the one that had convinced Connelly that Emma was in the Dominican Republic. Emma's eyes were glassy and blank, the eyes of someone sick or drugged, maybe both. Her face was slightly bruised. There was nothing in the background of the photograph, except the ground. The photo had been taken from above, with Emma reclining on the grass. Perfect grass, every blade uniform in color and size. Too perfect. It reminded her of the grass at her father's club. Resorts had perfect grass. So did golf courses. They had both of those in the DR, but might there be anything unique about the grass that might prove Emma was still in the area?

She sent Sam the picture. He would be able to tell her.

With so many things on her mind, Victoria needed a colleague to bounce ideas off, like she and Rivera had done on past cases.

Her mentor, retired agent Helen Bernard, was often her go-to person when she needed someone to talk about a case. Victoria called, and was glad when Helen answered.

"Hi, Helen. Can you talk for a bit?"

"I sure can. Where are you, girl? What's going on?"

"I'm in Charlotte, North Carolina."

"For the Football Festival? Good for you. It's about time you got away from that big empty mansion of yours."

"God, no! No!" Victoria laughed. "Everyone keeps asking me that. I'm here to help on a case."

"Just sayin' my Tigers are going all the way. Speaking of wild animals—"

"I know where this is going, Helen. There's nothing wild about my dogs. They know more tricks than you."

"Ha! Now that's cute. How many are you up to now? Twenty? Thirty? You know, be careful. Cat lady is a thing, but dog lady can be one, too."

"It's still just seven. Ned is taking care of them. In fact, you'd be proud of me. He spent the night recently. With me at the house."

"Proud? I'm in shock. How was it?"

A teenager arrived at Victoria's table with her food. He set everything down and Victoria mouthed "thank you." To Helen she said, "He still slept in the guest wing."

"That bad, huh?"

"Stop. We're . . . taking our time."

"Well, tick tock, honey. He ain't gonna be patient forever. What's the case you're working? You a consult?"

"Consult and sort of a favor because Murphy knows someone involved. I'm pretty much relegated to the outside of the investigation thanks to the lead detective."

"Oh, Victoria, Victoria, you know by now how this game can be played. So much territorial bullshit. Why can't everyone just get along, right? And it's not just men. Powerful women can be the absolute worst about not letting anyone steal their thunder."

"At least he's civil about it. It's all very politely disguised."

"Same crap no matter how you package it. What's the case?"

"An abduction. Possibly for sex trafficking." Victoria filled her in on the case without mentioning that Emma might be out of the country and their chance of finding her greatly reduced.

"Thought we had a good lead to check out a building. But whoever was staying there got the jump on us."

"Like they knew you were coming?"

"Yes. That's my gut feeling." Victoria took a sip of her sweet tea. "I know these operations don't stay in one place very long, but there were a bunch of things left behind, my sense is they left in a hurry."

"Sex trafficking rings are constantly moving to the next big event. They follow the demand. With another big game and all the events being advertised to draw crowds, seems a little strange they'd pack up now."

"I thought the same."

"You know, for a ring to work over the long haul, there's got to be people of influence in each city who are paid to look the other way. City council, mayor, local cops. Hell, even lawyers and judges. Could be anyone."

"Yeah, but it's gotta be someone."

"Pretty much. Or all of them. These things don't operate in a vacuum."

"I know."

"You want the girl back. But you might not find her if someone with power is thwarting your efforts. So, you improvise until you figure out who to trust. Basically, until you know who you can trust, you trust no one."

"It's not even my case though."

"Of course it is. Maybe not officially, but why are you there if it's not? Look, if you were the missing girl or her parents—"

"Her parents are another matter. Don't get me started on them. And their PI. They're all making things more complicated."

"My point is—if you were one of them, would you give a crap about who owns the case?"

"Nope."

"Call Murphy and tell him what you told me. Then call Ned."

"Ned's fine."

"He sure is. I looked him up on the internet, found a picture of him all sweaty after one of his races—whoa and wow—a whole lot to admire there. That's why you should call him. Whatever happened to Rivera? He still around?"

"I was actually thinking about calling him, too."

161

"What? I think I'm going to have a stroke. Did you just go from warming the bench for every game to starring in the field?"

"I was going to call him for input on the case. We work well together."

"Uh huh. Well, whatever you decide there, just know that the right guy will appreciate you for you. It might take some time, but he'll embrace all your weird quirks and that stoic personality of yours."

"Weird quirks? What–?" Victoria didn't know if she should laugh or be offended. *Count on Helen not to beat around the bush with anything.*

"You have a big heart. I've seen it. Big enough for your dogs and a special someone. Once you figure out who he is."

"Helen—"

"Okay, darlin', it's almost kickoff. Get your input and call me back if you want my help with anything else."

Victoria finished her meal, left a generous tip on her table, and another on the table where the four girls had been sitting, since they left without doing so. She headed back to her hotel. She missed Ned and her dogs, but the case in Charlotte needed her.

Inside her hotel suite, she did a bit more research, and decided on a plan. If Murphy okayed it, she'd only have to wait one more day. She hoped Emma Manning could, too.

Her phone beeped with a message from Sam.

Grass expert responded. Your pic shows a hybrid of Centipede grass that grows primarily and almost exclusively in the Southeast United States.

She still couldn't prove anything, but she knew something wasn't right.

She called Murphy and told him her plan.

Chapter Twenty-One

Anastasia tugged on her ear as she climbed the basement stairs. "I don't think Ms. Bois ever came home."

"I sure hope not." Sofia gripped the flashlight she'd found behind the bar. "But Svet and Stephen might still be here."

Sofia stopped on the landing. Her free hand wrapped around the door handle.

The girls stared at each other until Anastasia looked back down the stairs. "We are so very in trouble if we get caught."

"We're not going to get caught." Sofia placed her hand on her friend's arm. "We'll be fast and we'll be quiet. Look on all the walls and all the tables. Then in drawers. If you find a phone, come get me and we'll take it back here."

"And then we must put it back." Anastasia's lip trembled and Sofia was tempted to tell her to stay put, but her friend had a better chance of spotting a phone than she did.

"I'll bring it back up." Sofia closed her eyes to say a quick silent prayer. *Help us find a phone. Don't let them catch us.* "Are you ready?"

Anastasia nodded.

Sofia flicked the switch and the light above the stairs went off. Slowly, she nudged the door open, then listened.

Silence.

A light shimmered somewhere down the hall. Visibility was dim, but far from total blackness. Without turning on the flashlight, they tiptoed into the first room off the hallway.

"What is realtor?" Anastasia whispered, staring at a plaque on the wall. "There is picture of Ms. Bois. It says 'Top Ten Realtor of the Year.' There are prizes for what she do with us?"

Frowning at Anastasia, Sofia placed a finger against her lips. She turned to creep around the dim room. Worried she might miss something sitting in plain sight, she slid her hand over table tops and into drawers.

She was heading into another room when something creaked. Sofia held her breath. She strained to listen over the thumping of blood rushing past her temples. Were her nerves playing tricks on her? A quick glance across the room at Anastasia told her otherwise. Her friend stood frozen; elbows lifted at an odd angle by her sides like she was doing a chicken dance.

Another creak and then heavy footsteps approached. A loud burp echoed into the room.

Svet is up!

A soft suctioning noise came from the kitchen. Bottles clinked together.

Sofia pressed her back against a wall, trying to become invisible. *Don't breathe, don't breathe. If he finds us hiding in the dark . . . that will be the end of using the tip line.* She didn't let herself imagine what he might do to them. She was afraid enough already.

A carbonated drink popped open with a quick hiss. The rustling and crinkling of a plastic bag followed.

If Svet finds us, I'll tell him we got hungry . . . we couldn't find the bathroom . . . we needed a glass for water . . .I'll tell him Emma needs something.

Sofia pointed back toward the basement door. Anastasia's eyes were already on it, her face scrunched with fear. With each slow and meticulously controlled step, they inched closer to safety. Sofia braced herself for what might happen as she pulled the door open and they slipped inside. Once the door was closed behind them, she allowed herself to breathe again.

They hurried down the carpeted stairs, panting.

They were safe. But they hadn't found a phone. *Tomorrow.* They had to find one tomorrow. Before Emma disappeared for good.

Chapter Twenty-Two

In the late morning, Adams found the funeral home that handled the burial of Linda Wood. The business hadn't reached the modern ages in terms of information storage. After a long wait, while an elderly man shuffled through papers, Adams left with the address of the person who had paid in cash for the funeral. The paperwork had been signed *friend of Linda Wood*. No name. Just an address. He drove straight there.

Adams followed directions to a neighborhood with large homes built around a golf course. At the end of a private cul-de-sac, he pulled up to the curb in front of a stucco house with a stone-facade. A chimney rose from each side of the brown-tinted roof. Purple and lavender flower beds decorated the front. Whoever lived there could pay for a nice funeral.

Adams walked to the front door. He knocked. He waited. The door remained closed. He stepped to the edge of the stoop and peered through the nearest window. He walked to one side of the house, stopping at the side gate without going through to the back yard, and then did the same on the other side. He was about to get back into his car when the front door opened.

A trim, middle-aged man wearing a gray suit stuck his head through the opening. "Can I help you?" He spoke with an accent.

"Yes. I'm looking for someone who knew a woman named Linda Wood. Specifically, someone who might have paid for the woman's funeral."

"I don't know anyone by that name. When was this funeral?"

"Five years ago."

"Sorry. Can't help you. I think you have the wrong address."

Adams apologized and walked back to his car. The man watched him go.

On the side of the house, two girls appeared behind the tall, black-rail fence. They looked very young because of their slender frames, but poise and grace characterized their movements. One girl arched her back and tipped her face up to the sun. The other spread her arms wide and twirled around. Their long, flowing hair swayed with the breeze. At exactly the same time, they jerked their heads toward the house and ran off, disappearing again.

◆ ◆ ◆

Victoria pulled the blinds to block out the afternoon sun coming through her hotel room windows. Someone knocked on the door. She peeked through the spyhole before opening it. Her smile quickly spread. "Welcome to Charlotte, Rivera! It's really nice to see a familiar face."

Agent Dante Rivera smiled back and stepped into the room. A dark shadow of stubble covered his cheeks and chin. He looked handsome wearing jeans, boots, and a button-down flannel shirt. "Always happy to be of service."

"You won't be tonight." Victoria slumped into the corner chair. "Happy, that is." She and Rivera had worked closely together on several cases. He was a man of few words, and she appreciated anyone who valued silence. Even when they were together, his presence allowed for time alone with her thoughts. But now, it was she who could hardly keep quiet. She was fired up about the case and glad to have someone to discuss it with. "Between following people around, I've been doing a lot of research on sex trafficking in our databases. Sorry to say this, but right now, men make me sick."

Rivera stood close to the wall and looked around the suite. "What men? Johns?"

"Yes. Remember the grad student in our last case who was a . . . companion? To put herself through school."

"Olivia Something."

"Right. So, I know not every prostitute is a victim, but these girls are young. It's entirely different. The average pimp makes around three hundred thousand dollars a year off of each girl."

"Whoa. That's . . . a lot."

Victoria huffed in disgust. "Makes me sick. Johns can pay up to five thousand to have their way with a terrified or drugged child for an hour. I mean, who does this? Who?"

"Well, it's a sick and expensive fetish, so sick bastards, that's who. But you got to have extra cash to throw around, so it'd be a pool of rich guys. Any sick deviant who has money to throw away."

"Think of the good they could do with that money instead of using it to hurt others."

"Right." Rivera rubbed his knuckles and cracked them. "Just because a few men do this, doesn't mean the majority—the overwhelming majority—aren't just as horrified as you."

She sat up and scooted to the front of the chair. "Fine. Just wish I had a list of who was horrified and who was exploiting them." She sighed an angry sigh and turned to look at the wall. *For now, I need to narrow my focus on whoever is responsible for Emma's situation. And whoever is responsible for locking people in an abandoned building with a bucket for a latrine.* She took a deep inhale. "Did you get the file with the pictures I sent?"

"Yeah. I studied them." Rivera took a seat in a chair across from Victoria. "I'll recognize her."

"She'll be different. They'll have done something to change her. Different hair. Heavy makeup. Or maybe no makeup at all if they want her to look young."

"I know." Rivera set his hands on the sides of his chair.

"Good. So, you have a time and meeting place?"

"Nine thirty tonight. I used an anonymous browser and an email from an old cover. It's solid. I specifically requested the girl in the school uniform with long straight hair. We're set to go."

"It was that easy?"

"I had a whole creepy exchange prepared, just in case. But it was easy. They were very trusting."

"Just proves no one is looking for the girls they have and they know it."

"True. And why is that? I should know but . . .never worked a sex trafficking case before."

"Most of the girls were already troubled runaways and their family and friends have already given up on them. Some came from poor families overseas. Maybe they're told they're coming to work as housekeeping in a motel, and then they find out they're being sold for sex. Some come from families so poor, with so few options, they have to sell one child to feed the rest."

Victoria let the harsh facts sink in before continuing. "There isn't enough time and resources for sting operations. If the girl is over eighteen—and I'm sure the pimps get fake ids for most of them—she has to identify herself as being sex-trafficked. Most of them don't. They won't."

"Because?"

Victoria ticked off reasons on her fingers. "They're being manipulated. They're terrified. If they take the stand against their pimp— do you know how many girls are killed after they take the stand? With some of the gang-based sex-trafficking, there's a hit on them as soon as they agree to testify. They don't want to die. And even if they do take the stand, the defense attorney's job is to try and rip the girl apart—try to prove she's an addict, that she "chose" this life-style. It's very, very difficult to successfully prosecute."

"So, I can probably get fifteen big drug busts done in the time it takes me to prosecute one sex-trafficker, and any girl who does help me put one away might die as a result."

"That's the gist of it. Look, I'm sorry about giving you a hard time. I'm really glad you're here."

"I go where the boss sends me. And I'm honored you requested my help. But, if I can catch the NFL game before I go, that'd be awesome. Gotta figure out how to get a ticket last minute."

Victoria rolled her eyes. "I don't really care about the game."

"That's practically un-American." He chuckled. "You know, once I saw a bunch of dogs doing tricks at a half-time show. You would have loved that. Anyway, I didn't say I'd try to get a pair of tickets."

"Good. Right now, I only care about bringing Emma home. And once I have some assurance that will happen, I want to get back to Virginia and my own life as soon as possible."

"I've been wondering, are we sort of going rogue on this?"

"Rogue? No. Murphy knows. He approved this. It's hardly going rogue if our boss condones it. Like you said, I asked and he sent you."

"Yeah, but it's not his jurisdiction."

"The motel address is in South Carolina, right?"

"Yep."

"Then they've crossed state lines with the girl to bring her there. It's an FBI matter. Potential kidnapping." Victoria lifted her chin. "But for right now, no one else can know we're doing this. Not even the local FBI. Not until we've figured out what is going on. Detective Connelly thinks I went home."

Rivera grinned. "Like I said, we're going rogue on this."

"You can call it whatever you like." Victoria held up her hands. "We could be running out of time. Murphy asked me to see what I could do here. This is what I came up with. This is what I can do. With your help."

"I didn't say I wasn't in. I'm all in. But it's good to be aware of who we might be pissing off. Was there a briefing today for everyone working on the case?"

"One that I know of. They forgot to include me."

"Doesn't seem right," Rivera said, rubbing his eyes.

"I know. That's why you're here." Finally, she smiled, though it was more of a knowing smirk. "So, let me tell you everything I know about the people involved with the case."

Chapter Twenty-Three

"Your layers are almost entirely grown out. It's been a few months, hasn't it, ladies?" Armando the stylist had the usual flourish to his voice. "And, I must say, this is a beautiful place you're staying in now."

"Yes," Sofia replied from the chair. *A major step up from some of the basements and slums where you've met us in the past.*

Anastasia sat nearby, legs tucked underneath her, chewing on the hem of her sweatshirt, waiting her turn.

Armando froze, one hand clasped a section of her hair, the other gripped his scissors in mid-air. "What's that noise?"

Emma's sickly moaning just barely traveled through the walls, sounding like there might be a trapped animal in the next room.

"It's nothing." Sofia kept her eyes on her reflection in the bathroom mirror.

The stylist frowned but returned to combing and cutting Sofia's long hair into flowing waves. Eventually he stepped back, scrutinizing his work like a true artist. "Finished. Now, you said you need an elegant updo for tonight?"

"Yes." Sofia responded, her voice deadpan. "That's what I was told we need."

"Somewhere fancy to be, then." The stylist was always good about not asking questions and pretending everything was normal. He wasn't stupid or evil. He was simply a coward who chose to stay in denial. Might have something to do with the wad of cash he received after each visit.

Armando turned to Anastasia. "Two of my most beautiful customers," he said with a twinkle in his eye. "But where's your third amiga?"

Anastasia squirmed in her chair. "We don't—"

"Sasha's just not here," Sofia said to protect Anastasia, uncertain of what her friend had been about to say. They couldn't trust Armando. They didn't know what he might report to Stephen.

"Oh." The hairdresser busied himself with creating an elegant updo and said nothing more. His forced jovial attitude had disappeared. Some things were harder to pretend through than others.

◆ ◆ ◆

Armando left and they checked on Emma. She was propped up on her elbows in the bed, her face flushed, surrounded by tangled sheets. She sat up and looked right past them. "In the closet, in the closet," she cried, pawing at the air. Her eyes opened wide like a wild animal, she gasped, then sunk back onto her elbows.

"We have to make her take her pill," Sofia said, holding one out for Anastasia.

Anastasia took the pill and crossed the room holding a bottle of water. "She has fever still."

Sofia stayed in the doorway and crossed her arms. "She's delirious but it might just be the drugs."

173

Anastasia put one hand behind Emma's head to gently lift her up, parting her lips with the rim of the plastic bottle. "Here, drink this and swallow pill." Anastasia's voice was soft, coaxing.

Emma shivered. A sheen of sweat coated her skin.

"Being really sick is one sure fire way to get out of working," Sofia said. "If she can keep it up without dying, she might be on to something."

Anastasia shot a frown at Sofia as she lowered the bottle. She sat down next to Emma and stroked her hair. "It's going to be all right."

Sofia rolled her eyes. "Why tell her more lies?" But just below the surface, she was grateful for Anastasia's kindness. At least one of them could still feel compassion. Sofia only wanted to return to reading in the comfortable armchair. From one of the shelves in the hallway, she'd chosen a book about a nurse who time-traveled into 18th-century Scotland. Absorbed by the book, she could pretend none of this was really happening.

Anastasia stared at Sofia. "Why being so mean to her?"

Sofia shrugged, but the answers came to her nonetheless. "Well, for one, she took Sasha's place."

"You don't know Sasha isn't coming back. You don't know it."

"I'll be shocked if she does. But that's not all—people are looking for Emma, like… like she's more important than the rest of us. And here she is, a weak, drugged, deliriously babbling baby and . . . and we could end up just like her if we're not careful."

"You're scared and taking it out on her. That is all it is."

"I'm not scared." Sofia turned away, biting into her lower lip.

I need to stay tough for all of us.

174

She called to Anastasia as she walked away. "Don't mess up your hair. This one's not earning for Stephen, and that means she's costing him. Don't give him more reasons to be upset."

Chapter Twenty-Four

A few miles after crossing the state line into South Carolina, Agent Rivera exited I-77. He drove down a nearly-deserted business road and past an adult-only store with a billboard-sized sign. A mile further, the red, white, and blue neon lights of a motel sign illuminated the words 'No Vacancy'. He drove around to the back of the building, where the motel rooms weren't visible from the street and the doors were shaded in darkness. *Convenient construction.* Whoever designed the place might have known what it would be used for.

The motel had twenty rooms. Five other vehicles were parked behind the building. One was Victoria's rental. Two cars looked like they were on their last legs, one with rusted siding and one with a patchwork DIY paint job. Two were luxury sedans. All but the junk heaps had backed into their spots. In a state that didn't require front license plates, parking so the plate wasn't visible was often a sign of someone with something to hide.

His clock said nine fifteen, so he waited. An old man exited a room on the second floor with his head down. He zipped his coat and hurried to one of the nicer vehicles. Rivera took a picture of the license plate as the car pulled out. Unless the people behind

Carolinafestivalsexygirls.com had lied, which would be the least of their legal and moral offenses, girls were being exploited for sex right now inside the hotel. Like Victoria, he wanted to take down anyone helping to keep the operation in business.

He popped two pieces of gum into his mouth, glaring at the motel and chomping aggressively.

What a coincidence that the last case Victoria and I worked on involved another hotel and a prostitute had been our most valuable witness. He allowed himself a slight smile, glad to be working with Agent Heslin again, glad she had asked for him. Unfortunately, he had an inkling that she and her dog walker-private-vet might be having more than just a professional relationship. A heavy feeling weighed on his chest with the thought. He wasn't going to ask her. Or maybe he just didn't want to hear the answer.

A few minutes before his appointment, he tucked his weapon under the front seat, in case they checked him before letting him inside with Emma. He exited his vehicle wearing a cap pulled low over his eyes.

There was a dead calm to the night and no trace of a breeze as he headed up the stairs to the second floor. He knocked on the designated room. A large man in his late twenties answered. The muscles bulging under his shirt made Rivera think of a bouncer or bodyguard.

"Put your hands up." The man's accent was thick. "Keep them up."

Romanian? Russian?

He patted Rivera down. All the while, his bulk blocked Rivera's view of the room. The agent caught glimpses of a small, female figure lying on the bed, but the lights in the room were off and the curtains were drawn, so he couldn't tell much more.

177

The bodyguard held out his hand. "Give me your phone."

Rivera grunted. "That necessary?"

"Is if you want to go in there."

Rivera grumbled and gave up his phone.

The bodyguard took a step back. "Five hundred."

Rivera handed him a stack of folded twenties.

After counting, the gruff foreigner slid the money into the inside pocket of his coat. "Thirty minutes. More time costs more."

"Don't need more. I'm going to catch one of the game parties."

The man stepped aside. Rivera went in, closing and locking the door behind him. He checked the window to make sure the shades prevented anyone from seeing inside. Then he walked to the bed, expecting to see Emma Manning.

The girl wore a silky negligee. She was lying on her left side, one arm draped across her chest.

Under other circumstances, he might think she was napping peacefully. She reminded him of his fifteen-year old niece, who had fallen asleep watching a movie on his couch a few weeks ago. But a closer look revealed the relaxed, loose-limbed floppiness of someone on drugs.

Her skin had an unhealthy grayish pallor. Strands of yellowish-blonde hair covered most of her face, but her eyes were open. Emma's hair could have been colored, but this girl was thin, emaciated almost, her collar bones jutting from her fragile frame above small budding breasts. In her recent pictures, Emma was a healthy, athletic girl. No way could her body have changed so quickly. It wasn't her.

His head spun with anger. He wanted to wrap the girl in a blanket and take her to the hospital. He wanted to haul the bodyguard off to the worst jail he knew of, a place where the man would have plenty of time to feel the wrath of his crime.

Rivera lowered to one knee next to the bed. "I'm not going to hurt you," he whispered, glancing toward the door. "Can you tell me your name."

She stirred but didn't respond. Her lips moved, just barely, but no sound came out. In slow-motion, she lifted her head up above the pillow before settling it back down. She didn't have the strength to hold her head up. Maybe she didn't even speak English. There wasn't much he could say anyway. The room might be wired to keep the girls from asking for help.

Anger and disgust churned in his gut. This wasn't what he had expected. He hadn't found Emma Manning, but he'd discovered a girl who looked like she'd needed rescuing for a long time.

He walked to the door and stopped, rubbing his chin, thinking for a minute. He opened the door and found the bodyguard leaning against a wall, smoking a cigarette.

"Hey. This here isn't the girl I asked for." Rivera put his hands on his hips. "This isn't the one in the plaid skirt."

The man shrugged. "Looks like her."

"Doesn't look at all like her. Is this all you have?" He checked his watch, trying to reinforce his story about the after-game party.

The man grunted. He stared at Rivera, shoulders tensed and ready to beat the crap out of him, but then turned to unlock the door to the adjacent room. "Here." He turned on the lights. Another girl was lying on the bed, also too slight to be Emma, curled into a fetal position. Her hair was jet black.

Rivera hid his revulsion and channeled his anger into his cover. "Not even close. I paid my money, and I want what I paid for. The one in the school uniform. Where's she?"

The man stared and shrugged.

"Are these two really all you have to offer? How old are they?"

"Just turned eighteen. Have proof." The bodyguard stepped closer, getting right in Rivera's face. "They're all I've got for you. You pay for the time you booked either way. Take one or leave." His accent was stronger when he was riled up. Rivera sensed his excitement—shoulders tensing, fists curling into balls. This guy lived for opportunities to pulverize someone. Apparently, there was a low threshold to customer satisfaction in the world of prostitution.

"No." Rivera widened his stance and leaned his head back.

"You take her or I take you outside and crush you." The big man stepped closer. "Yes?"

"Not for five hundred." Rivera's heart raced. "I thought you were advertising a virgin. They're obviously not. I want what I paid for. She's not five hundred."

Flexing his jaw muscles, the guard leaned forward. "Four hundred or you end up in dumpster. Then you miss party after game."

Rivera glanced at the frail girl on the mattress. "Okay. Have my refund waiting when I'm through." He stepped into the new room and closed the door. He expected there was at least one other girl at the motel, because the old guy had left from the next room over, but he couldn't push his luck. He studied the girl. Her pupils were glassy and dilated, unable to focus on him. Scabs covered one slender forearm. She looked younger than eighteen, but it might have been because she was waif-thin. The longer he stood, the more an overwhelming mixture of anger and sadness ate away at him.

He picked up a glass from the bedside table and filled it with water from the bathroom sink. *How can I leave her? But if we arrest the pimp and rescue the girls here, we might lose our only chance at getting the Manning girl back. That's what we're here to do. That's what we should do. Or should we? Why was saving her more important than saving these girls? Because Emma was definitely a minor?* He pressed his fingers hard against his temple. *Waiting might mean we save them all, or it might mean we save none.*

He remembered what Victoria had told him. If these girls really were eighteen and he took them now, it was unlikely they would do what needed to be done to free themselves, but very likely he and Victoria would lose their chance to rescue Emma.

"Here, drink this," he said in a gentle whisper, lifting the girl's shoulders, and putting the glass to her lips.

She lifted her head from the mattress and Rivera caught a glimpse of something on the back of her neck. Markings darker than her skin. He leaned in closer and made out the scar, a brown medallion. Where had he seen it before? It only took a second for him to remember. It was a brand just like the one Dr. Boswell had sent him a few days ago. The girl Dr. Boswell autopsied in Virginia had the same brand. His hand tightened around the glass. He wished he'd checked the girl in the first room, but he hadn't expected to find a brand and hadn't thought to look. It was safe to assume she also had one.

Stooping, he removed the phone he'd hidden in his shoe, took a photo of the marking, then texted Victoria.

Two girls. Not Emma. Drugged and in bad shape. Guard says they're 18. I can't tell. They look younger.

It's possible they were adults. Addiction could make a young person look old or an older person so emaciated they appeared childlike. There was no way to know for sure. Their whole situation seemed too sad and too sick to be real.

Waiting for Victoria to respond, he found Dr. Boswell's contact number, typed her a quick note, and sent it with the photo of the brand.

A row of "message in process" dots appeared and disappeared on his screen. Victoria was typing her reply. The dots on his phone started and stopped again. Victoria wasn't sure either. He studied the girl. Her eyes were closed now. Strands of her hair covered her cheek and nose.

Victoria's reply arrived. *Anywhere to put a tracking device on them?*

The girl was barely dressed, with no shoes. He pressed a hand against his stomach as he typed. *No.*

He glanced around the dark, nasty room, waiting for Victoria's response.

Make another appointment for tomorrow. Ask for Emma again. If she doesn't come, we'll take whoever does.

Exhaling through gritted teeth, he stared at the girl he would leave in hell for at least one more day.

He typed. *If I distract the guy, can you put something on all the cars?*

Her reply was quick. *Don't have trackers. I'll take pics of the plates if you can distract the pimp.*

He stared at the door. The big guy was on the other side. Rivera had already provoked the bodyguard about wanting the American. Too much more might get him put in the dumpster. Besides, if they argued, he might not get to return. On the other hand, asking for Emma after he finished with this girl—possibly offering more money for the privilege—that could be just what the Hulk would want to hear.

He typed into his phone. *Give me exactly ten minutes, then take the pics.*

Rivera set an alarm on his phone and waited, killing time by listening to the girl's soft but labored breathing and the hum of cars on the nearby road. Suddenly he wanted to be anywhere else than the dingy, warm room with its stale smell of cigarettes and body odor. He fought the urge to gag, wanting instead to burst out, carrying the girl with him.

The alarm vibrated. He opened the door and motioned for the bouncer. "Hey, I need a word." He stepped back into the darkened room, drawing the man with him.

"What?" the bodyguard grunted.

"I'm in the area one more night. I want to come back. Same time?"

"I don't make the appointments," the guard said, turning.

"Wait." Rivera extended his arm. Big mistake.

The man spun around. His nostrils flared. Rivera took a step back, held up his hand. "I'll make the appointment through the website. But there's another three hundred for you if you bring me the right girl. Here's half of it now. I'll trust you."

This time, the pimp slid the cash into the front pocket of his pants. The bribe money wasn't going to the same place as the other cash. Which meant the big foreigner wasn't the one in charge. "No promises. The one you want is new. In demand. Young."

Rivera fought the urge to try and kill the monster with his bare hands. Instead, he stuffed his hands in his pockets and grunted, forcing his snarl into a lecherous grin. It was all he could do not to throw up. "I have money and I want the girl in the school uniform. Tell your boss to think of a price."

183

"You want a girl like that, you're going to pay more. If I can get her, it's going to cost you another five-hundred tomorrow night."

It wasn't a promise and the man couldn't be trusted, but it was enough to give Rivera hope that Emma was still around.

Chapter Twenty-Five

Rivera paced on the carpet. While they'd been gone, the couch in Victoria's suite had been pulled out and made up into a bed. Smooth white sheets, a blanket, and pillows were arranged into a very inviting layout.

"You should have seen these girls." He ran his hand over his head and chewed hard on two new pieces of gum.

"I know." Victoria pressed her hands over her mouth and slowly shook her head.

"It bothered me even more than I expected. I feel sick about leaving them for the next guy to have his way with. They were drugged, could barely sit up." Rivera leaned against the wall and stared at the floor in front of his boots for a few seconds. "Before I left, when I was still in my car, someone else drove up to the motel. I watched him go into the first room I was in. I got his license plate."

"Good. Let's run it now with the others." She woke up her laptop. "I want to bust each of the customers as much as the people running this show. Maybe more."

"So do I." He pounded a fist into his other hand. "One of the girls had the same brand Rebecca asked me about earlier this

185

week. A Jane Doe in Virginia. Dead for less than a day before they found her."

Victoria's jaw dropped. "Really? How big is this ring?"

"Exactly."

"Did you tell Rebecca?"

"I sent her a picture of the brand."

"Good." Victoria looked down at her computer. "Okay. I'm ready. Read me the numbers."

"North Carolina. SRV7T94"

Victoria typed on her keyboard. "The plates are registered to a Volvo S90—"

"Yep. That was the car."

"The name on the registration is Thomas Stanton." She switched to another app and typed his name. "He's an attorney."

"He went into one of the rooms. But I can't prove anything. Aside from him, we don't know if any of the plates belong to people who were actually with the girls."

"Unless a girl can pick him out of a line up."

"Not likely…not the two I saw. Even if the threats and manipulations didn't come into play, they were too out of it." He stopped pacing. "Send the info to Murphy. See how he wants us to handle it." Rivera pointed to the pull-out bed. "You expecting company?"

"Yep. You. Unless you want to sleep on the floor in the lobby. There's not a room to be found in the area. Big game weekend, remember?"

"Yeah. I think I'll take your offer and bunk up with you. Thanks."

"Not 'with.' Near."

"Near works for me." He laughed. "Think your dog-sitter guy will be okay with it?"

"Ned knows. He said to remind you he does neutering for a living."

Rivera smiled and shifted toward the door. "I was thinking I'd grab a beer. Want one?"

"No, thanks." She stood up and grabbed her coat out of the closet. "Listen, make yourself at home, or . . . whatever you need to do. I'm going outside for a while, maybe take a short walk around the hotel." She stopped by the door and put on her coat. "What else did Rebecca say when you called her?"

"She said no one has claimed the Jane Doe yet. Is that what you mean?"

"When we get back home, how about a double date? Me and Ned. You and Rebecca? We could go to dinner. Have a nice time." She smiled. "As an investigator, I happen to know she'd really like that."

"Oh, uh . . . sure. Sounds good." His answer was more polite than convincing.

"Unless you've got someone else in mind?"

"Huh?" He stared at her. "No. No one else."

"I'd have everyone to my house, except I don't cook, and I know you'd need to down a bottle of Benadryl to come inside."

Rivera gave her a half-hearted smile.

"Rebecca is an amazing woman, a gorgeous, confident physician, and for some strange reason, she's got her eye on you." Victoria laughed. "Guess she likes the strong, silent types. Anyway, we'll talk about it more later. I won't be long."

◆ ◆ ◆

He waved as the door closed. *Some strange reason?* She had to be teasing him.

He'd lied to her face. There was someone else all right. Had been for some time. But now, with whatever Victoria had going on with Ned . . . she'd pretty much just confirmed it—and with him staying in her room, it wasn't the time to tell her how he felt. If she didn't reciprocate his feelings, it would be beyond awkward staying there. He didn't want to ruin their friendship *and* possibly get booted out of the bureau for sexual harassment in one swoop. He'd already tried to tell her once, on their last case. He could wait. Although—it was her that made up the bed for him. He hadn't asked and hadn't expected to stay there.

Outside the window, Victoria passed by, walking briskly. Rivera followed her with his eyes until she was out of view.

He decided to take a quick shower while she was gone. After hanging up his wet towel, he dressed in a t-shirt and shorts, the same clothes he'd brought to work-out in if he got the chance. He turned off the living room lights but lamps remained on in the bedroom. Their illumination carried through the suite. He sat down on the make-shift bed and heard the click of the door opening.

Victoria came in and hung up her coat. "I'm back."

"How was the walk?"

"It helped. I'm just having a hard time with this. Dealing with kids and a kidnapping."

"Remember our last case with the spree killer? You asked what could make me angry enough to go on a rampage?"

Victoria closed her eyes. "I do."

"Do you remember my answer?"

"You said pedophiles, anyone who hurts children."

"I feel that way even more after today."

"It's going to be okay," she said from the bathroom doorway. "If we do this right, we can save all of them."

"Right."

Victoria stepped into the bathroom and shut the door behind her.

Rivera closed his eyes and prayed she was right.

◆ ◆ ◆

"Rivera, are you still up?" Leaning against the pull-out bed, Victoria spoke in a raspy whisper. Her lace nightgown just barely covered the top of her thighs. She wore her FBI cap and bright blue running shoes.

Rivera sat up. "Yeah, I'm awake."

"Good." She sighed, and there was something there that sounded like contentment. "I know it's really late, but I can't sleep. Guess I'm just too wired."

"Oh. Well, I brought a bottle of wine. It's a thank you gift, for letting me stay in the room, but we could open it now."

"That sounds wonderful. It's been a long day. A glass of wine would be perfect."

Rivera poured the wine into water glasses. Victoria sat down on the pull-out bed, crossing her gorgeous, long legs. The cap and running shoes had disappeared and her toes were covered in a light pink polish.

"Remember our last case?" She laughed. "What an oddball, right?"

Rivera drank his wine, poured another glass, laughed along with her, but it occurred to him that there really wasn't anything funny about the case. His laughter felt off. It didn't matter. Whatever was happening with them, he wanted to ride with it. Work had no business intruding.

Victoria rested the rim of her glass against her bottom lip. "I always feel like you've got my back, Rivera."

"Yeah. I feel the same way. We're a good team. You know, Tori . . . Rebecca and I... I'm not really interested in anything beyond a professional relationship."

"No? Oh, I just thought . . .Why not?"

"There's kind of someone else."

Victoria lowered her voice. "Kind of?"

"She . . . doesn't know. Well, I haven't told her . . ." *Am I imagining things, or is she leaning closer?*

"Maybe you should." Her voice was so low, he could barely hear her. Her pink toe-nails nudged his ankle.

It's not my imagination. I haven't moved and our legs weren't touching before. "It could be awkward. We work together occasionally."

"Do you think that's just a coincidence, the working together?"

"No. It's not. I've asked to be assigned to cases with her before. But she also requests my help. She could have asked for anyone to help her, but she asked for me."

"She must trust you. She must know she can count on you."

"She can."

They gazed into each other's eyes. Everything seemed to be happening in slow motion. Victoria placed her hand on his arm, the tips of her finger moving in tiny circles. An electric current ran through his body.

"I'm sure any girl would be flattered to hear you're interested."

"I think she might be interested in another guy, though."

"You know what they say, Agent," she whispered. "No guts no glory." She stroked her hair and smoothed it around her ear, then let her fingers trail down her neck. "You should tell her. If you really do like her, she needs to know."

"Maybe… get together, talk for a while over some wine first? Something like that?"

Her eyes were focused solely on him. "And then, when you're alone together and you're both relaxed, you could say something like, I think you're an amazing FBI agent, and a really great person. I have so much respect for you. I've also been attracted to you since the very first time we met, and I'd love to take you on a real date sometime."

Rivera couldn't take his eyes off her. *Is it okay to touch her back? Is this what she really wants?*

Her breath tickled his ear. "Sounds… nice, doesn't it?"

There was no mistaking what she wanted. He turned to kiss her.

Victoria's mouth opened and a sickening, high-pitch wail erupted. Rivera's hands shot up to cover his ears.

What the hell?

Victoria vanished into thin air, as if she'd never been there at all, but the shrill, wailing sound continued.

The relentless noise jolted Rivera to a sitting position. He opened his eyes, suddenly wide-awake. *What's going on?*

The bedroom door opened and Victoria rushed past him wearing a t-shirt and shorts, stuffing her laptop into her bag. "Wake up, Rivera. Fire alarm. Let's go."

Chapter Twenty-Six

In Ms. Bois's basement, Sofia and Anastasia sat curled up in chairs eating some of their stash from the previous day. There had been no other opportunity to go upstairs and search for a phone.

A whirring noise traveled through the ceiling.

"That is garage door opening." Anastasia grabbed the remote and silenced the television. Sofia hid their food wrappers inside her suitcase.

In less than a minute, the shouting began.

Ms. Bois's sharp voice was clear. "I told you to get them out of here! You had no right to bring them to my house!"

"You, of all people, of all women, I might say, lecturing me about rights?" Stephen's laughter rung out, crazy and scary. "That's very funny. Very, very funny."

"Shut up, Stephen." Her voice rose to a shrill height. "Where are they now?"

"They're in the basement. You won't have to see them."

"She already pretends we don't exist," Anastasia said, wrapping her arms around her knees. "She can't even look at us."

"Yeah. Like we got ourselves trapped here all on our own and she had nothing to do with it," Sofia said. "Or maybe the cold-hearted bitch actually feels guilty and that's how—"

"No. She doesn't. She won't like Emma being sick. At least Emma is sleeping now." Anastasia had spent much of the day watching over Emma, giving her sips of Ms. Bois's fancy bottled waters and reporting her condition to Sofia. "Maybe feels better when she wakes up."

Above them, Ms. Bois screamed and something shattered.

"Did that make you feel better?" Stephen asked. "I think someone's had a bad day."

"He likes making her much angry," Anastasia said, gripping her earlobe.

"Maybe they'll kill each other," Sofia whispered with a wishful smile.

Anastasia didn't smile back. "He is going to come down here and be angry on us."

Sofia's gaze flew to the small closet next to the bathroom. Just large enough for one person. She couldn't bear the thought of being locked in a space that small.

The voices upstairs grew quieter, Stephen and Allison's hostility channeled through snide remarks. Sofia stood near a ceiling vent directly under the kitchen, craning to hear them. "Ms. Bois said the place near the stadium isn't going to work out and 'they'—you and me—aren't coming back here after Winston-Salem. Or else." Winston-Salem was a few hours away. She'd been there enough times to know. Would the tip line number work there? And if so, for how long? Maybe it was only a temporary phone number.

"Or else what?" Anastasia asked. "What place?"

"I don't know. Shush." Sofia listened. "Now she said Emma has to get out of the country immediately and she's making it happen."

"If Emma leaves country and we don't know where she is," Anastasia cried, "what good is number?"

"Shhh," Sofia warned.

Footsteps with a clicking heel struck the hard-wood floors above.

Anastasia's eyes followed the sound across the ceiling until it disappeared. "I think she went to second floor."

Only Stephen's voice echoed down through the vents, singing something about don't stop him now because he was having such a good time. "Nothing irritates Ms. Bois more than his song outbursts. That's why he's singing so loudly now," Sofia said. *Please don't make her angrier.*

The door at the top of the basement stairs opened and footsteps descended on the carpet. Too light to be Stephen or Svet. The girls jumped out of their chairs and stood up straight with their backs against a wall, terrified of seeing Ms. Bois.

Sofia's eyes darted around the room, worried something might have been overlooked and one little thing might be out of place, even though they'd been so careful since they arrived.

Ms. Bois appeared wearing yoga pants and a tight gray jacket for exercising. Her red hair was gathered in a bun on top of her head. She spotted them cowering in the corner, and scowled. "Where is she?"

Sofia pointed to the bedroom.

Singularly focused on getting to Emma, Ms. Bois passed without another glance at them. She disappeared into the room and closed the door behind her.

Sofia and Anastasia exchanged looks. Sofia wasn't sure what to do, other than stay out of the way.

Only minutes later, the door opened and Ms. Bois stormed out, head held high. "She's not even pretty. All that she has and she's not even that pretty, is she?"

She didn't look at the girls, so Sofia wasn't sure if Ms. Bois was asking them a question that required an answer or just talking to herself. Sofia stayed quiet.

"Don't give her anything," Ms. Bois said, headed back toward the stairs. "She needs to learn to take care of herself. Life isn't always easy." Ms. Bois stomped up the stairs, but yelled back, "And don't you dare ruin anything in my house with your grubby little hands."

Sofia couldn't help but look down at her hands. They were clean. Her nails were lightly polished. Her cuticles smooth.

Anastasia's shoulders drooped forward. "She is worst person in whole world."

"Maybe," Sofia answered. "It's a tough contest if we're picking winners." She tried to lighten the mood but was still shaken from seeing Ms. Bois. *Thank goodness she's already gone.*

"Leaving in thirty minutes, ladies," Stephen yelled down in a strangely cheerful voice. "Evening dresses. Pink and red. Be ready."

Anastasia hurried toward the bathroom.

Relieved he wasn't coming down too, Sofia got ready. When it was almost time to go, the girls stood in front of the bathroom mirror, clean, smelling nice, and wearing dresses with some simple jewelry.

"Do you remember the number?" Sofia asked Anastasia, speaking to her reflection.

195

"Yes." Anastasia set her jaw in an expression as serious as Sofia had ever seen.

They said it together several times.

"Something important is going to happen tonight," Sofia whispered. "It has to. That number is our ticket to freedom. All we need is to get hold of a phone."

"Come on! Get going!" Svet shouted in a way that sounded like he'd had to ask repeatedly. If Svet was there, it meant Stephen had left to check on the motel girls.

They jogged up the stairs, carrying their heels through the beautiful house to the van waiting in the garage. Sofia's heart beat fast and she was a little lightheaded, but it wasn't from lack of food. For once, her stomach was full from eating everything they'd taken from the pantry and fridge. She was weak from a combination of nerves, excitement, and fear.

They drove in style. The silvery gray Mercedes Sprinter had black tinted windows and a handicap plate, although none of them were disabled.

Svet fiddled with the radio dial. "How's that new girl doing?"

"I think you made her sick." Sofia was careful to disguise the hatred in her voice with a flat monotone.

Svet laughed. "Too much of a princess, she is. That needs to change. Oh—almost forgot." He alternated his gaze between the road and looking into the rearview mirror at the girls. "I have something for you."

He tossed a small object onto Anastasia's lap. At first, Sofia thought it might be a lipstick. A client once wanted their lips colored black. Another insisted the girls' hair be worn in two French-braids. One wanted Sofia to pretend she was blind. Whatever the party girls' customers wanted—they got, because they paid the big bucks. The package might contain someone else's whim.

Sofia pressed a button on the ceiling, casting light on a wad of wrinkled tinfoil. As Anastasia peeled back the foil, Sofia caught Svet's sadistic grin. His eyes gleamed with delight as he waited for their reaction. A cold, foreboding shiver ran down her spine and she braced herself for whatever the package held.

Anastasia jerked her hands away and stared. A small, rounded object nestled inside the foil, pink and brown with dried, crusty blood. "What is it?"

"A parting gift from your friend." Svet's grin was even bigger now. "No matter how long you've been around, or how valuable you *think* you are, this is what happens when you don't keep your mouth shut."

Anastasia grabbed hold of her ear lobe and tugged. She turned to Sofia. "What is it?"

"Nothing." Sofia's heart sunk. "It's nothing." She pressed the tinfoil closed around the object and tucked it under her seat.

"You don't recognize it, Anastasia?" Svet laughed. "Some friend you are."

"What is it?" Anastasia pleaded with Sofia, her voice a mere whisper. "Tell me." She sounded afraid and desperate. She twitched her ear back and forth at record speed.

In the rear-view mirror, Svet watched, laughing like a frightening lunatic.

Sofia didn't want Anastasia to know. She needed her friend to be strong. But if she didn't tell her, Svet would. Somehow, he would find a way to make the situation more heartbreaking than it already was. Sofia shielded her mouth with her hand and leaned close to her friend. "It's Sasha's tongue."

Anastasia stopped tugging and instead, squeezed her ear so tight it turned bright red. She stared down at her lap. Tears rolled down her flawless skin.

Svet slapped the steering wheel repeatedly like it was a drum. "And for the finale, someone in Sasha's family is going to disappear to pay for her misbehavior. That's what happens, ladies. Get it? Play by the rules or die. You die, and then something very bad happens to someone you love."

Still grinning, Svet turned his heavy metal music up and bobbed his head to the beat.

Sofia reached for Anastasia's hand and squeezed it. "Don't cry," she whispered. "You'll mess up your makeup."

She glared at the back of Svet's head. *This has to end.*

The van turned into a neighborhood and slowed. Sofia whispered into Anastasia's ear. "Do you see a street sign? And can you read it?"

"Old Sycamore," Anastasia whispered back, massacring the pronunciation.

They arrived at a stately brick home with black shutters, still clutching hands. The house was familiar. They'd been here before, but Sofia couldn't remember the details. This time, she hoped and prayed, would be the last. "Memorize the street name and the house number," she whispered. "We'll need that information for when we find a phone and call the tip line."

Svet escorted them to the front, pretending to be a gentleman with his dates. They looped their arms through his like they were taught to do.

Wreaths made of bright fall leaves decorated double doors forming a tall arch.

"Oh, no." Anastasia turned pale. "Please, no." She reached for Sofia's arm and tightened her grip.

As Svet rang the doorbell, Sofia searched her friend's face for the source of her fear.

A silver-haired man in a sports coat opened the door. He greeted the girls warmly, like they were actual friends invited over for a dinner party. Sofia cringed. A coil of panic tightened inside her stomach. She remembered the stories Anastasia told her about the owner of this house. He was someone important—a politician or business executive—and he had sadistic penchants. He didn't want to have sex with the girls, he wanted to do things to them. Things that made her stomach turn.

Sofia squared her shoulders. The man stared longingly at Anastasia's neck, then turned his back and went into the house. "Don't worry," Sofia murmured. "I'll go with him. You went last time."

Svet suddenly dug his fingers into Sofia's arm. She gasped.

"Whoever he wants is who will go. Got it?" Svet snarled, his voice low but threatening.

Inside, a small number of guests were also well-dressed, mostly overweight, all of them old. Their laughter was loud and frequent, evidence they'd been drinking for some time from their etched crystal glasses. Their eyes roamed over the girls, making Sofia feel like Hansel and Gretel—one of the more disturbing stories from her childhood—before the witch decided to eat them. There were no other women in the room.

Sofia took hold of Anastasia's wrist and gently pulled it away from her ear. They had important work ahead of them and needed to focus.

Under Svet's watchful eye, Sofia flitted from room to room pretending to admire large pieces of framed art and leather furniture while she searched for a phone. She needed to lean close to the carved mantels over the glowing fires, close to the grand piano that had a room to itself, and close to the shelves lined with leather-bound books because her eyesight was worse in the dim light. Anastasia was supposed to be doing the same, but Sofia knew in her heart that when it came down to it, if anyone had the guts to pull this off, it would be her.

She turned sideways to pass a leering man with a gray beard and moustache, trying not to get too close. *Surely he's too old.* He lurched forward and pulled her onto his lap. He had one long and errant gray hair protruding from his eyebrow.

"Can I get you a cocktail?" His voice was hoarse and gravelly.

"Thank you, sir, no." While he stared at her cleavage, she eyed his suit coat and pants pocket for the outline of a phone.

"Come with me." He pushed her up.

From across the room, Svet met her eyes and gave an almost imperceptible nod.

Hobbling, the decrepit man led her down a hallway, away from the rest of the guests, and into a bedroom.

She squinted at the dresser and the tables next to each bed. When she finally spoke again, she used her thickest accent over poor English. "Room very nice."

He grunted and pushed her toward the bed. "Take off your dress."

A wave of panic hit and she rubbed her damp palms against her dress. When he finished with her, someone else might take his place. *If I'm stuck in here all night, we won't have a chance.*

He started removing his belt and a quick glimpse of his flabby, hairy stomach repulsed her.

She screwed up her face into a grimace. "Excuse me. Powder room?"

The man frowned, holding on to his belt buckle. She didn't think he was going to let her go. With an irritated puff of breath, he finally pointed a gnarled old finger. "There's one down the hall. Hurry up because I'm ready now."

She knew all about men waiting for their pills to take effect. She hurried into the hall. It was now or never. She had to find a phone.

Svet frowned and stepped in front of her, blocking her way. "Where you going?"

"I have to pee first, or I might wet myself. And no one here tonight has asked for that . . . yet." She smirked to hide her hatred.

"Hurry up," he grunted. "There's only the two of you now. You need to keep busy."

Maybe you should offer to service some of them. But she dared not say it.

Svet didn't know where the bathroom was any more than she did, so Sofia hurried into the first doorway she came to and locked the door behind her. She turned and took in a large master bedroom.

Quickly, she opened and closed each drawer in a dresser that ran almost the length of one wall. Her search came up empty. She darted across the room to check a giant closet with men's clothing. Nothing. Across from it, an even bigger closet held women's gowns, sweaters, an entire wall of shoes. The door of a safe was slightly ajar. She opened a polished-wood box inside. Jeweled earrings, bracelets, and rings stared back at her from compartments and slots. Above the safe hung gold and silver necklaces.

But no phone.

She hurried back to the bedroom door, opened it a crack, and peered into the hall. Svet was talking to one of the old men,

201

but not the one Sofia had left. She didn't think she'd been gone more than a minute, but any second Svet might come looking for her and drag her back to the other bedroom. In a frenzy of emotion, her hope was draining as if her wrists had been cut and left to bleed out.

She flew into the bathroom in the back of the master and yanked each cabinet drawer open and shut, so desperate and rushed she wasn't even trying to be silent anymore. *Don't rich people keep cell phones around their homes in case of an emergency? Or does each person only have one?* She didn't know. In Ukraine, only children of very wealthy parents had cell phones. But not here.

Frantic, her face tight with worry, she ran her eyes over everything again. A shower with three glass walls. A clawfoot tub in front of a large window.

If that window opens, I could fit through.

Trembling with anticipation, she hitched up her dress, climbed into the bathtub, and pulled a lever on the window. Jammed! She threw all her weight against it and pushed instead of pulled until the lever flipped to the opposite side. She pried her fingers under the sill and tried to hoist it up. It didn't budge. Forcing her fingers deeper into the miniscule crack, she pushed again with all her might. Her pink nails shattered. With a squelching release and the snapping of old paint, the window let go its hold and nudged upward until it was higher than her shoulders and tall enough for her to fit through.

Giddy with fear, she peered into the darkness below. She was on the first floor with maybe seven feet from the bottom of the window to the ground. She couldn't see well enough to be sure. Chills flared through her body. She hoped the darker objects under the window were bushes that would break her fall. And was there a fence around the yard? She couldn't remember.

Her pulse pounded. She pulled off her heels and dropped them into the tub. Where would she run to? If she didn't get far away, and fast—if she failed—if the microchip was real—Stephen would murder her. He would make it long and painful, do it right in front of Anastasia and the new girl so they wouldn't even dream of trying to escape again. And what might happen to her family then, if she didn't get away? An image of her younger sister, Katya, popped into her head, making her already queasy stomach drop and clench. Katya was so young and innocent. Not near as tough as Sofia. She'd never survive.

Her hands shook as they gripped the window ledge, her mind racing. *It's now or never.* A chance to see her family again was hers for the taking. If Ms. Bois shipped Emma to another country, the opportunity would slip away. Sofia might never have another number to call with people who wanted to know the truth. As long as she could make a deal about leading them to Emma, she and Anastasia had a fighting chance at freedom.

The overwhelming desire for change had finally outweighed all the risks now that she had a branch of hope to grab hold of.

But how can I go home empty-handed after all this time? Nothing to show for all I've endured.

She spun around, leaped out of the tub, and ran back to the woman's closet. Yanking the jewelry box open, she pulled out everything she could grab then snatched some of the necklaces down from the wall. Her sheath dress had no pockets, so she flung beads around her neck, slid bracelets over her wrists, and jammed rings on her fingers.

She raced back to the bathroom, slammed the door, and twisted the lock just in time.

"What you doing in there?" Svet was through the locked bedroom door.

Her heart was in her throat, pounding fear and adrenaline through her body so she could barely think straight. "I'm not feeling well. I got sick." She flushed the toilet for effect. "I just need a minute to clean up and I'll be back out." Her whole body was shaking like she'd caught Emma's fever. "Just let me get cleaned up."

The bathroom door handle rattled.

"Open door now, Sofia!" His voice was a low, sinister growl. "Don't screw with me or you'll regret it with every ounce of your whoring body! Open door now!" He pounded against the wood.

She scrambled over the tub. *I'm so sorry for leaving you, Anastasia. I'll come back for you. If I'm alive, I'll come back for you.* Before she could change her mind, she heaved herself into the open window and leapt out. Her dress tugged, caught on something. It ripped as she fell to the ground, hitting the bushes. She jumped up. With branches grabbing for her and scratching at her skin, she ran for her life.

"Hey!" Svet's angry voice came from somewhere behind her. He was shouting now, all pretenses abandoned.

I'm out! I'm free! I'm running!

She could scarcely believe it was happening. Under the full moon, she yanked her dress up and ran faster, feeling like an Olympic sprinter who had no other choice than to win the race.

Just need to get somewhere safe and dial the number. Faster! Faster! Keep running!

Aiming for a house brimming with light at the top of the
street, she pumped her arms harder, eating up the sidewalk like her
life depended on it.

A man and woman exited a house with a small dog on a
leash.

Sofia screamed through gasping swallows of air. "I need
your phone!"

The roar of a gun permeated the silent night.

Her body jerked violently. A searing pain roared over her
shoulders, sliced through her nerves, and exploded across her back.
Hitting the ground face first, confused and angry, her ragged
breath still loud and rapid, was the last thing she remembered.

Chapter Twenty-Seven

Stephen opened Allison's wine refrigerator, selected a bottle, and held it up. "Nice."

Allison winced. "That's a very expensive vintage."

"I know." He unwrapped the top. "That's why I'm opening it." She was still angry about the girls being in her home. He didn't care.

"Fine." Allison sat on a leather-topped barstool, scowling. "Just make yourself at home why don't you?"

"I have." He enjoyed Allison's less than humble abode. "Just need a cork screw."

"Top right drawer." Allison pressed her hands flat against the marble counter while Stephen found what he needed and opened the bottle.

He sniffed the top. "Very nice." Grabbing two glasses from her shelf, he set them on the counter.

Allison watched him pour the wine. "Busy night, I presume."

"Petar and Damian are at the motels. Svet has Anastasia and Sofia at a house party for McCullen."

Still frowning, Allison accepted her glass. "Our client arrives in Charlotte in a few hours. He'll smuggle Emma out and sign the papers for the new building. So, let's get this done, make sure we're in agreement."

"First you wanted us to buy the place, then you didn't." He sang the words to a tune only he could hear. "Now you do . . ."

"Don't start, Stephen. Focus."

"Who is the client?"

"One of our contacts in Japan—"

"What's his name?" Stephen took a drink of his wine, staring at Allison from the other side of the kitchen island.

"Yusaku. The one who bought Camila last year."

"The freak with the toe fetish."

"Yes. He'll lease the building through a holding company. I'll order some supplies and cots, and you can have the girls move in when you finish in Winston-Salem. The whole Carolina crew. All of them in one location."

"Hmm." He swirled his wine. "I don't know if that's a good idea."

"Think about it—"

"I will. We'll need a name for the business front, if it's going to work. Massage something."

"Calling it a spa would be better." Allison smoothed her hand over her hair and pulled it forward over her shoulder.

"Spa something. Okay. How do we keep people from coming in to get an actual massage?"

"Train the girls to do massages?"

"There's no chance in hell of the motel girls giving a real massage. You know that. They don't have the strength to wipe their own asses most of the time."

"Sofia and Anastasia—no reason they should lie around sleeping all day."

Stephen smirked. "Right? The two of them together don't have the muscle to do it. I go to this woman . . . the arms on her, she could wrestle an—"

"I'll figure it out. We wouldn't be reinventing the wheel. These places are everywhere. It's going to be much easier than continuing to find new places every time they're in Charlotte. This is our best market."

Stephen picked at the wine label, creating small tears across the top. "About the American girl—her parents actually do have money. I'm thinking of orchestrating a ransom."

Allison huffed. "No. Ransoms never work. People get caught picking up the cash. Besides she's seen all of us. It's out of the question."

"I didn't say we'd give her back after we got the money."

"Okay." Allison took a sip of wine. "I'm listening."

"Damian will do the pick-up and hold on to the money until it's safe. If he's caught, he can be replaced with a new spotter. He won't give up names. Never. It's his fault the whole city is looking for this girl anyway. All because Martinez asked for a prep school girl. I can make anyone look like a prep school girl. Can't believe he snatched a real one."

Allison ran her red-tipped finger around the rim of her glass. "Just when you think the extras are with the program, you find out how brainless they really are."

"Damian is the least stupid of the lot."

Allison shrugged one shoulder. "Have you confronted him yet?"

"He just got back in Charlotte. I'm still deciding how I'm going to do it." He grinned. "Lots of options. If I only had one hand that worked, I'd be quite worried about protecting the other."

"Damian is too nice for our operation anyway. Always bringing the girls presents or whatever the hell he buys them."

"Disfigured Damian has checked in, but can never leave. Not alive anyway." He silently entertained the chorus from Hotel California but refrained from sharing it with his colleague. He returned his thoughts to the matter at hand—what to do with Emma and Damian.

"Don't waste your time talking to him about it." Allison rested her forearms on the counter. "Just get rid of him. I'll tell Svet to do it. Give him a bonus."

Stephen flung his arms open and broke into song. "You're a monster, Ms. Greenwood. Your heart's—"

"Enough. I don't want your stupid songs stuck in my head." She waved her hand to the side. "And forget about the ransom. It will backfire. I told you, I've got it all arranged. It's good money. He's taking her tonight from the truck stop. She's caused enough trouble already." Allison downed the rest of her drink. "We don't need to find out how much more."

"Hey, didn't the Japanese guy like girls much younger?" Stephen asked.

His phone rang. "It's Svet." Frowning, he answered.

Svet hesitated before speaking and Stephen knew something had gone wrong.

"We've got problem," the bodyguard said. He always dropped his articles when he was angry or anxious.

"You know I don't like problems. Is it a big one I'm going to care about, or a small one you can take care of without involving me? Is it really our problem, or is it your problem?"

"Sofia is . . . gone."

Stephen hissed through clenched teeth and set his wine glass down before he snapped the stem. *Definitely a big problem. Now I have to find out just how big.*

Allison crossed her arms. "What happened? Why is he calling?"

Stephen gripped his phone against his ear without answering her. "How did it happen?"

"I shot her."

A cold tightening sensation spread across Stephen's chest. He slowly inhaled, needing all the patience he could muster. He enunciated each word slowly. "Why did you shoot her, Svet?"

"She escaped from house. Out bathroom window."

"*The* house! *A* bathroom!" Correcting Svet's grammar gave him time to process the news. He could hardly believe Sofia had attempted to escape. He'd been too lenient with the girls lately. He hadn't done enough to keep them scared. Svet should have murdered Sasha in front of them, not somewhere off in Virginia. He had believed the girls were sufficiently brainwashed. He hated finding out he was wrong. Now, with his nails digging into his palms, he needed to listen to the consequences; find out the full story.

"She had a big head start. I didn't want her to get away, or run to someone's house, so I shot her."

"You shot Sofia in front of McCullen's house?"

Allison stood, staring intently at Stephen and gripping the edge of the counter.

"Not in front. Down the street."

"And what did you do with her body?" Stephen could feel an artery twitching in his forehead. An irritating sensation made worse, so much worse, by Svet's responses.

"Um—"

"Um? Did you just say um, Svet!" Stephen jumped out of his seat and paced, shaking his hand in the air. "Where the hell is she right now? And this better be a damn good answer."

"People with dogs ran over to her. More came out of homes. I couldn't kill them all, yeah? I took Anastasia and disappeared a different way before police came."

"Do you know for sure that she's dead? She better be dead." Stephen rested his forehead against his hand. "That girl better be deader than a doornail."

On the other end of the line, the big man swallowed loudly.

"You don't know! Where are you now?"

"I'm with Damian and the motel girls. And Anastasia. Didn't want to bring her back to Allison's house in case . . . in case . . ."

At least he was thinking. "Stay there," Stephen ordered. "I'm coming."

"This is bad," Allison said. "We need to get everyone out of Charlotte. Except Emma. Petar needs to bring Emma to meet Yusaku."

"Can't you do it?" Stephen sneered.

"No. I'm staying here. I already have the police and FBI poking around in my business. I'm not going anywhere near those girls!"

Stephen rushed out through the back exit, slamming the door behind him.

Chapter Twenty-Eight

A persistent jostling sensation forced Sofia awake. She was on her back, moving.

In the van again?

A wailing siren filled her ears.

She struggled to force her eyes open, squinting to focus on the strangers shrouded in bright light. Snatches of orders and instructions volleyed through the air around her.

"En route . . . young female, gunshot wound . . . lost consciousness . . ."

Punches of tension-filled voices and words faded in and out.

"Blood loss . . . pulse tachy . . . morphine administered . . ."

She couldn't feel her body. She'd been drugged, her brain rendered thick and foggy like the helpless motel girls.

""IV fluids, normal saline, wide open. . . ETA less than five minutes."

There's something I have to do. Something urgent. What is it?

Blinking, she tried to understand what was happening around her. And there was something else, something important spiraling away from her in a jumble of racing thoughts.

". . . inserting another line . . ."

The tip line!

She tried to recall it, but the numbers floated just outside her grasp. She prayed Anastasia remembered them. "Anastasia?" she whispered. "Anastasia?" She wasn't sure if she was saying her friend's name aloud, or simply dreaming that she was. In any case, Anastasia didn't answer. *Where is she?* Sofia tried to sit up, but didn't have the strength.

I'll disappear just like Sasha. Poor Anastasia will get my tongue.

Images of Sofia's family floated by. An overwhelming sadness descended. *I'll never see them again. They'll never know what happened. Never even know I missed them.*

Gray clouds nudged her frantic thoughts away, making room for the darkness of nothing, until she was pulled back from consciousness.

◆ ◆ ◆

The nurse assistant was tired, but she couldn't wait to share the interesting news with one of her friends on the next shift. That was the beauty of pulling a double, you had the full scoop from the last eight hours.

She refueled with black coffee as her friend clocked in. "Here's the big excitement you missed. Young female, GSW."

"Another? Where was this one shot?"

The assistant followed her friend into the locker room. "Back of her shoulder. Dr. Chaudhry said a millimeter to the side and she'd be dead."

"I meant, where was she?"

"That's what makes it real interesting. Ready for this? She was in the Myers Park neighborhood. The ritzy part. One of the streets right off the main street with the multi-million-dollar houses and those gigantic trees. Outside. Right on the sidewalk."

"Seriously?" The aide grabbed a set of scrubs from the top of a pile and unfolded them.

"Yep."

"That's not business as usual out there," her friend said, opening a locker. "Did they catch who did it?"

"Nope. Cops went door to door asking people. No one saw the shooter. And—get this— no one knew who the girl was or what she was doing there."

"Ha! They said they didn't anyway." The nurse assistant began to undress. "Can't trust rich people. They're the best liars. They're not worried because they always get away with it. That's what makes them lie so good."

"The girl—she was rich all right. Just a teenager, but really beautiful, something special. She came in wearing a fancy dress, her hair all done up like she was going to prom, but there's no proms going on tonight. And she was wearing lots of jewelry. A few of the things were fake, but most of it—very, very real."

"How would you know what was real?" She pulled her top down over her abdomen.

"One of the doctors said so."

"And you said the girl had no identification?"

"Nope. And she was alone. But I think they'll figure out who she is. Might be in a gang."

"A gang? She don't sound like a gang member to me."

"I know. But . . .I was getting to this—she has a brand on the back of her neck. Dr. Chaudhry took a picture and sent it to the FBI. They have a database with marks and tattoos to help identify gangs and things like that. If it's in there . . .the FBI will know who she is, maybe, and can figure out what happened."

The nurse's aide tucked the last item of her clothing inside the locker and slammed it shut. "Sounds like that girl's gonna have an interesting story."

◆ ◆ ◆

Rivera pulled into the motel parking lot for his second appointment. He'd failed to return to sleep after the fire alarm had kept the hotel guests outside for an hour, but the lack of sleep hardly mattered. He was fully alert from adrenaline.

Moonlight illuminated the seedy motel making it look like the setting in a horror movie. Something was different. The No Vacancy sign was unlit and there were only two other cars in the lot behind the motel. One was Victoria's rental. She'd left the hotel wearing a Georgetown sweatshirt and jeans, looking beautiful in spite of her efforts to downplay her looks.

His phone buzzed with a new message and he checked the screen. Dr. Rebecca Boswell's message asked him to call her. He might have thought it had something to do with the double date Victoria mentioned, except it was marked priority. He tightened his bullet- proof vest. It was time to get out of his car and head up to the motel room.

I'll call Rebecca as soon as this is all over.

His dream from last night was a little embarrassing. Thank God he didn't talk in his sleep, as far as he knew. A romantic relationship with Victoria was off limits right now. One—they were colleagues, and two—she was with her dogwalker guy. But a persistent voice wouldn't stop reminding him—*she asked for you*

215

to come out here. Anyone could have done this—any guy—but she asked for you. Sure—she trusts you. But is that the only reason?

The wind picked up and whipped the tree tops around. A piece of trash swirled past his feet.

Agent Rivera walked calmly to the designated room. He slid his key fob into his pocket and pulled on the rim of his cap. This time, Emma or not, they were taking the girls with them.

He knocked.

He looked around, gripping his wrist. *Please don't let them be gone.*

"Answer the door," he growled, pounding on it. "I don't want anyone to see me out here."

He leaned in, listening for anything to indicate there was someone inside. Hearing nothing, he moved on to the next room, and then the next, gritting his teeth and shaking his head. *Did I tip them off somehow? Where the hell are they?*

The door opened in one of the rooms Rivera had been in the previous night. A middle-aged woman backed out pulling a supply cart with one hand and pushing the door open with the other. *Strange she was cleaning the rooms at night. Had something happened inside this one?* Rivera took hold of the door and held it open.

"Gracias," the woman responded without making eye contact.

As the cart moved past him, he scanned the rumpled sheets and towels for signs of blood. He saw only white. He peered inside. The room was tidy and empty.

Keeping her head down and giving no further acknowledgement of Rivera's presence, the woman slid a key into the next door.

"Here, let me get that for you." Again, he held the door open while the housekeeper pushed her cart inside. He followed her in. The door closed behind him with a clink of the metal latch.

The woman's eyes shot to the closed door. She gripped the handles of her cart.

Rivera felt guilty for causing her fear. He showed his badge. "You're not in any trouble, I promise. I'm looking for a missing girl."

The woman stared down at her shoes. Rivera could see uncertainty eating her up inside.

"Can you take a look and let me know if you've seen this girl around?"

"Disculpa. No hablo Ingles." Again, her eyes moved toward the door and back.

He tapped his phone until Emma's picture appeared. "She's missing. Have you seen her around here?" Rivera repeated the question in Spanish. "Elle está desaparecida. La han visto por aqui?"

The housekeeper glanced at his phone and shook her head.

"Thank you for your help. Her family is very worried. Gracias por su ayuda. Su familia esta muy preocupada."

His disappointment weighed heavy as he left the room. It was impossible to know if the woman was simply fearful for herself and her own situation, whatever that may be, or if she knew anything about Emma but was afraid to disclose it.

A sedan beeped as a man locked it and headed toward the motel. He was middle-aged, wearing jeans and a jacket. Didn't look like he hit the gym much. Average looking in all respects.

Out of desperation, Rivera tried a different tactic. "Hey, um, excuse me. Can I ask you something?"

The man stopped walking. He studied Rivera and quickly looked around. "What?" He pressed a hand against his side. Either he was carrying a weapon or protecting something like a wallet in his coat pocket. Rivera sensed it was the latter.

Rivera moved closer. "I'm here looking for a fresh piece of ass—this is what she looks like." He held his phone where the man could see Emma's picture, the one in the school girl uniform. "I was with her a few days ago and I really want to be with her again. Do you know if she's here?"

As realization clouded the man's features, he shook his head. "Look, buddy, I'm just here for the football games. I don't know anything about a girl." He resumed walking, glancing back at Rivera with disgust.

Rivera believed him.

Sick about the missing girls and the way he'd just represented himself, he sent Victoria a message.

They're not here.

Victoria responded almost immediately.

Just talked to Rebecca. We have a new lead.

Chapter Twenty-Nine

Sofia's eyes fluttered open. She was lying on her back.

White ceiling. White walls. Machines with blinking lights. Strange contraptions with colored wires.

Where am I?

"Oh. Hello, there. You're awake." A woman hovered above, staring into her face, wearing a green top and pants—*hospital clothes*. "Let me get the doctor."

Sofia shivered even though beads of sweat coated her brow. She'd heard Stephen address men as doctor, right before they forced her to do disgusting things. Once a client wanted to "play doctor." Svet had to approve of the creep's toys first, which he did. Doctors couldn't be trusted any more than other men. *Wait, don't go,* she tried to say. Her words came out as a whimper of gibberish that made no sense at all.

The woman left. Sofia fought to stay alert, but drifted back to sleep.

"Hi. I'm Doctor Chaudhry. I heard you were awake."

219

Sofia forced her eyes open, relieved to hear the doctor was a woman.

Dr. Chaudhry had shiny, black hair and big brown eyes. Her teeth were very white against her dark skin.

Sofia tried to pull the sheet up to her neck but had to stop short. There wasn't pain, exactly, but she could barely move her arm. Being compromised left her feeling exceptionally vulnerable. An image flashed through her mind— Emma, passed out and helpless on Ms. Bois's guest room bed.

"Careful now." Dr. Chaudhry held up her hand. "You're waking up from surgery."

"W—what happened?" Sofia sputtered like Petar and her throat ached when she spoke.

"A bullet entered through your shoulder and damaged your axillary artery." The doctor stood at the end of the bed, studying the chart in her hands. "We repaired your artery, cleaned up the surrounding tissue, and put you back together."

Sofia remembered the pain exploding across her shoulder, the mental agony of falling, the anguish of being unable to run another step. She pressed her dry lips together, relieved to be alive but afraid of what would happen next.

"You're going to be fine. There will be considerable soreness for a few days, and you'll need physical therapy to get your arm functioning at one hundred percent, but you'll be good as new in a few months." The doctor moved to Sofia's side. "How do you feel? Do you want something to help you with the pain?"

Do I have a choice? Sofia licked her lips and wished she had a glass of water. "I don't want any drugs, if that's what you're asking." The last thing she wanted was to end up like the motel girls who had no idea what was going on around them.

"Okay, then. You're quite a trooper. Usually I hear just the opposite." Dr. Chaudhry smiled. "I'm going to do a quick examination, now that you're awake."

The doctor turned on a pen light. "Follow my finger." She moved her finger slowly to one side and Sofia did as she was told

"Good. Now this side."

Again, Sofia followed her finger until the light went out. She used the time to try and think through her options. *Does she know who I am? Does she know who I ran away from?*

"I'm going to help you sit up now, not all the way, just enough so I can check your bandage, make sure there's no bleeding."

Dr. Chaudhry placed her hand on the back of Sofia's neck and lifted her forward, just barely.

"Everything looks as it should." The doctor stepped back. "Now that I'm sure you're on your way to healing nicely, there are some people here who want to speak to you. Do you feel up to it?"

Stephen? Ms. Bois? Sofia's heart beat faster. She struggled to sit up against a wave of dizziness.

"Whoa. Not so fast. It's all right."

It's not all right until I know who's here. She kept her eyes on the doorway, afraid of who might be out there waiting. "Who are they?"

"Well, your first visitors were police detectives. But they've been replaced by FBI agents. They have to figure out what happened to you. They're here to help."

Help who, exactly? That was the important question. It was unlikely they wanted to help her, and she wasn't about to be tricked again. She needed to speak to the people looking for Emma. They might be willing to make a deal with her in exchange for information. She needed a phone and she needed to remember the number. She dug her fingernails into her palms and lifted her chin as tears brimmed in her eyes, threatening to fall.

The doctor moved to stand by the door and two strangers entered. Sofia couldn't see their features clearly, but she sensed the casually dressed, blonde woman was attractive by her fit figure and the way she carried herself. The man looked solid and strong in his flannel shirt and jeans, but not a giant beast like Petar and Svet.

Sofia's heart beat faster. She flattened her sweaty palms against the sheet. She was so close to being free, closer than she'd ever been, but she was also weak and could barely sit up in the bed. She couldn't run. Maybe in a few days, but not now. She needed help. But how could she know who to trust?

"Hi. I'm agent Victoria Heslin." The woman sounded confident and in charge, but not harsh. "And this is Agent Dante Rivera. We're with the FBI. We're here to help you. We want to find out who shot you."

Sofia's throat tightened and she had a hard time swallowing. Stephen had law enforcement officers on his payroll. Did he have FBI too? If she trusted them and was wrong, they would send her right back to him. She shuddered and her empty stomach heaved with fear. Stephen would be furious that she'd tried to escape. But maybe, just maybe . . . if she fed the agents the story she was supposed to tell if she ever got separated from Svet or Petar—*I'm visiting my uncle. I can't remember his address right now, but I'm sure he'll come for me soon*—maybe Stephen would forgive her.

The female agent held a black book or a computer tablet, Sofia wasn't sure which. "Can you tell us your name?" the woman asked.

Should I pretend I don't understand English? Pretend I have amnesia? Sofia pressed her lips together, twisting the edge of her hospital gown between her fingers. *I've got two options— trust them, or stay quiet until Stephen finds me here. He always said he would find us anywhere.*

"Do you know your name?" Agent Heslin asked. "Are you having trouble remembering?"

The room seemed to be shrinking in size, the air stifling. "I know my name." Sofia responded in perfect English, although anyone could tell from her accent that she wasn't American. "Sofia Domitrovich."

The male agent responded, "That's a start." His voice was authoritative but kind.

Anyone can pretend.

"Do you remember why you were running and do you know who shot you?" he asked.

Sofia shook her head.

"We're trying to piece together what happened. No one seems to know what you were doing in the area when you were shot."

Sofia looked down at her hospital bed.

"Okay," Agent Rivera conceded. "Let's see what you do remember. Where are you from, Sofia?"

"Ukraine. I'm here visiting my uncle."

Maybe he was making faces that would tell her more about what he was thinking, but from where he was standing, his face was mostly a blur of skin color topped with dark hair and offered Sofia no clues. "And your uncle's name is?"

"I'm—he's—I've always called him Uncle." She looked away from the agent. "I'm not worried. I know he'll come for me soon." The knot in her stomach grew with those words.

"We saw a picture of the mark on the back of your neck," Agent Rivera said. "Can you tell us what it means? How it got there?"

Sofia hadn't expected that question. She stared ahead, trying to focus on the wires coming out of some sort of medical contraption. "It's just a tattoo," she whispered.

Agent Rivera cleared his throat. "Earlier this week, we found a girl with the same mark in Virginia. And yesterday, I saw the same mark on a girl in a motel, here in Charlotte."

Sofia had questions she didn't dare ask. *Why was he at the motel? Did he save the girl or not? If he's going to help me like he said he would, he would have saved her first.* Now she really didn't trust him.

"We know you've been through a lot." Sofia had to give the agent credit for trying her best to say all the right things. "It's over now. All of it. And we want it to be over for the rest of the girls, too. Can you tell us what happened to you?"

Sofia remained silent, straining to remember the tip line number, still wondering if all of this was a trick or a test and if Stephen was standing outside the door listening to see what she said.

"You are an incredibly strong person." There was warmth and assurance in the female agent's voice. "You're safe now. No one is going to hurt you. We just want to help you."

Torn between wanting to trust the woman, and not letting herself fall for anyone's lies, Sofia counted to twenty-two before the agent spoke again.

"We can protect you and get you back to your family, if that's a safe place for you. But we can't help you until you help us first with some information."

The statement reminded her of Ms. Bois when they arrived in America. "No money until you earn back the cost of your travel." Total BS. *I should know better by now.* Sofia stared down at her lap. "If you work with Stephen, then you must know everything already. I shouldn't need to tell you." *There, Stephen should be pleased with that response. I told them nothing.* But then she thought of Sasha's tongue wrapped in foil under the back seat of the van. *What did Sasha do or say to deserve that? What will Svet do to me?*

Agent Heslin moved closer to the bed, close enough for Sofia to see her well-defined bone structure, her perfect nose, and her long-lashes. *What is her beauty hiding?*

"We heard you were shot running away from someone or something." Agent Heslin dipped her head. "You took a huge risk because you're brave. Fear is not a reason to give up now, not after you've come this far. But . . . I understand that trusting someone now might be your biggest leap of faith. Take all the time you need, but please, let us know what we can do to earn your trust."

The agent's blue eyes contained something Sofia hadn't seen in a very long time—empathy. She had occasions to see pity, and even mild concern from men after they were done with her, but no one besides Anastasia and Sasha had ever understood what was going on in her head. No one in America had spoken to her as if she was strong and intelligent.

Agent Rivera poured a glass of water from a pitcher. Sofia had noticed it previously, but with her vision, she thought it was some sort of decorative vase. He handed her the glass and she gulped the water down. It was pure heaven on her parched throat.

225

Something shifted inside Sofia. *Isn't freedom worth taking a big risk? Even if it means sacrificing my life?*

She summoned her bravery. *It's now or never.*

But if I'm wrong . . .

She sputtered out the words before she could talk herself out of it. "I know where the missing American girl is. Emma. I know who took her and where to find her. But you better move fast because they're about to smuggle her out of the country." She shut her eyes and tensed her body, half-expecting Stephen to burst in, grab her by the neck, and slam her head against the wall.

"That's great," Agent Rivera said. "There are a lot of people looking for her, her family is worried."

Ignoring a pang of jealousy, Sofia opened her eyes. "I know. I saw it on television." She struggled to sit up straighter and a pulling sensation around her stitched shoulder made her wince. "But I can't remember the number to call."

"What number?" Agent Heslin asked. "Are you talking about the tip line that was on the news?"

"Yes."

"That's okay," Agent Heslin said. "You don't need it. You can tell us."

Sofia wrapped her good arm around her chest. She met Victoria's eyes, and held her gaze steady, summoning every last ounce of her strength. "But I won't tell you unless you help me, too. That's the deal."

"Of course, of course, we'll help you." Agent Heslin's imploring look said *why wouldn't we?*

"And Anastasia," Sofia said.

"We don't know who Anastasia is, but we want to help free all of the girls in this operation." The female agent looked and sounded sincere. But Ms. Bois could also look and sound sincere. Three years ago, she'd looked Sofia's mother in the eyes and promised to take care of Sofia as if she was her own daughter. But whether the agents were tricking her or not, none of it mattered now anyway. It was done. She had betrayed Stephen. There was nothing left for Sofia to do except wait and see if she'd made a fatal mistake. The tears began to flow. Tears of relief—the decision was now out of her hands. She hadn't cried in a long, long time.

"If you're ready," Agent Rivera said. "I want to show you a picture and see if you can identify someone else for us."

Sofia wiped at her tears, biting down on her bottom lip. "I'm ready."

He held up a photograph. "This is the girl we found in Virginia."

"Bring it closer," Sofia said. Agent Rivera complied.

Sasha looked to be sleeping in the photo, although her lips were a troubling bluish-gray color.

Sofia pressed her hand against her cheek. She held her breath for several seconds before exhaling. Of course, she knew there was a good chance Sasha was dead even before Svet presented her tongue. Yet she'd tried to convince herself the tongue hadn't really belonged to her friend. The proof in the photograph hit her hard. She had to overcome her disorientation and focus. "That's Sasha. Svet gave us her tongue last night."

The agents quickly turned to look at each other. They were close enough now for her to pick up on their sympathetic expressions.

Sofia stopped her tears and told her whole story from the beginning.

"We were supposed to be models. Ms. Bois saw us walking home from school. Me and Sasha. She said we were strikingly beautiful and it would be a crime not to share us with the world. Stephen found Anastasia at another school in our town and told her the same."

The agents listened without interrupting as she recounted bits of her sad and sordid story about Stephen and Ms. Bois, the brothers, and the parties with the men. She ended by describing the house from which she escaped. She was mentally and physically exhausted.

Dr. Chaudhry came in and did a quick exam. "She's been through a lot," she told the agents. "We need to give her some time to rest." The doctor's expression left no room for negotiations.

"We'll be back in a few hours," Victoria said. "We still need specific information—names, locations."

Sofia was struggling to keep her eyes open. "Okay. I'll just rest for a few minutes."

She immediately drifted into a sound sleep.

◆ ◆ ◆

Victoria had a heavy feeling in her stomach as she and Rivera walked down the hospital corridor.

"We don't have enough information to go after the sex traffickers yet," Rivera said. "But we can get a search warrant and send police to the house she ran from."

"What she just told us—it's so heartbreaking—I couldn't interrupt. And the 'motel girls.' I can't imagine how any of them survive. We've got to find them fast."

"I told you."

"We have to protect her. That was huge for her to trust us." Victoria placed her hand over her mouth, covering a yawn. "I wouldn't trust anyone if I were her."

"She's tough."

"And smart. Came speaking little English, and now she's fluent."

"But did you pick up on the way she talks about Emma and the other girls? Everyone except Anastasia. There's no compassion. Like their weaknesses disgust her."

"Three years as a sex-slave—how is she supposed to learn about compassion? Not from the people exploiting her. Not from the men paying to rape her. People don't go to prison and come out kinder and nicer. They get tougher in order to endure." Victoria lowered her voice. "She's going to help us bring down this sex trafficking ring. And then, if necessary, I'm going to help get her the best psychologist out there. But right now, we need to keep her safe."

They walked the rest of the way to the nurse's station in silence. A few of the hospital staff were busy typing on computers and sorting through charts.

"Excuse me." Victoria cleared her throat. "May I have your attention?" She held up her badge, waiting until one of the doctors put down her phone and a nurse looked up from a computer. "I'm Agent Heslin with the FBI, and this is Agent Rivera. The patient in room 302 needs a private room. There's no one else in there now, and we need to keep it that way. We'll have a guard posted outside the door at all times."

The woman on the computer nodded.

"And we cannot have her listed in your database," Victoria continued. "Change her name and age, whatever you need to do so she becomes invisible here. Can that happen immediately?"

"Yes," Dr. Chaudhry responded. "We have a protocol in place for that."

"Might she have any visitors?" a nurse with glasses asked, shifting the chart he carried to the opposite side of his body.

"No visitors." Victoria made eye contact with each of the workers as she spoke. "Until you hear otherwise from me, no one other than her doctor and the nurses can see her. Her life is in danger and anyone attempting to visit her is a potential threat, no matter what they tell you."

"Are the other patients on the floor in any danger?" the same nurse asked.

Victoria didn't answer, exactly. "As soon as she can be safely discharged, we'll be taking her to an isolated location. Until then, we'll have agents or guards on the floor. Please make sure everyone working on this floor is aware and each next shift is informed."

There were nods and murmurs from the staff.

"Thank you," Victoria said. "I'm going to talk to security now. Agent Rivera will be outside the patient's room."

She headed downstairs to meet with security. *Better try to find some coffee, too.* Almost two nights without sleep was beginning to take its toll.

The elevator doors slid apart as she approached. Detective Connelly stepped out.

Victoria offered a tight-lipped smile of acknowledgement.

"Agent Heslin. You're still in Charlotte." Connelly stood directly in front of her. "Heard there might be a girl—?"

"Yes, there is."

"Have you determined if she's connected to Emma Manning's disappearance?"

Victoria studied him. "She just had surgery. We can't talk to her yet. Doctor's orders. We're going to handle this from here out."

A flash of resentment narrowed his bloodshot eyes. He rubbed his hand over his face. Circles of sweat stained his shirt under his arms. "Who is 'we'?"

"The girl in the hospital is now my responsibility, detective. And so is Emma Manning."

"Since when?"

"Since yesterday."

"Who gave you jurisdiction? I didn't hear anything about it." Connelly raised his voice and one of the nurses turned to look their way.

"No one, yet. I thought you'd be grateful, seeing you're getting pulled into other work. Excuse me. I have a meeting." And then, probably because she was sleep deprived, she couldn't resist adding. "I'll give you an update as soon as I can." She stepped around the detective and walked away. *Better wake up Murphy before I meet with security, since I'm going to tell them no cops or investigators allowed on the floor. At least not without Rivera or me present.*

Chapter Thirty

Stephen backed his BMW between the faded lines of a parking spot. *I hate this dump.* The motel reminded him of starting out in the business. He supposed the dark and dingy place perfectly matched his mood since he found out Sofia had been shot and was now unaccounted for.

He knocked on one of the doors to signal his arrival. Svet answered, shirtless, with a beer in his hand. There were empty bottles on the nightstand and on the table holding the television. Trash from fast food restaurants littered the floor.

Nadia was sprawled across a bed, sleeping like a limp doll. Maria was lying on her side on the stained carpet, obsessed with scratching her arm and chest. Stephen slapped her hand away from her body to stop her from clawing at her skin.

Still wearing her dress, jewelry, and elegant but mussed hair-do, Anastasia huddled in a corner chair looking like she didn't belong. *One of these things is not like the others.*

"Just gave them a fix," Svet said, tipping his head toward Maria and Nadia.

Heroin and meth rendered them confused but compliant, barely able to stand on their own, mostly wanting to lie around and sleep. When the drugs wore off, they turned desperate, crying and clawing, like rabid, feral animals. They gave Stephen the creeps. No way could he bring them to Allison's house, just in case a nosy neighbor came over to borrow something. These girls had to stay hidden from all but the customers, who rarely complained.

"Petar was at the gym." Svet picked a bag of trash off a chair and sat down. "But he's on his way here, now."

Stephen had to endure less than a minute in the room before Petar trudged in.

"Glad you got my message." Stephen glared at Petar. He deliberately paced to let them all see how angry yet how in control he was. He stopped at Damian. "And it started with you."

"Me?" Damian looked to the door and then his shoes, blinking. He knew not to look at Stephen when he was mad.

Never show fear. Stephen pounded his fist into his hand. *Give them a glimpse of your crazy. Kill whoever they care about. That's how to keep them in line.* "I've had a very bad few days, or we would have had this conversation much sooner."

Stephen locked eyes with Svet and signaled toward Damian. Svet knew exactly what to do. He moved quickly, wrapping one arm tight around Damian's neck and gripping Damian's hands behind his back. Damian was strong, but no match for Svet.

Stephen stared Damian down. "Why? Why? Why, Damian?"

"Why what?" Damian struggled to get the words out through Svet's chokehold.

"Why did you take the American girl?"

Damian grimaced under Svet's grip. "You said one of your best clients wanted a white prep school girl."

233

"Really, Damian? If a client says he wants a girl who reminds him of a pirate, do we go to the damn ocean and smuggle one off a boat? No! You stupid little . . . we buy a damn pirate costume! What were you thinking? Little princess Emma's family wants her back and they have friends in high places."

Stephen nodded at Svet, who responded by twisting Damian's arm.

Damian moaned. "But—" He struggled to speak. "Allison told me to."

"What the hell are you saying?" Stephen poked his finger into Damian's chest. "Allison asked you specifically to get Emma Manning? She said, get Emma Manning and bring her to me?"

Damian's face was red and growing brighter. His eyes bulged.

"Let up on him. I want to hear this." Stephen leaned forward. "It's been a night of unexpected events."

Svet loosened his grip. Damian gulped air as his color returned to normal. "Yes, what you said—that's exactly how it went down. Allison paid me extra. She paid me a bonus to get Emma Manning. She showed me pictures and gave me the girl's address."

Stephen rubbed his chin and paced with his head down. "See, what you're saying doesn't make sense. Allison was furious about the attention the girl is drawing. And you expect me to believe she asked you to kidnap her?"

"It's the truth. Why else would I go after her?" Beads of sweat covered Damian's forehead and slid down his temples. "I thought it was messed up, not how we do things, but it's not my place to argue with Allison. And it ended up being easy. She told me to contact Emma through the ChatEasy app, which I deleted from her phone and laptop before we dumped them."

Stephen studied the young man and tried to figure out who was playing him, Damian or Allison. Who was the better liar? That was an easy question to answer. "Let him go."

Svet released Damian. He stumbled away, chest heaving. His useless hand dangled at his side, the other rubbed his neck. "Allison wanted to get Emma out of the country and sell her. I wasn't supposed to tell you Allison was involved."

Stephen cackled. "No, I imagine that you weren't. And that was another mistake." He waved him away. "Get out. You and Svet are taking all the girls to Winston-Salem. Two different motels. Same as last time. Don't leave any of them alone for a second. Petar, you're staying here until I tell you otherwise."

"N-n-not bringing Emma to the truck stop to get rid of her, like Allison told me?" Petar asked.

"No. You're not." Stephen didn't trust Allison anymore. He'd set up his own deal to make Emma disappear.

Svet moved toward Stephen. "What about the rest of today's appointments?"

Stephen didn't like Svet standing so close and he didn't like the brothers questioning him. "The only thing happening tonight is you and Damian getting all the girls out of Charlotte and Petar waiting here until I tell him otherwise!" *Things are separating at the seams. It's my job to tie them back together. Then Damian will pay for crossing me.*

While he waited for confirmation that Sofia was dead, he could at least get to the bottom of this new development. Time to drive back to Allison's house and figure out why she abducted Emma Manning.

Chapter Thirty-One

Following Dr. Chaudhry's orders, the agents let Sofia get some rest. They took turns sitting outside her room, anxious for another chance to talk to her. Victoria called her boss, grabbed something to eat, and bought another coffee for Rivera.

She caught Sofia's doctor in the hallway.

"We really need some more time with Sofia," she told the doctor. "It's urgent."

Dr. Chaudhry glanced toward the room she was about to enter and sighed. "All right. Let me check on her first."

They returned to Sofia's room together. Victoria handed Rivera his coffee. He wasn't quite as fresh looking as when he'd arrived in Charlotte two days ago, but he was wide awake, tapping his foot.

Dr. Chaudhry knocked lightly as she entered. "Sofia?"

Sofia pulled the sheet up to her neck and squinted toward the doorway. "Who's there?" Her voice trembled.

"It's Dr. Chaudhry. I'm with Agent Heslin and Agent Rivera."

"Sofia, are you . . . nearsighted?" Victoria asked. "Do you normally wear glasses?"

Sofia shook her head. "No."

"How many fingers am I holding up?" Victoria held up one finger.

"Three," Sofia answered immediately.

Victoria extended all five fingers. "Now how many?"

"Two." Sofia sounded certain, but her hands were busy twisting her bedsheets.

Victoria wasn't sure how to respond at first. The poor girl wouldn't allow herself any weaknesses, but there was an easy fix to her problem. "I'm going to look into getting you some glasses." She glanced at Dr. Chaudhry. "Surely there's an optometrist who can make a visit."

"I don't know if that's possible here." Dr. Chaudhry sighed. "They would need—"

Victoria gestured toward the hallway. "Let's step out and talk about this." She led the way. "It might be unusual, but let's make it happen. If it's a matter of costs, I'll pick up whatever it is personally. You have my word. If you could just find someone to get her a prescription and bring some frames for her to choose from, we can have her seeing again in a few hours. I think it would really help her to trust us and to feel more comfortable if she can see us."

"I . . . I'll see what we can do."

"Thank you so much, doctor. I know it's not normal, but nothing about her life has been what it should be. This would be a good first step."

Dr. Chaudhry went back inside the room. She smiled at Sofia. "Doing okay?"

Sofia tried to straighten her shoulders but the pain stopped her. "I'm fine."

"I'm going to check a few things and make sure. Have a look under your bandage."

"I'm fine," Sofia said, her voice firm. "We have to save Anastasia. And Emma, before they send her away. Their lives are more important than my rest."

Victoria's heart surged with admiration for the girl.

"I see your point. But your health is my main responsibility. Remember, you have some serious healing to do." The doctor stepped back, studying her patient. "Tell these agents what you can, and then make sure you get some rest. A nurse will check on you, soon."

Victoria took the chair next to Sofia's bed and pulled it closer. "Ready to talk some more?"

"Yes." Sofia sat up straighter, with only the slightest wince. "We need to hurry."

Victoria smiled. "Good. We agree. What we need are names, locations, vehicles, anything we can use to help us arrest the people who were holding you and your other friends captive."

"They're not my friends." Sofia clutched the neck of her gown. "Only Anastasia. I have to look out for her. I'm worried about what's happened to her since I escaped."

"Then let's figure out how to find her." Victoria took out her tablet, ready to jot down whatever information Sofia provided. "I have faith that you know more than you think, and it will be enough for us to go on. Can you tell us the names of the people who held you?"

"Yes. The leaders are Stephen and Ms. Bois. I don't know his last name, and I know that's not her real name. But her first name is Allison. He's Romanian. She's American. And then there's Svet and Petar. They're brothers. From Ukraine, like me. They're strong. And cruel. Petar stutters. And then there's Da—"

Victoria waited until it became clear Sofia wasn't going to finish her sentence. "I didn't catch that last name you were about to say. What was it?"

Sofia twisted her hands in her bedsheet. "There might be a few others that watch over the motel girls or spot new girls. I don't know their names."

"I'd like you to describe each of them to me as best you can," Victoria said. "How old is Stephen, about, and what does he look like?"

"Stephen is older. Forties or fifties. Almost always wears suits during the day except for when he goes to yoga classes. And always carries a gun."

Good to know. Victoria made a note of it. "And Allison Bois?"

"Ms. Bois is thin and beautiful. Pale skin with freckles, red hair. Do you know who Nicole Kidman is? From the magazines?"

"The actress. Yes."

"Ms. Bois looks like Nicole Kidman. With long, straight red hair. She usually wears nice dresses and high heels. She looks like a business woman. Oh . . . I know she won an award from the City of Charlotte. You know they have police they pay to help them?"

"We suspected," Rivera said. "Do you think you'd recognize any of them if you saw them?

"I don't know. Maybe not. It's hard . . ." She glanced toward the window. "I'm not safe yet, am I?"

Victoria followed her gaze, but there was nothing to see. "We're going to get you out of here as soon as your doctor says it's okay. And then no one but us will know where you are until this is over and we catch the people responsible. Meanwhile, we're not leaving you. How about cars? Do you know what kind of cars they drive?"

"Stephen drives us in a dark silver Mercedes van or sometimes in his BMW. A black BMW. Ms. Bois's car looks a lot like his, but it's a black Mercedes."

Something pinged in Victoria's brain. She set her tablet down and hurried across the room. "Hold on. I'll be right back." It was just a hunch, but her intuition was suddenly on fire.

The Charlotte magazine she'd thumbed through earlier was no longer by the chair in the hallway. She flew down the stairs to the hospital lobby where she'd seen a stack of them. She grabbed one and flipped through the pages. Sure enough, just a few pages in, under the headliner Celebrating Success—a two-page spread featuring twenty or more attractive Charlotte Realty Max realtors. The perfect line up. Carrying the magazine, she ran back up the stairs and straight to the nursing desk. "Do you have a black pen?"

The nurse looked around the desk area.

"Never mind." Victoria spotted a marker under a white board and grabbed it. "This will do." Pressing the magazine against the wall, she inked out the name under each photo.

She hustled back to Sofia's room, offering Rivera a smug smile as she entered. She rested the open magazine on Sofia's lap. "Do any of these women look familiar to you?"

Sofia had no problem seeing close up. Her finger moved quickly below the headshots and stopped exactly where Victoria expected—middle row, second from the left. "That's her. That's Ms. Bois."

Victoria smiled. She could have pulled up the realtor's image on her tablet, but the magazine spread had made for an infallible line up. "Great job. Thank you, Sofia." She turned to

Rivera. "Allison Greenwood. The realtor who owns the listing for that building I searched."

"That's right." Sofia fiddled with an elastic hair band, wrapping it around her finger then pulling it off and starting again. "I forgot. The award at her house was for Allison Greenwood, but it had Ms. Bois's picture. If she and Stephen get away, they'll just move somewhere else, get more girls, and start over."

"We have more than enough to find her now. We're going to give this information to some people we work with. People we trust."

"And they'll go after her now?"

"Yes," Rivera answered. "Our boss is already on his way here to help organize the teams that will arrest them. What you've gone through, the risks you've taken to help others—you're a hero. You really are. So now, we need to heed your doctor's orders and let you recover. Is there anything we can get you? Are you hungry or thirsty?"

"Is there any way I could get . . . a Smoothie King Smoothie?"

Victoria smiled. "You can have anything you want. Just name it."

"I'd like chocolate with banana and peanut butter. Please."

"I'll call and see if they'll deliver it," Victoria suggested.

"No. I'll go get it," Rivera said. "I need some fresh air and I saw one across the street."

"But you're staying with me?" Sofia looked toward Victoria, her face earnest, her question more of a plea.

"I'm just going to step out to call my boss. He's on his way to Charlotte to help us catch the bad guys. I'll be right back. And there will be a guard in the hallway."

"Okay." Sofia let herself slump back against her pillow.

Chapter Thirty-Two

Stephen stopped at the back gate, gripping the post with one hand, his phone with the other. He growled into the phone. He ended the call and crossed the back yard. Using the key he'd borrowed earlier, he opened the back door.

In the kitchen, Allison greeted him with a glare. She was barefoot but still dressed in a sexy black sheath dress. "What the hell, Stephen? Why did you come back?" She peered around him. "You don't have any of the girls with you, do you?"

"I'm alone." He closed the door and leaned back against it.

"Did you find Sofia?"

Stephen glared at her. His fingers stroked the gun at his side.

Allison grabbed a dishtowel and wiped hard back and forth against the counter. "Shouldn't you be on your way to Winston-Salem?"

"Soon. I have to clear something up first."

"I'm on my way out. You should have called ahead."

"Why did you want the Manning girl?"

"What are you talking about?" She pulled the dishtowel tight between her hands. "Why would I want her?"

"You paid Damian to snatch Emma Manning. We don't touch girls like Emma. Too big a risk."

Allison stepped backwards towards the door without taking her eyes off Stephen. "I don't know what you're talking about. You're way too paranoid."

Stephen removed his gun, holding it casually, and strolled toward her. "The business we're in, it's not pretty, is it? But we've always behaved as professionals. We've never lied to each other, as far as I know. We've never kept decisions from each other. At least not decisions that could destroy our entire business and take us down with it. So, I'm going to ask you one more time, why did you want the girl?"

"I don't know what you're—"

Stephen cocked the gun.

Allison flinched but regained her composure.

"Sometimes we need a little incentive to tell the truth. Here's yours." He inched closer and pointed the gun at her shoulder. "Why did you pay Damian to take Emma Manning?"

Allison squared her shoulders. If she was afraid, she wasn't letting it show. "I had a score to settle."

"With a high school girl?"

"With her father."

"Her father? Was he one of your conquests, but you wanted more and he spurned you? Is that what happened?"

"No." Her eyes were dark as she stared at the counter. "Nothing like that."

"Then what, Allison? I'm getting tired of asking. What is he to you?"

He wiggled his finger in front of the trigger. Her eyes widened, but only for an instant. She sat on the bar stool with erect, defiant posture, still watching Stephen's every move. Her haughty anger had returned, erupting from every pore. "You wouldn't."

"I will."

She let out a deep breath. "Her father is also my father."

Stephen was genuinely surprised. "Really? He's the big, bad, demon who knocked up your mother and left her nothing?"

"Yes." Allison's gaze didn't waver. "He's always had money and did nothing to help us."

"So, let me see if I'm understanding this." Stephen kept his gun on Allison, turning it in small circles. "Your father, who may not even know you exist—hell, he must have been what—eighteen? He screwed you out of a nice country club life with ballet recitals and horseback riding lessons—so your way of cheering yourself up is to steal his privileged little girl? Even if it's a surefire way to get us locked up for life?"

"He knows I exist, all right."

"Why the sudden need to ruin this man's life?"

Allison's face flushed with embarrassment. It didn't happen often, but when it did, her pale skin gave it away. "Someone in my office saw Emma's picture in the newspaper. Jokingly said she looked like she could be my daughter. I agreed and took a closer look. I always believed my father was somewhere in this city."

"Your mother never told you who he was?"

"She didn't tell me, but I had the sense that she knew exactly who he was and where to find him. A few months ago, I finally looked through some of my mother's belongings, the few items I kept after she died. I discovered some things."

"Like?"

"Letters. She wrote him letters. They were returned unopened. I hired an investigator. It didn't take much to find Tripp Manning and to learn he's paying child support to two other women. Is that fair?"

Stephen threw his head back in a laugh. "You're complaining about fairness? Come on, Allison. Surely this is beneath you. I thought you were so much stronger. Immune. You don't even know for sure that he's your father. Just because the girl looks a little like you? That's pathetic."

"I do know." Allison glared at him. "The window cleaning company the Mannings use—I've used the same one for some of my clients. I paid one of their employees to take what I needed to do a DNA test. Tripp Manning is my father. Emma is my half-sister. And she's living an incredible life—"

"Was. I think she would beg to differ with you now—"

"Her life was nothing like the way I was forced to grow up."

"That's certainly changed." He cocked his head and swirled his gun around. "You're doing pretty well for yourself these days."

Allison cackled. "This—paying off informants and hiding stolen girls in my basement—this is not an ideal life."

Stephen's phone rang. He ignored it and focused on what to do about Allison. In a few more years, he planned to take his spoils and disappear to a remote island with the best yoga studios and live happily ever after without a care in the world. Everything he'd built was now in jeopardy, and so was his future. Allison needed to face consequences.

On the fourth ring, he glanced at the screen. "I have to answer this. It's perhaps the only person I'm more disappointed in than you right now. Although all of you are giving me a good run for the money."

He picked up the call. "Did you find her?"

"She's at the Charlotte Center Hospital. She hasn't given them her name, so it was hard to find her."

If she hadn't given them a name, it meant she wasn't talking. Stephen was relieved. "It's about time you did some successful investigating."

"She had surgery yesterday. She'll probably be there one more day. She doesn't have insurance. They'll want her out of there as soon as possible."

Stephen cursed under his breath. "I don't want her alive with the ability to speak for another hour, never mind another day." He didn't think she would say anything. He'd always told the girls if they got away, he would find them and make them pay. But the more time that passed without him coming, the more she might doubt his resolve. The more confident she might become.

"There's nothing we can do about—"

Stephen tightened his fingers around his phone. "There's nothing you can do? Don't you dare say that to me. What good are you? If I did my job as well as you, we'd all have much, much smaller bank accounts and you wouldn't be driving that Maserati I've seen you in." Stephen let that settle in. "That's right, I'm watching you. Bring me Sofia or you'll be sorry for the rest of your life."

"Once she's out of the hospital. Right now, there are guards and FBI agents there."

"Once she's out of the hospital it might be too late." Stephen growled. His operation only worked as long as everyone he was paying did what he told them to do. Their willfulness, negativity, and incompetence were becoming a problem.

"My advice to you is for you and Allison to get out of town," the man said. "Leave your girls with the brothers and hop on a plane to another country as soon as you can. Like today."

"I don't take advice from you," Stephen said.

"You should. Listen. If you expect me to help you, I need to know. Is Emma Manning still in the country?"

"No." Stephen hung up. The men he paid to protect his operation might look the other way with runaways and girls from poor foreign countries, but the daughter of a prominent businessman might test loyalties. Now was not the time to find out.

"What was that about?" Allison asked.

"I know where Sofia is. I'm calling Petar." He was already making the phone call.

"This situation with Sofia has nothing to do with Emma Manning, you know. Nothing. So, don't try to blame it on me."

"I don't believe in coincidences." Stephen closed his eyes briefly, getting a hold on his emotions as he waited for Petar to answer. "Change of plans, Petar. You've got a job to do here. An immediate priority. Get your ass to the Charlotte Center Hospital and drag Sofia out of there. You know the story."

"S-s-say I'm her uncle and sh-how them the papers."

"And if anyone gives you trouble, her religion doesn't allow for hospital stays and you're taking her home."

"B-but what if she denies I'm her—?

"She won't."

The stuttering beast would do as he was told, regardless of the risk or consequences. His dumb loyalty was worth its weight in gold.

Stephen hung up and turned to Allison. "I'm calling Svet and Damian with a change of plans, telling them to take all of the girls to the Garden Courtyard. Go pack your bags because as soon as I know Petar has Sofia, you're coming with me."

I'll punish Allison later. She doesn't get to double-cross me and live.

Neither does Damian.

But Sofia needs to die first.

Chapter Thirty-Three

Victoria left Sofia's hospital room with Rivera. She passed the guard sitting outside Sofia's door and ducked into a nearby alcove.

"Be right back," Rivera said, continuing on.

"Okay. I'll call Murphy and see if he's in Charlotte yet."

One of the hospital staff hurried past, wheeling equipment in front of him. Then the guard tapped her on the shoulder. "I need to take care of something. Back in a second. Okay?"

"Okay." She kept her eyes on Sofia's room. She was only a few yards away.

A tall, muscular man with a military-style haircut entered the hall. Tattoos covered his upper arms. Something about him was familiar. He entered the nearest hospital room.

Victoria's first thought was of Sofia, in case the man hadn't come alone. She rushed back to find Sofia squinting at her from the bed.

"It's just me, Agent Heslin." She peered out the door, just enough so she could watch without being seen. A hospital employee strolled past, reading from a chart. The tattooed man stepped back into the hallway, looked both ways, and went into the next room. He had to be an idiot not to realize how suspicious he appeared. His size would always get him noticed and the tattoos weren't helping him blend well either.

Heart racing, Victoria called Rivera. "Where are you?"

"In front of the hospital."

"The guy I chased out of that basement is here. He's going in and out of rooms. I don't know that he's alone. I'm going to stay with Sofia."

"I'm coming. Hold tight."

"I'm calling for back up. I doubt he's here to talk. Take the stairs. They exit right next to this room. I'll call you back."

"Someone came for me, didn't they?" Sofia scrambled out of the bed and moved into the corner of the room. She leaned against the wall. "Who is it? Svet? Petar?"

"It might be one of them. I'm not positive." Victoria kept her voice calm and level, but it was just above a whisper. "Go into the bathroom and lock the door. Get on the floor and stay as low as you can, especially if you hear . . . signs of trouble." No one else was going to hurt Sofia. Victoria was there to make damn sure of it.

Cradling the arm on her injured side, Sofia hurried to the bathroom. No questions. No complaints. But her eyes were wide with fear.

"It's going to be all right." Victoria's gaze left the door to the hallway only long enough to see where Sofia was. "This is what I do for a living. I'll protect you."

Sofia gripped the edge of the bathroom door with her good hand. "Be careful. Please don't get killed."

"I'm not planning on it." She waved at Sofia to step back and close the door.

Victoria called for backup and alerted hospital security. She opened the door a crack and peered into the hall as she called Rivera again.

Rivera's breath came short and fast. "On my way up the stairs."

"I'm going to get a location on him. If he gets here before you do, I'll handle him."

Before she moved, the door to Sofia's room creaked as it opened a few inches. Victoria tensed and made sure her gun was cocked and ready. Her adrenaline had her prepped for whatever would happen next.

The door burst open.

Victoria raised her gun and yelled "FBI! Stop!"

A commotion of flying feet and grunting breaths erupted. The man at the door jerked his head to the side as someone slammed into him. They both disappeared from sight. The soft snap of a silenced gun went off.

She raced into the hallway. Rivera was lying on his back, a stunned look on his face. Victoria gasped. Next to Rivera, a large man was lying on his stomach, forcing weight on his arms and pushing himself up. Victoria pounced onto his broad back, pressing her knee into his spine with all her weight. The hospital security guard darted to her side, helping to hold the man down. A male nurse ran over to help them. It took the three of them to overpower the intruder and get him cuffed.

Rivera groaned.

"Rivera! Are you shot?" Victoria yelled, breathless, craning her neck to see him.

"Yes." Rivera moaned through gritted teeth. His body shook violently.

Victoria moved away from the intruder, who had stopped struggling. "Don't let him up," she told the security guard. She knelt beside Rivera, searching for blood and the location of his wound. Shouts and hurried footsteps buzzed around her like white noise, none of it fully registering. She pulled the buckles apart on Rivera's vest, tossed it to one side, and tore open his shirt

"We've got this. You need to move." Victoria heard the woman's voice, but couldn't register her request.

A blazing red burn glared from the center of Rivera's chest.

But no hole.

And no blood.

"You're okay," Victoria said, barely able to breathe, eyes unblinking. She took hold of his hand and squeezed it. Aware of her racing heart and the chill tingling down her spine, she stepped back, letting his hand go as the hospital staff surrounded him. She covered her mouth with her hands and whispered again, "You're okay."

Chapter Thirty-Four

Outside the makeshift interrogation room, Victoria checked her watch. Rivera was supposed to join her as soon as a nurse finished wrapping bandages around his bruised torso. Petar was waiting inside. His hands were cuffed to a large pipe. A red lump had formed on the side of his head where he hit the floor. Hopefully he'd concluded that his game was up and it was in his best interest to talk. She'd give Rivera a few more minutes before she went in to interrogate him.

For the second time in less than thirty minutes, Victoria called Murphy. The first call had been a little emotional, coming right after Rivera got shot. Murphy's flight had just landed in Charlotte. She'd relayed the information they'd gathered. Now, she'd calmed down and was more herself.

"Allison Greenwood's home is surrounded," Murphy informed her. "I'm almost there."

Victoria now experienced a pang of fury each time she pictured the cool-as-ice realtor.

Murphy continued. "We've got agents positioned across the street. They confirmed she's inside. They'll use a battering ram and tear gas if needed. They're just waiting to hear we've located the girls before they bust in there. Once we have them, she won't have a bargaining chip. We can lock her up and throw away the key."

"And Stephen?"

"Still tracking him down."

"Make sure they know he always carries a gun. And from what Sofia says, he won't hesitate to use it. She's seen him commit murder."

"They know. What's the latest on Rivera?"

Remembering the horror of thinking he'd been shot sent another shudder down her back. She was still overwhelmed with relief that he had been wearing a vest. The uncertainty had lasted mere seconds, but it had rocked her world. She wasn't sure if she understood why. "He's okay. Two fractured ribs. I'm waiting for him now. I'll give him another minute before I go in."

"Good, good. And you?"

"Me? I'm fine." She'd finally stopped shaking.

"Then get your suspect to cooperate immediately. Let him know we're not playing games. They're all going down, it's just a matter of how far. We need the girls' locations so we can move. Call me once you have them."

There wasn't time to waste. Victoria had her hand on the door when Rivera walked around the corner, his gait slow and stiff. He smiled. "Sorry to keep you waiting."

"Better late than dead, Rivera." Her tone was snappier than she'd intended. Whatever she was feeling, now wasn't the time to sort it out.

She stared at Petar through the window in the door. "Check out the twitching eye. He's worried. Let's see if we can't make him sweat."

Rivera took a deep breath. "Walking hurts. I'd like to give him a taste of it. Let's get in there."

Victoria's phone buzzed as they entered the room.

Rivera moved with his usual athletic grace and gave no indication he'd been hurt. "Good thing I wear Kevlar, big guy. Or you'd be facing the death sentence. If you aren't already for something else."

Petar glanced at them, then back down at the handcuffs securing him to the table. "You took me down."

"You reached for a gun." Rivera eased into a chair. "What were you doing sneaking in and out of hospital rooms? What did you think you were going to do? Shoot someone and walk on out of here? Threaten Sofia not to talk? Either way, is your boss really that stupid? Or just that desperate? And what does that say about you?"

Petar didn't look up.

"Answer me," Rivera shouted.

"I was only going to talk and take her with me. I'm her uncle. The gun went off by accident."

"Maybe it did." Rivera huffed. "Clearly, you're not very smart. We know you're not her uncle, Petar."

Victoria's phone buzzed again. This time she took it out of her pocket and glanced at the screen. It was a 911 from Murphy.

She turned to Rivera and lowered her voice. "Give me one second."

She shut the door behind her and raised the phone to her ear. "Murphy. What is it?"

"Allison isn't alone in her house. She's with a Caucasian male, six feet tall, late forties. We got a picture of the plates on a black BMW through the garage window. The car is registered to Stephen Petrovich."

"It must be our perp. We've got them."

"They've been in there for over an hour. Allison wheeled a suitcase by a window not too long ago. Agents will have to move on both if either tries to leave. Do you have the location for the girls?"

"We need a few more minutes. We just started talking to him."

"You need to talk faster."

Victoria hurried back into the room. She wasn't able to tell Rivera what had transpired, but he would trust her lead. She remained standing, holding on to the back of a chair.

"Let's cut to the chase here. We know you're not the mastermind of this operation. We're not sure how you and your brother got involved, but we know you couldn't just leave, just like the girls couldn't leave. Maybe they threatened to kill your family if you did. That's how it always works with these types of rings, isn't it?" She didn't know if it were necessarily true in his case, but it allowed him an angle in case he wasn't smart enough to think of one himself. "The faster we can catch everyone, the safer your family will be. You cooperate now, and we'll make sure prosecutors know how helpful and remorseful you were. Tell us where to find Svet and the girls you're trafficking."

With the mention of his brother's name, Petar lifted his head and pinned Victoria with a look that said, *how do you know that?* He would get destroyed in a game of poker.

"We have Sofia," Victoria said. "She told us everything. The only thing she couldn't give us was the address of where the other girls are right now. That's the only thing we don't know. But we will find them. Once we do, it's all over for the rest of you.

You're going to do time for kidnapping, prostitution, and a bunch of other stuff. Life in prison. Do you want to know what inmates do to guys who hurt children? It's not pretty, that's for sure. Brutal and sadistic is what it is. Or . . . you can help yourself and make a deal. If you help us, and help us right now, we can tell the prosecutor you've been helpful and argue for leniency."

Petar shifted in his seat. "I d-don't know what you're talking about."

"You took a loaded weapon into a child's hospital room!" Victoria's voice rose with her anger. "You and your brother kidnapped girls. You made them use drugs and forced them into prostitution—underage girls! Stop acting tough and start acting smart. How many people?"

"He'll kill me."

"Not if we get him first," Rivera said. "You've seen your last glimpse of sky outside of a federal penitentiary, but we need your help. We want to move fast, and we're willing to make life a lot easier for you if you cooperate. We can help protect you in prison. But while you're taking your sweet time deciding, if the people you work with get scared, they might do something stupid like kill the girls—which means you're an accessory to murder. But it might not be too late if you start talking right goddamned now! So, how many people, other than your brother, are with the girls?"

Petar lowered his head and whispered. "J-j-just one. Damian."

A jolt of exhilaration shot through Victoria. He was going to talk.

"Tell us where they are," Rivera said. "And maybe we won't shoot your brother in the head when we find him."

Petar's phone vibrated and lit up on the table.

"Speak of the devil." Rivera snorted. "Bet he's wondering where you are."

Petar stared at Stephen's name lighting up on his phone.

"So, here's what you're going to tell him." Victoria leaned forward, speaking quickly. "Tell him Sofia is alive. She just left the hospital. She's going to a safe house."

Petar stared at the vibrating phone.

"Hurry up," Rivera said. "And don't forget that we can help you or we can make your hell even worse than it otherwise will be."

Victoria accepted the call and then pressed the speaker button. She prayed Petar wasn't loyal enough to his boss to give them away.

Petar spoke. "S-S-S—" He swallowed, closed his eyes, and tried again. "S-S-Sofia's alive."

"I know. That's why you're there. Bring her to me. I want to kill her in front of the other girls."

Victoria cringed. The man was a monster.

"Yeah. B-b-but the cops have her. Th-th-they're taking her somewhere safe."

Victoria mouthed the word "Good."

Stephen sighed. "I'll find out where she is. You be ready and waiting by your phone."

Rivera waved to get Petar's attention and mouthed. "Where are the girls? Ask him."

"Uh, w-w-where are the other girls now?"

"They're at the usual hotels. You're going to focus on getting Sofia. Do you understand?"

"Y-y-yes."

Stephen hung up.

"Do you know which motels they're going to?" Victoria asked.

"D-d-don't I get a lawyer to help me?"

"Absolutely. I'll have one sent over." Rivera pushed a pen and notepad across the table. "Now, write down the information about the motels."

Victoria wrapped her fingers around the necklace under her T-shirt. Beside her, Rivera capped and uncapped a pen. Time passed at an impossibly slow pace as Petar held the pen over the notepad. He was silent for several seconds before scribbling down the names of two motels: the Winston Express and the Garden Courtyard. As soon as he finished, Victoria snatched the notepad and stood. She was as energized as if she'd gone for a fast run.

She took a few steps before stopping in the doorway. She had one more question. "There are several hospitals in Charlotte. How did you know Sofia was at this one? Or did you?"

"St—St—Stephen told me."

"And how did he know?"

Petar shrugged.

◆ ◆ ◆

With the rescue operation and arrests in motion, Victoria had more time to think about loose ends. She also wanted to buy toothbrushes and toothpaste for her and Rivera from the hospital's gift store. On her way there, she called Sam.

"Sorry, I never got back to you, Sam. Things got . . . busy, but Murphy's got them under control. I know you still have some info to give me on the private investigator I asked you about."

"Yes. Hold on. Let me switch to another file. Wait . . . here it is. Got it. Okay . . . this is specific to what you told me about him and the boy at the apartment complex. Jay Adams has been a mentor with a big brother program for years. Turns out anything he does with his mentee needs to be documented in their database. Everything is confidential, but it provides a record and ensures the person in charge knows what's going on. Or at least knows what is being reported as going on."

"And you were allowed access to this database?" She entered the gift shop and looked for the personal hygiene section.

"I wouldn't say that, exactly."

"I'm sorry." She walked to a corner of the store. "Please continue."

"The boy Adams currently mentors has a history of being beaten by his mother's boyfriend. It happens every time the guy goes on a drinking binge. And Adams has a history of taking the boy and his older sister to a hotel to keep them safe so they can get their homework done without being knocked around. You saw him with the boy. Apparently, the sister drove there and joined him after her work shift. Adams pays for it. Quite generous of him. He's hoping the boyfriend will move on or the sister can move out soon and take the boy with her. Adams also reported taking a small baggie of drugs from the boy when he picked him up."

"Okay. Not what I expected, but it all fits. He was just taking the kid somewhere safe to spend the night while the mother's boyfriend cooled down. Adams helps troubled kids." *Or does he?*

"Sounds like he might be a good guy," Sam said.

She selected a tube of Crest. "Maybe." *Maybe he's not a pedophile, but . . . troubled kids are the biggest targets for sex traffickers.* "We'll bring him in for questioning. Then I'll decide."

Chapter Thirty-Five

Svet blasted heavy metal music, slammed the brakes at a stop light, and floored the gas on green. Anastasia had spent the past ninety-minutes feeling carsick and praying Sofia was still alive. Her friend's absence, so soon after Sasha's, left an aching void in her chest. She still wasn't sure what had happened. After Svet dragged her half-dressed from the house and backhanded her hard enough to send her spinning, she'd pieced together important parts of the story. Sofia escaped and Svet shot her. But where was Sofia now? Had her brave friend died trying to save them? Or had she found a phone and called the tip line first? Were people coming to get Emma and free the rest of the girls?

Svet turned the music down and pressed a few buttons on his phone.

"Call me back now, bro! This is not cool."

The voice mail messages he'd been leaving indicated something might have happened to Petar.

On the seat next to her, Maria scratched and picked at scabs on her arm. Anastasia was equally saddened and repulsed. Emma and Nadia were sedated and sleeping in the third row, both snoring loudly. Emma's beautiful hair had been colored black, leaving her skin looking washed-out and pale. At least she hadn't been shipped away to another country yet.

Svet swore, threw his phone onto the passenger seat, and turned his music back up. He sped around a corner, sending Emma and Nadia tumbling toward one side of the van and then tossing them back together. Emma's eyes flickered open. She made a garbled noise and struggled to sit up.

Svet pulled into the parking lot of the Garden Courtyard motel, drove to the back, and turned off the engine. "Get out," he growled.

Damian arrived and parked his car alongside the van. He got out at the same time Svet slid the van door open.

"I'm going in there, too?" Anastasia asked with a tremor in her voice.

"What does it look like, princess?" Svet shot her an evil look. "It's just you and them now. And if anything happened to my brother because of your little friend, you're going to be sorry. I don't give a damn if I hurt you and it shows. I'll whip you with a wire hanger until your skin falls off in bloody chunks. I'll yank your hair out by its roots so hard your eyes will pop out. No one who comes here will care what you look like as long as they can spread your legs and then stick their—"

"He still hasn't responded?" Damian asked. "Is that why you drove the whole way like you were begging to get pulled over?"

"He's not answering his phone," Svet snarled. He pushed against Emma's shoulder to wake her and dragged her out by her arm. She moaned as her head flopped to the side.

"Get a hold of yourself, man," Damian said. "If anyone sees you . . ."

"Shut up," Svet responded, yanking on Emma.

Damian gave Anastasia a look of sympathy, at least she thought he did. He helped a frail girl with long brown hair from his car, putting his arm around her as she stumbled out and then letting her lean heavily against him.

The wind sliced through Anastasia's thin jacket as she stood next to the van. She shivered and glanced at the beckoning woods behind the motel, then toward the dark road they'd turned from. What would happen if she ran? Would Svet shoot her, too? Did she care anymore?

Svet jerked Maria out and called her disgusting.

"Um, I should get the room keys?" Anastasia asked Svet. *There's got to be a phone at the check-in counter.* She hadn't forgotten the number, but she scarcely believed that it was real anymore. It was more like a far-fetched fantasy she and Sofia had concocted to give them hope.

"We already have keys." Svet barked and pointed toward the stairs. "Move."

The other girls shuffled along toward the stairs like zombies, barely noticing where they were. Maria's arm dripped blood onto the dusty ground. Anastasia walked behind them, her mind racing through her options—every one of them futile.

On the second floor, near the end of a dirty passageway littered with cigarette butts, Svet told the girls to stop. He pushed them aside so he could open one of the rooms. Damian slid a key into the door to the room next to it.

Svet shoved Nadia forward and walked in, pulling Emma along behind him. Under his shirt, his gun created a bulge against his hip.

Anastasia stood on the landing, looking over her shoulder, fighting a strong urge to vomit. *Am I one of the motel girls now?* She couldn't go in there, but she didn't know where else to go.

Who would believe her even if she got away? Not that she needed to worry about that. She'd be shot before she got very far. At this point, with Sasha and Sofia both gone, wouldn't that be the most merciful way to go? *A few bullets through my back while I'm running away—it would be quick, quicker than so many things I've endured—and all of this can finally end.* Trembling, with tears streaming down her cheeks, she crept backwards towards the stairs.

A loud and sudden commotion erupted inside the room. Svet shouted. The girls screamed. Something crashed to the ground. Anastasia froze in her tracks.

Three armed men wearing metal vests and helmets with shields emerged from other rooms. Anastasia hurried forward, into the room with the other girls, unsure of who was the bigger threat, Svet or the men carrying guns. Inside were three more armed men wearing the same black uniforms. In the back of the room, Svet struggled in handcuffs and screamed, "This is my sister's birthday party, assholes!" He glared at Anastasia. "Tell them!"

Anastasia kept her mouth shut, shrinking back against the wall as the strangers stared at her.

One of the men raised his face shield and spoke to her. "It's okay. You're safe. We're not going to hurt you. Are you Emma Manning?"

Anastasia shook her head and pointed across the room. Emma cowered on the floor, arms wrapped around her knees, with unfocused, bloodshot eyes. The man looked at Emma and then back at Anastasia. He didn't believe her. Emma was almost unrecognizable from the girl Anastasia first met a few days ago. Anastasia was the only girl in the room who didn't look deathly sick.

Svet continued to scream and swear like a raging bull. In the next room, visible through the adjoining door, Damian stood with his head bowed, silent, also handcuffed with a gun trained on him. The motel girls he brought were huddled together in the corner, looking terrified and confused.

The man nearest Anastasia pushed a button on his collar. "This is Delta forty-four. We have two men in custody. We found seven girls. One of them has been identified as Emma Manning."

A rush of static and then a woman responded. "There was no one at the other motel. That's all of them. We have medics on the way to take the girls to a hospital."

Shaking, Anastasia pressed her back and shoulders against the wall, unsure of her emotions. More than anything she wanted to reach for Sofia's hand.

Sofia did it. She saved us.

◆ ◆ ◆

The front and back doors of Allison's house crashed open simultaneously, shattering the silent tension between her and Stephen. By the time he processed what was happening—*an actual SWAT team busting in like we're part of a damn action thriller*—there were two guns targeting his body and two focused on Allison.

"FBI. Hands up and don't move," one of the men shouted.

"Drop your gun," another yelled.

Stephen set his gun down. It suddenly looked pathetic and small. "I think there's been a serious misunderstanding," he said calmly as he lifted his hands.

"Yes. A big misunderstanding," Allison echoed, reaching for her phone.

"Don't move!" The shout came from several of the men at once, their aim steady. "Keep your hands overhead."

Allison lifted her hands. "Okay. I'm Allison Greenwood." She spoke with the eloquence of someone leading a meeting full of important clients. "I'm not sure what this is about, gentlemen, but I think I should ring my attorney so he can help us clear up whatever this is."

One of the men stepped forward and yanked the phone from her hand. "You're under arrest for the kidnapping of Emma Manning."

"Kidnapping?" Allison laughed, her voice inappropriately light and pleasant. "I assure you, Emma Manning was not kidnapped. She was visiting."

Stephen would have preferred to deny all knowledge of the girls, but he had to admire Allison's uncanny composure, her cool lies under pressure. And now he had to play along. "Emma is Allison's half-sister," he said. "She was just telling me about her."

"That's right." Allison's surprise at their predicament was genuine, as was his, but nothing in her demeanor suggested guilt, only confusion and shock. "Emma came to stay with me, hoping to get acquainted, get to know each other. She's at a friend's birthday party right now. Wait—are you saying she didn't tell her parents? She promised me—"

One of the agents looked at their leader, the man in charge.

Stephen knew it was working. Whatever intelligence the FBI possessed; they were now questioning its validity. The girls would back up any stories he and Allison told. They wouldn't dare turn on them.

"Murphy," one of the men said, "this one lies like the best of them, doesn't she?"

Murphy strode past one of the men to get to Allison. "Put your hands behind your back." He snapped cuffs around her wrists. "Stop talking and start walking. No one's buying your stories."

"This is preposterous." Allison glared at Murphy. "Do you know who I am?"

"Yep. You're Allison Greenwood, previously Allison Wood, aka Allison Bois. Part of an interstate-sex trafficking ring, and you're on your way to prison."

Stephen dropped his head and surrendered his wrists to handcuffs. Two agents escorted him through Allison's front door.

Chapter Thirty-Six

With the shades drawn and the television on in the Charlotte safe house, Victoria sat on the couch cradling her phone in her hands. Sofia's jacket was strewn across a chair, and pink running shoes were lying in the middle of the floor.

With Ned finishing up a shift at the vet clinic and her father busy with a dinner and board meeting, she'd passed the last few hours keeping herself updated on every miniscule new piece of information in the investigation. A few questions still needed to be answered before she was satisfied with her work in Charlotte.

Five arrests had been made so far. All played a part in the sex trafficking. More would come. Someone was helping the ring thrive by providing protection and inside information.

One step at a time. She smiled. That was one of Ned's sayings. *One step at a time,* he told her when Tallulah broke her leg and needed surgery and months of recovery. *One step at a time,* is how he told her he finished each triathlon, which wasn't quite accurate because there was no stepping once he was in the ocean or on his bike. But the point remained.

269

Right now, Ned would be—oh crap, I almost forgot! She typed "livestock transportation in North Carolina" into her phone's browser and then made a few phone calls.

A message from Rivera popped onto her screen. *Hey, what's going on there?*

For some reason she didn't understand, hearing from Rivera made her sad.

She typed her response. *Still nothing.*

Victoria went into the kitchen and poured herself a glass of water. Her phone rang. Ned's name appeared on the screen. She set her water down and accepted his call.

"Calling to say hello," he said.

She took a satisfied breath. "Hello. Where are you now?"

"At your house. Just got all the dogs fed. I'm going to put you on speaker phone so you can say hello to everyone. Hey dogs, it's Victoria."

"Hi, babies. I miss you. I'll be home soon and the first thing we're going to do is go for a long hike." After cooing to her dogs, her normal speaking voice returned. "I can't wait to get home. You patched up that area of fallen fence on the side of the house a few weeks ago, right?"

"That old corral? Yes. It's fixed."

"Great. I—" She thought she saw a shadow pass outside the door, but she hadn't heard a car. "Hold on a sec."

Through a crack in the blinds, she spotted Detective Connelly. She might have let it slip that she was alone with Sofia near an older establishment touted as having the best barbecue.

"I have to go," she whispered.

"Sure thing, be careful—"

Outside, Connelly looked around before approaching the safe house. He stopped on the landing. Looked around again. Then he knocked.

With no idea of what might happen next, Victoria flipped the locks. She opened the door a few inches, leaving the security chain still attached. "Hold on, Connelly. Be right there." She walked to the other side of the small home and stopped outside the closed bathroom door. "Sofia? It's me. Just making sure you're still okay in there." She returned to the front and unlocked the chain with a smile.

Connelly stepped inside, running his hand through his hair. The door to the bedroom was open. Some casual teen clothes—a pink T-shirt, a white sweatshirt, and a pair of jeans—were strewn across a chair and the bed. "Where's your partner?"

"Rivera? He's not my partner. He just went out to grab some food. He'll be right back. Glad you came, actually."

"How's it going?"

"Fine. Not much to do here. I'm catching up on some reading."

"Where's the girl now?"

"She's in the bathroom. In the tub, I believe. Poor girl. What she's been through."

"I know." Connelly lifted his hands toward the ceiling. "Listen, why don't you take a break and join Rivera. I'll wait here until you get back."

"Hmm. I'm not sure how I would ever decide between the best burgers or the best pizza or the best wings."

The detective chuckled, but his laughter had a sharp, nervous edge. "Actually, I was giving Rivera the same food advice at the hospital, and he told me you were a vegetarian."

271

She grinned. "So, now you have a whole new list of recommendations?"

"Nope. Not a one. I'm a carnivore."

Victoria stretched her arms overhead. "Okay. I am a little hungry. Let me just tell Sofia I'm going." She walked to the bathroom and knocked on the door. "Sofia?" She waited. "I'm just going to get something to eat and come right back. Detective Connelly is here. He'll take care of you. Okay? I'll be back soon. You have my number. Let me know if you want anything. The detective can call me and I'll pick it up on the way back."

She returned to the living room and lifted her coat off the back of a chair. "Thanks. I appreciate this. I'll just let my boss know you're in charge for a bit. Shouldn't be more than forty-five minutes, or an hour at the most."

Victoria stepped outside into the night and walked around the safehouse, taking the side with no windows. On the road behind the house, she spotted a white Maserati and made the connection. *The guy who almost hit me at the airport. No wonder Connelly looked so familiar when I first saw him.*

She broke into a run for a half block, stopping at a gray van marked 24 Hour Emergency Plumbing. She tapped on the back in code. The door swung opened. She climbed inside, joining three agents wearing armor and readying guns—Murphy, another man, and a woman. They were crowded around a television monitor.

Victoria drew closer to the monitor and the clear image of the safe house's interior.

On the screen, Connelly was standing outside the bathroom door. His hand rested on his gun.

"Sofia?" he called. "It's Detective Connelly. We have a small problem. I need you to get dressed and come with me."

He slid the gun out of his holster. "Sofia?"

He banged his forearm against the door. He waited.

"Sofia! Get out here! I'm not playing games with you." He banged on the door again. When he looked around, Victoria could see the desperation in his eyes. "You shouldn't have run away from Stephen. You knew what would happen if you talked." And then, his voice changed, as if he'd just considered trying a new angle. "He's paid people to kill you and they know where you are now. I need to get you away from here to protect you. If you want to live, you need to come with me now."

"Unbelievable," Murphy grunted. "We've got enough and it's all on tape. Let's go get him."

The agents jumped out the back of the truck with Murphy in the lead. "He better be the only sleaze-ball with a badge in on this."

Victoria stayed behind, unable to take her eyes off the screen as Connelly burst through the bathroom door, confirming all her suspicions.

He lowered his gun, staring around the empty bathroom. He turned and lifted his head toward the ceiling. His eyes roamed until he found the camera and his gaze seemed to settle right on Victoria. A chill coursed through her.

"He knows we've got him. Come on," the female agent said, holding the door open for Victoria. "You see the car he drove here? No cop on the up and up drives something like that. And he kept it hidden from his colleagues."

Victoria jumped down from the van, her stomach suddenly queasy. "At least he didn't unload a round of bullets through the door. I guess that's . . . something."

"He'd never kill her here, but after she left with him? Absolutely. Maybe he was paid to do it in the event one of the girls ever got arrested."

"But how would he think he'd ever get away with it," Victoria wondered out loud.

"How did any of these sex traffickers get away with what they were doing? Who knows what he would have tried to tell us! Either way, you just saved that girl's life again, Victoria."

◆ ◆ ◆

"This is like the walking wounded suite at the Hampton Inn. You know, with both of us injured," Rivera joked.

Sofia's injured arm rested in a sling to immobilize her shoulder. She offered a slight smile in return. Either he wasn't at all funny, or she didn't trust him enough to be in a laughing mood.

The hospital had given her some novels to read and some clothes to wear, and whatever else she owned sat below her chair in a duffel bag from the hospital's lost and found. She looked nothing like the pictures he'd seen of her with makeup and an evening dress entering the hospital soaked in her own blood. Occasionally she touched her good arm to the bridge of her new glasses. She'd acted like a different person since she got them. With delight and confidence, she pointed out everything she could see—from signs on the wall to birds in the trees. Now, she sat in a chair watching television from a normal distance, nibbling at candies she'd selected from the lobby.

Only Victoria and Rivera knew where she was.

Rivera had the strange sensation of being under surveillance from across the room as he worked on his laptop. Every time he turned to check on her, she was already watching him.

Room service arrived with their dinner. He made sure to give her as much space as possible while they took their trays off the cart and returned to their respective corners. Nibbling at her french fries, she continued to watch television.

"You're sure they have her?" Sofia asked suddenly, surprising him by initiating the conversation.

"Anastasia? Yes, she's safe and sound. She's with a colleague of mine, another FBI agent. The raid was a success. No one got hurt. There was one man with Anastasia, Emma, and—"

"Did he have one hand that doesn't work? It's burned?"

"I think I heard something like that." Rivera bit into his hamburger.

"That's Damian," she said, and unless he was mistaken, her words carried a hint of sadness.

"Well, Damian is in custody now. So is Petar's brother."

"Good. And Petar is still in jail?"

"Yes. He can't leave."

"And Stephen and Allison?"

"They're not going anywhere." *If we do our jobs right.*

"What will happen to Anastasia and the motel girls?"

"They'll be in the hospital a few days for assessment and care while we contact their families." He wasn't sure where they were going to go if they didn't have families. Most would end up with social services.

"I can't believe I'm going to see my family again." Sofia said, massaging her hands.

How would they deal with what happened to their daughter? "They're going to be thrilled to see you. And amazed that you speak English so well."

"Yes, they will be surprised. It will be their first time in America. The land of the free and the brave, except this is my first week here with freedom."

Rivera swallowed his anger and tried to appreciate her new situation. There would be plenty of time to help ensure those who were responsible for her suffering paid for their crimes.

"Agent Rivera, I have to ask you something." Sofia's voice took on a whole new tone.

"Go ahead." He crumpled a napkin on top of his empty plate and leaned back in his chair.

"I have some jewelry." She lifted her bag off the floor and onto her lap.

"And?"

"I want to sell it. You know how I told you my mother believed she was sending me off to begin a modeling career?"

"I remember."

"I wanted to earn money so I could help my family. But I've been here three years, working all that time, and I have nothing to give them that would help. They don't need jewelry. So, do you know a place where I can trade my jewelry for money?"

Rivera didn't know whose jewelry she had been wearing when she was picked up by the ambulance, or how she had come across it. If she'd stolen it from a customer, he doubted that person would have the nerve to claim she had been anywhere near his home. If she'd stolen it from Allison Greenwood or Stephen Petrovich—good. He only hoped it was a small fortune. "I'll help you sort it out. I might know a guy. Don't worry."

Chapter Thirty-Seven

Victoria was sitting at a table in the hotel lobby when Adams spotted her and walked over.

"Hey." He remained standing. "Thanks for meeting. Hope I didn't interrupt anything."

"I'm just getting ready to go home."

"Tripp asked me to give this to you." He handed her a sealed envelope. "To give to Sofia. There's a check inside. He wants to thank her. If she hadn't escaped, he might not have gotten his daughter back."

"That was considerate of him. I'll make sure she gets it. It's really wonderful that Emma will be home soon."

"Yeah." Adams rested his hands against his sides. "I can't imagine the relief for her parents."

"And now we won't be digging into their personal life anymore." Victoria smiled.

"Right." Adams' expression turned serious. "I hope I was able to convince your colleagues when they interviewed me—for all Tripp's flaws, he didn't know Allison Greenwood existed and he definitely didn't know what she was doing."

"Well, it's his own fault for not knowing she existed."

277

"Agreed. Turns out he worked with her on a business deal a few years ago. Neither realized their connection."

"Imagine that. What a world. How is the boy you're mentoring?"

"He'll be okay once he can get a job and live on his own. Right now, it's day to day, depending on how drunk his mother's boyfriend gets. I put him and his older sister up in a hotel near his school for a few days when the boyfriend was on a drinking binge. Sad thing is, the mother didn't even notice either of them was gone. The kid is selling drugs to try and buy the stuff he needs for school. It's just sad. There are worse things than having parents like the Mannings."

"I know," Victoria said. "Glad your mentee has someone like you to help him through tough times and help keep him off the streets."

Adams looked over his shoulder then back to Victoria. "Just making sure no one is following me or anything." He held Victoria's gaze.

She pretended to scan the room. "I don't think so. Not today." She finished her sentence with a straight face but broke into a smile.

Adams chuckled. "Thought I'd have a better sense of something like that when it happened, but apparently not."

"Well, I'm pretty stealthy." She laughed.

"It was nice working with you, Victoria. I hope our paths will cross again."

"Same."

Adams waved and she watched him walk away.

She was glad she'd waited before condemning Adams based on what she'd witnessed—the boy and the hotel. She'd certainly seen enough to jump to conclusions, but all of it made sense now. *Things aren't always what they appear to be. And neither are people.*

◆ ◆ ◆

Victoria waited in the lobby of the Hampton Inn to say goodbye to Sofia. Murphy and Rivera were talking. Victoria studied Rivera. When he caught her staring, she quickly looked away.

A woman from social services walked in with Sofia behind her. Dressed in jeans and a loose sweater, her hair up in a bun, and her horn-rimmed glasses, Sofia looked like a young ballerina. She could easily pass for a normal teenager, but strikingly beautiful, with a measure of grace beyond her years. Victoria hoped that after what Sofia had been through, and the tough wariness she now possessed, she would never let anyone take advantage of her again.

Sofia clutched a book in one hand, and in the other, the carry-on suitcase Victoria bought her. By her feet rested another duffel bag filled with clothes and toiletries they'd recently purchased at the mall.

"All set?" Rivera asked. "You've got your savings account info?"

"Yes." Sofia offered a quick smile and regripped the handle of her bag.

"Remember, that's your money. You can take it out whenever you need it, for you or your family. You can access it from any country. No one else can touch it." Helping Sofia sell the jewelry wasn't protocol, but too bad.

"Your mother and grandfather will be here on Thursday," Murphy said. "Their tickets have already been purchased."

"Thank you." Sofia rubbed her hands together. Victoria didn't blame her for being nervous. So much had changed since

Sofia left her family three years ago. How much of it would she want to share?

"Thank you again, for all your help," Victoria said. "You're the reason all of the girls are safe and the adults who harmed you are going to prison."

This time Sofia's smile was complete.

Victoria hugged her goodbye. "If you ever need anything, you have my number. From Ukraine, you can call me collect if you need to. Okay?"

"Okay."

Rivera stepped forward. "I wish you all the best, Sofia."

"Same." Sofia shook his hand.

The agents watched them walk away. Victoria sighed. "I hope she'll be okay."

"Gotta be better off anywhere than where she was," Murphy said. "And she'll have some protection until she leaves the country." He started walking. "Come on. Lunch is on me."

"I know a few places that Connelly *didn't* recommend." Victoria snickered. "But I'm going to pass."

"I bet you're ready to fly out of here," Murphy said. "See those dogs of yours."

"Yes. But I'm not flying, I'm going to drive back."

"You're driving up to Virginia?"

Rivera also looked surprised. "Did you buy a car here or something?"

"Not a car, exactly." She couldn't repress her smile. "Something bigger."

"I don't think I want to know," Murphy said. "I might be a little jealous."

"Nah." Rivera chuckled. "Victoria isn't your typical rich person. Whatever it is she bought; we probably wouldn't want one."

Victoria smiled. "To each his own."

Murphy gave a last wave as he got into his car.

Rivera and Victoria continued walking. She couldn't help but feel like something had changed between the two of them. She wasn't as comfortable as she used to be with Rivera by her side.

"Everything okay?" Rivera asked. "Because I'm kind of sensing I might have done something to upset you."

"No. Of course not."

"You sure?"

"I'm sure." She sighed and rubbed her hand down her neck. "I'm sorry. It's just . . . when you tackled that piece of crap—"

"I knew you and Sofia were in that room."

"I know. And when I heard the shot and saw you on the ground, I was worried I'd lost you. Really worried."

"And?"

"And . . . I don't know." She glanced at him and then looked off toward the horizon. *Why do I feel guilty?* "I don't know."

Rivera offered a sad smile. "It's okay. You don't have to explain. Not now. But think about it while you're driving to Virginia and let me know what you come up with."

She thought of her last conversation with Helen. What had she said? Something about the right guy taking the time to embrace her. There'd never really been a man before, and now, if she could trust her feelings, there seemed to be two.

"Goodbye, Rivera. Hope to see you soon." She held out her hand. "You're a good guy."

He took it between both of his. "Maybe. But I don't intend to finish last."

She stared at their hands, unsure of how to respond.

◆ ◆ ◆

Victoria placed her phone in the center console and hit the speaker button, waiting for Ned to pick up on the other end.

"Hi! On my way," she said. "Shouldn't be too much longer."

"Sounds like you're in a good mood."

"I am. I can't wait to get back."

"So, your case wrapped up?"

"It did. Wrapped up with a really good ending. A major bust. Hey—just want to give you a heads up that I've got a special surprise with me."

"Let me guess, you found a dog who needed a home."

"Nope.

"Two dogs, then?"

"Nope. You'll just have to wait and see."

She smiled at the sound of braying donkeys coming through the open window from behind her. "Almost home, fellas."

The End

END NOTE

I'm grateful to all the women and men who shared trafficking stories and information that helped me write this book. Tammy Harris, founder of the URSUS Institute, a non-profit that works to combat human trafficking, especially amazed me with her knowledge and passion.

The events and characters in *Pretty Little Girls* are fictional, but everything about human trafficking in the novel is grounded in reality. The United States is ranked as one of the three worst countries in the world for human trafficking. If you think someone is being human trafficked, call the National Human Trafficking Hotline. The number is 1-888-373-7999

NOTE TO READERS

Thank you for reading my book! If you have the time, I would deeply appreciate a review on Amazon or Goodreads or Bookbub—wherever you bought this book. I learn a great deal from reviews, and I'm always grateful for any encouragement. Reviews help authors like me to sell a few more books.

READY FOR BOOK 3?

WHEN THEY FIND US

A commercial airliner disappears without a trace.

Stranded, injured, and freezing. What happens to the survivors next will haunt them forever.

After breaking up a sex trafficking ring, FBI Agent Victoria Heslin wants nothing more than to visit the rescue shelter she sponsors, a trip that also offers a much-needed European vacation and a chance to figure out her new relationship with Ned. Comfortable in first class, she drifts off—only to be shocked awake when her plane crashes.

Lost in a frozen wasteland, Victoria and a few other survivors battle extreme temperatures, as each day brings more tragedy. One by one, the desperate group is winnowed down. The remaining passengers must decide if they'll stay with the wreck, waiting to be found, or brave the harsh elements and venture out in search of help.

When Agent Dante Rivera learns of Victoria's fate, he puts all his energy and expertise into finding her plane, which seems to have vanished from existence. As he unravels a technological mystery and layers of scheming, he fears his worst nightmare will be realized: that he won't find his coworker and friend alive.

ABOUT THE AUTHOR

Jenifer Ruff is a USA Today and international bestselling author of thriller novels who writes in three series: The Brooke Walton Series, The Agent Victoria Heslin Thriller Series, and the FBI & CDC Thriller Series.

Jenifer grew up in Massachusetts, has a biology degree from Mount Holyoke College and a Master's in Public Health and Epidemiology from Yale University. She worked as a management consultant for Price Waterhouse Coopers and IBM before discovering her love for writing. An avid hiker and fitness enthusiast, she lives in Charlotte, North Carolina with her family and a pack of greyhounds. For more information, visit her website at Jenruff.com where you can join her newsletter to find out about new titles, promotions, giveaways and more.